"Nancy Herriman's vivid characters, tender romance, and enduring themes of hurt and healing make this richly woven story set in nineteenth-century England a perfect read."

MARGARET BROWNLEY
AUTHOR OF THE ROCKY CREEK SERIES

"The Irish Healer is a wonderful debut novel. I enjoyed watching James and Rachel fall in love and heal their wounded hearts. I'll be watching for more books from Herriman."

ROBIN LEE HATCHER
AUTHOR OF BELONGING AND HEART OF GOLD

"First-time author Nancy Herriman knows how to engage readers and win their hearts! Set in 1830s London, The Irish Healer is the tale of Rachel Dunne, a simple Irish healer accused of murdering one of her patients, and James Edmunds, a wealthy, high-born physician in the process of closing down his London practice and retiring to the life of a gentleman farmer on his country estate. Though painful secrets, personal crises of faith, and differing social standings threaten to keep them apart, you can't help but root for these strong yet vulnerable characters struggling for a new and better life. If you enjoy historical fiction, you won't want to miss this engrossing, heartwarming story. Nancy Herriman has penned a winner with The Irish Healer!"

KATHLEEN MORGAN
AUTHOR OF A HEART DIVIDED AND A LOVE FORBIDDEN

"The Irish Healer charms readers with rich historical details and endearing characters that capture the heart."

DOROTHY LOVE
AUTHOR OF BEYOND ALL MEASURE

THE IRISH HEALER

The *Irish Healer*

A NOVEL

NANCY HERRIMAN

WORTHY
PUBLISHING

Published by Worthy Publishing, a division of Worthy Media, Inc., 134 Franklin Road, Suite 200, Brentwood, Tennessee 37027.

HELPING PEOPLE EXPERIENCE THE HEART OF GOD

eBook available at www.worthypublishing.com

Audio distributed through Oasis Audio; visit www.oasisaudio.com

Library of Congress Control Number: 2012931879

Scripture quotations are taken from the King James Version.

Published in association with Natasha Kern Literary Agency.

For foreign and subsidiary rights, contact Riggins International Rights Services, Inc.; www.rigginsrights.com

ISBN: 978-1-936034-78-9 (trade paper)

Cover Design: FaceOut Studio/Jeff Miller
Cover Photography: Dogleg Studios/Mike Houska
Interior Design and Typesetting: Cindy Kiple

Printed in the United States of America
12 13 14 15 16 17 18 SBI 10 9 8 7 6 5 4 3 2 1

CHAPTER 1

At sea, 1832

"*My name is Rachel Dunne.*
I am not a murderer."

Rachel tightened her grip on the ship's wooden rail, as if she might choke into silence the echo of her own voice. Better to focus on the receding sight of Ireland's blue-green hills, seek to memorize every bounding stream, every wisp of misty fog, every rubble-walled farmer's field, than to remember. For who knew how long—if ever—it would be before she saw her beloved homeland again.

"Oh, Mother," she murmured over the slap of the paddle wheels and the hiss of the steam, the scree of persistent seagulls skimming the boat's wake. "How did it come to this?"

This parting, this going. *Deoraíocht.* This exile.

Mother was not there to answer Rachel's question; they could only afford ship's passage for one, and Rachel was the one who had to leave. Mother and the rest had stayed behind in Carlow to mend the damage Rachel had never meant to cause. Restore the honor of the Dunne name in a town already prone to dislike them for their English ways. Once Rachel had been a healer, but she could not heal the scar upon her family. No more than she'd been able to heal poor Mary Ferguson, who had died so quickly and so quietly even Rachel had been at a loss to explain the how and the why.

I would never harm the ill. I am a banaltradh . . .

A healer. If the thought didn't hurt so much, Rachel might laugh. She had vowed never to let herself be a healer again.

Against the cool spray of the sea, Rachel knotted her fringed shawl around her neck, the charcoal wool warming her skin while her thoughts chilled her soul, and wrapped her arms about her waist. Cove of Cork dwindled, its pale stucco and limestone homes that snaked along the hillside becoming indistinct, its proud fleet of yachts bobbing at anchorage transformed into specks of white upon the cerulean blue waters. Two islands, bristling with storehouses, obliterated the last of the view. The paddle-steamer chugged past the looming stone forts that guarded the mouth of the bay, Forts Camden and Carlisle, names Mrs. O'Rourke had helpfully supplied when they'd set out. Next, according to Rachel's traveling companion, would be the lighthouse guarding the shoals, white-splashed with waves, and then the Irish Sea.

And England.

Mother's birthplace, but an alien land to Rachel.

She reached into the pocket hidden deep within the folds of her brown kersey skirts. Her fingers closed around the muslin bag tied with a grosgrain ribbon to keep the contents intact—dried leaves of mint, pennyroyal, and gentian. Mother had pressed the sachet into Rachel's hand when they'd parted in Carlow, a final gift as Rachel had readied to climb onto the post chaise bound for Cork Harbor. Her mother's soft green eyes had brimmed with tears, tears she'd kept at bay to stop the twins, clinging to Mother's skirts, from crying. Poor Sarah and Ruth. Too young to understand what was happening. And Nathaniel, trying hard to be the man of the family, straight-backed and sober, but at fourteen not truly ready for the role.

Rachel clutched the bag. The mixture of herbs was meant to help Rachel should she feel faint or dizzy. If she had not fainted in a stifling Carlow courtroom with her fate in jeopardy, however, she would not faint now. Lifting it to her nostrils, she inhaled, the aroma pungent and sweet. Right then, she would rather the herbs had been dried heather from the knoll beyond their house, or the lavender her mother used to scent the linens. Or maybe snippings from the peppery scarlet nasturtiums that grew by the kitchen door. The aromatic bits of her life.

"Ho! Stop now!" A proper English gentleman, coat collar turned up to graze his whiskers, shouted at a scrum of boys quick to turn the quarter-deck into a play field. They shouted back a string of Gaelic curses and chased each other along the length of the planking.

"Don't let those hooligans bother you, miss," the man said.

"They do not bother me, sir. I have a brother who is just as high-spirited."

His gaze made a quick assessment of Rachel's status as a lady. He could not fail to note her serviceable dress, well-worn shawl, and Irish-red hair—and find her lacking. "Heading for England for work, I presume?"

"I have a situation with a physician in London." She shuddered anew at the thought. At the irony. After all she had been through, to find herself in service to a medical man.

"You do?" The gentleman's tone curled upward with a cynical lift.

Rachel lifted her chin. "I do."

"Hm." He cocked a disbelieving eyebrow and shook his head. "What next."

The man tapped the brim of his hat and hastened off, his attitude a foretaste of the reception Rachel expected she would receive in London.

The boys taunted him as they tossed the bundled rags they were using as a ball over his head. They brushed past Rachel, boisterous, laughing. Seemingly untroubled that the sliver of earth they had called home probably all their lives was inching out of reach.

Rachel faced the dwindling shoreline. *Then I should be untroubled like they are. For what good does it do me to mourn what I have lost?*

Rachel looked down at the bag she clutched and felt hope for the first time in weeks. Months, actually. Slowly she unwound the ribbon and tucked it in her pocket. Turning the bag upside down, she released the dried leaves, flecks of slate-green caught by the wind. She dropped the bag after them.

"I have your strength, Mother. I do not need herbal remedies when your love bolsters my spine." Rachel watched the speck of cream fabric until it was dragged underwater by the churn of the float-boards. "I shall do very well in London, and someday we shall be reunited. I promise you that."

Because to do anything less was to fail, and she never wanted to fail again.

CHAPTER 2

London, three days later

"Well, Edmunds?" asked Hathaway, leaning across the bed to prop up his patient, too weak, too faint to sit up on her own.

Resting his ear against the circular ivory ear plate, James Edmunds moved the stethoscope down the woman's hunched back. Her breathing was shallow, rapid, and he could hear the thickness in her lungs. No sound in the low portion of the left lung at all, the tissue hepatized into a useless mass. Or much of the right lung, for that matter. She wheezed as she struggled to drag in air and expelled a shuddering cough. Acute pneumonia.

Death.

"Well, Dr. Edmunds?" echoed Mr. Bolton from the spot he'd taken up by the window. The family's surgeon tapped his fingers against his elbows. "Are you finished with that contraption?"

"It's a stethoscope, not a contraption."

"It's a bit of wood tubing and a bunch of poppycock, is what it is."

"What color has her sputum been?" James asked Hatha-way, ignoring Mr. Bolton's ridicule.

"When it comes up at all, it's rusty."

Blood. No surprise.

James set aside the stethoscope and released the woman's linen shift, the color of the material not much different than the gray pallor of her flesh. With Hathaway's steady help, he lowered her onto the stack of thick feather pillows. A relation—aunt? cousin?—sobbed quietly in the corner of the bedchamber. There would be more tears to come.

Separating the cedar stethoscope into its three pieces, James nestled them in their velvet-padded box and closed the lid. He caught Hathaway's watchful gaze and shook his head.

"*No,*" his young colleague mouthed, face falling.

"Can I get back to my leeches, Dr. Edmunds?" Mr. Bolton asked impatiently. The creatures squirmed in their bottles near his feet. "The only cure for her condition. Draw out the congestion in her lungs."

"You've had them on her since yesterday." The inverted-Y bite marks were still evident on her back. "If they haven't worked by now . . ." James wouldn't finish that sentence.

He swept back the woman's hair, a blonde the honeyed color of demerara sugar, her cheeks flushed from the fever that was burning her alive. He recalled seeing her at some social function long ago, in a teal silk gown with her hair dressed in pearls and feathers, smiling, charming everyone. Even Mariah had commented on her poise and her beauty. All of that lost, now.

In her half-conscious state, she muttered incoherently, drawing her relative to the bedside, who soothed, "Hush, my dear."

The older woman looked around the edge of her lace-trimmed cap at James. He saw the question form on her face, the one he had been expecting. The eight years he had spent doctoring hadn't taught him how to respond with cool indifference, like his father had always done. Instead, James only felt disheartened, the loss another chink out of his armor of confidence.

Soon, though, very soon, he would never have to face that question again.

"Doctor?" The relation's eyes, puffy and red-rimmed, begged him for a hopeful answer.

"I must consult with Dr. Hathaway, ma'am. He is her physician and will speak with you in a few minutes." James pressed her hand, the only reassurance he could offer, and stood, setting the stethoscope box inside his medical bag. "No more leeches, Mr. Bolton. If you agree, Dr. Hathaway."

"Whatever you say," Hathaway concurred.

"What?" The surgeon scoffed, drawing himself up to his not-insignificant height. "What am I doing here if you two are not going to listen to me?"

James snapped the medical bag closed and leveled an even gaze at the man. "I am sure I don't know, Mr. Bolton."

Nodding a good-bye, he left the bedchamber before the surgeon could compose a retort. Hathaway strode out behind James and shut the door.

"So the situation is bad," said Hathaway.

"Let's walk over there, away from the door." James inclined his head toward the far end of the hall, steeped in dark and a quiet so profound it was as if the entire house held its breath in anticipation of James's verdict. "It's definitely advanced pneumonia. She might only have another day."

"Dash . . . But I did everything I could think of." Hathaway scrubbed his tired hands through his hair. "She has two small children, you know, and she's only four-and-twenty. My age."

Cold tension spasmed along James's neck. Four-and-twenty had been Mariah's age as well. He pushed the memories back before they could rise, ugly like distorted fungi in a damp, dark corner. The memories of his ultimate failure.

"Edmunds, you all right?" Hathaway asked. "You've turned a funny shade."

"I'm fine." James waved away the query, letting the cool hush of the hallway still the tumult in his soul. Hard to believe more than three years had passed and the shock—and guilt—could still strangle. "No need to worry about me. Concentrate on your patient. She needs your full attention."

"I don't like to admit this, but I'm at a loss what to do next. Nothing, I suppose."

"All you can do is provide some comfort. A scruple of niter for the fever, keep her cool and quiet, laudanum for the pain." He glanced over at the door. "And get Bolton out of there. She can't handle any more blood loss."

Hathaway nodded briskly. "I just wish I had your fortitude, Edmunds. I've never lost a patient before, you know? I don't know what to do."

James felt his gut clench. He had precious little advice to offer. *Show a bold front, lad.* His father's favorite words. "Pray."

"Easy for you to say."

"Not really." James started down the carpeted stairs, his coattails slapping against his medical bag in his haste to depart. "Do you have an attendant to sit with her? That might provide you some relief and let you clear your thoughts."

"I've been so busy lately, I haven't had the time to hire one."

James glanced over his shoulder at his colleague. He remembered when he'd been like Hathaway—young, fresh, throwing life aside to plunge into medicine headlong and heedless. After eight years, though, that eagerness was already burned out of him. "I would stay to help you, but I've a woman coming from Ireland any minute now, and I have to get back home and see her settled."

"You've decided to hire a replacement attendant?" They rounded the landing, Hathaway hurrying to keep up. "I thought you were quitting your practice and leaving London, heading at last for your little farm in Essex."

"I am looking for someone to fill in for Miss Guimond for the next month, but this Irish woman isn't a nurse. I've hired her for what is only a temporary situation. A favor for a family friend." James descended the final steps. "It doesn't mean I have changed my mind about giving up medicine."

Hathaway uttered a sound halfway between a laugh and a grunt. "Which I still cannot believe."

At times, neither could James.

They reached the entry hall, and Hathaway shook James's hand. "Thanks for helping me here and good luck to you. You're a good man and will be hard to replace."

A good man. Am I? "You think too highly of me, Hathaway."

James bade the other man farewell, and Hathaway headed back upstairs to deliver his bad news. The maid, waiting by the open front door, held out James's hat and gloves along with his discreetly bundled fee. A young child hid behind her skirts; James could see a tiny hand clutching the edge of the maid's apron.

"Here you are, sir," she said to James. She twisted to pat the child on the head. "Come now, little miss. Stop hiding behind my skirts there. The doctor here's been to see your mum. She'll be up and about soon enough."

The child shuffled out from hiding. She smiled shyly, a lass three or four years of age, her eyes, her hair . . . James's chest constricted. The child was so like Amelia—nearly the same size, the same golden curls, blue eyes. In a day or so, the girl would be motherless too. Just like his daughter.

An impulse opened James's mouth to say hello, but he couldn't get the word to come out. Not when he could hardly breathe. Pulse tripping, he nodded to the girl and made a hasty escape.

A good man.

Dearest Lord. Help me believe it's still true.

⚘ ⚘

"Here we are, dearie." Mrs. O'Rourke brandished a hand in the air above the steamer's railing, the *thunk* of the gangway upon the stone pier nearly drowning out her words. "Londontown."

Rachel stared at the masses of people churning on the wharf like chickens fighting over a fresh throw of feed. "Oh my heavens."

"Truer words were never spoken," concurred Mrs. O'Rourke.

They had steamed up the Thames for several hours, the city approaching like an advancing storm cloud. Buildings pressed against the riverbanks in such quantity they blocked out the view of the alleyways beyond, so thick Rachel could imagine their steamer was chugging through a tunnel of brick and stone. A tunnel jammed with drifting barges and scuttling wherries and blackened colliers, thick as fallen branches choking a weir.

And now this.

St. Katherine's Docks were the greatest collection of buildings and masted ships Rachel had ever seen in her life. Ever dreamed she would see. She'd tried to count the boats, tucked so tightly against each other it seemed a man could jump from one deck to the next without fear of getting wet, and lost track after two hundred and forty. At the water's edge, yellow brick warehouses six stories high surrounded the basin, bristling with pulleys at open windows, bales and barrels and wine casks stacked to the vaulted ceilings. Men and boys clambered everywhere, thousands of them. They scrabbled for space between loaded carts and wagons, crates of chickens waiting to be loaded onto the next boat out, sacks of flour and coffee. Deafening shouts bested the rattle of boat chains and the squeals of pigs being toted off ships, the clang of ships' bells and a band on a foreign steamer heartily blowing unfamiliar tunes. All of it a noisy sea of flesh and commerce writhing beneath a hazy, reeking, smoke-heavy sky.

And not a blade of grass or patch of heather to relieve the oppression.

"It is not like home, is it?" asked Rachel, her heart hammering. *London will completely consume me.* But wasn't that what she wanted it to do? Let it hide her from her past?

"Nothing is like home." Mrs. O'Rourke sniffled, wiping a coarse woolen sleeve beneath her nose. "*Arra,* you'll make me cry, you will. And here I've held it back all this while."

"I am sorry. I did not mean to upset you." Rachel tucked

her carpetbag with its cracking leather handles against her hip and took her companion's arm. "Shall we go?"

Mrs. O'Rourke nodded. "'Tis nothing else for it."

Stiff-legged from three days spent in the cramped confines of steerage, they pushed their way into the throng tramping down the gangway and onto the teeming wharf. A dockworker knocked against Rachel and continued up the plank to become part of the stream of people moving on and off the steamer. If they didn't move speedily, they would either be run over or shoved into the oil-slicked water like so much garbage.

Mrs. O'Rourke found her bearings and Rachel followed the other woman in single file, their destination a set of rooms for departing and arriving passengers.

"Ho!" Mrs. O'Rourke cried out before they reached the dubious security of the grimy-windowed space carved out of a corner building. "Look then! Me sister sent her eldest to meet me, and there he is now, to be sure."

She made to move off toward a young man waving frantically over the heads of a hundred others.

Rachel grabbed Mrs. O'Rourke's elbow. "Are you not going to wait with me?"

"See all the guards? There be nothing to be affrighted of."

"I own I think there is."

"You'll be fine, Rachel. 'Tis a fearsome city, it is, but God watches over the least of His sparrows, does He not?" She patted Rachel on the cheek with dry fingertips. "*Rath Dé ort*, lass. You've had a stroke of bad luck, you have, but the good Lord will see you through."

"Right now, Mrs. O'Rourke, I simply wish He would help me find my employer's carriage."

"Ask for Dr. Edmunds in the passengers' office. And know I'll be prayin' for you." Mrs. O'Rourke hoisted her bag and melted into the crowd, her rust-red cloak soon swallowed up by all the bodies.

Snatching up her carpetbag, Rachel elbowed a path toward the passenger area and the waiting lines of wagons and carriages. She wished she still believed she could say a prayer that might calm her fears. Rachel pulled in a breath, sucking in the stench of sweating bodies and rotting fish, rather than courage. *I will be strong, Mother.*

For what else had she left?

"Now then, are you in need of lodgin', miss?"

The man's voice at her side startled her. "What?"

Dressed in a worn frock coat, the original shade of which was long lost to the jumble of fantastically colored bits of cloth sewn on elbows and cuffs and pockets, the man was squat, smelly, and leaning far too close. "I asked if you are needin' a lodgin'. Off the steamer from Ireland, are you?" he asked, his soft Irish lilt tugging at her already homesick heart as much as the sight of his *caubeen* tilted sideways on his head.

"Yes, but someone is meeting me here."

"You're certain, now? 'Tis a good lodgin' house, so it is. For the lasses, no more than six to a room." He gripped her sleeve. "And there's none of the fever or the cholera in me house. Not like the other places."

Cholera? "I am most certain I do not require lodging. Please, now, let go of my arm."

"Might be no other offers, you know. Lodgin' hard to come by."

"Let go. Now." She jerked her arm free of his grasp.

"Think you're too good, do you?" He muttered a curse and turned to another woman standing nearby. She must have come off the boat, too, though Rachel didn't recognize her. She looked barely past eighteen, yet she had two children with her, one clinging to her threadbare shift, the other cradled in her arms.

"Now, ma'am, you look in need of lodgin', you do," the man declared.

"That I am," the woman said, her voice barely audible above the noise on the wharf. Her face carried the marks of hard work and poverty, lines and freckles and dirt drawing a map of her desperation.

Rachel knew she should move away. This woman and her children were none of her concern. Then the smallest child coughed, her tattered woven blanket falling away from her head. Dark eyes peered out of a tiny face, glossy and fever-bright. Eyes so like Mary Ferguson's . . .

Rachel lurched as the pain and the anger and the guilt hit her again. She stumbled into the crowd, pushed her way through, her carpetbag banging into people, drawing shouts of "Watch where you're going!" and "Lousy Irish." She didn't care.

At last she broke through the stifling worst of it and reached the passenger arrival area. She found a spot in the queue and shuffled along with the rest until she reached a counter and a harried clerk.

His glance was brisk and disparaging. "Arriving or departing?"

"Arriving. Has Dr. Edmunds checked on the arrival of Miss Dunne off the *Somerville*?"

"No. Next!"

The man behind her attempted to muscle forward, trodding on Rachel's boot. "Then how am I to find him? There are hundreds of people out there."

The clerk frowned through his spectacles. "Next!"

Dejected, Rachel marched back outside the office and looked around. Not twenty yards off, a lad with a tattered cap peered down from a gig, the vehicle's wheels painted an eye-catching vermilion. His gaze danced over her face then scanned the dockside again. She wasn't who he sought.

Setting down the carpetbag, she waited. Carriages, carts pulled up, wheeled off. The crowds thinned, leaving Rachel quite conspicuously alone. Had Dr. Edmunds been confused as to the date of her arrival? Was she going to have to take lodging with that horrid man still plying the wharf?

As if he could read her thoughts, the lodging fellow looked her way, his thick eyebrows waggling, an open invitation to take him up on his offer. She glared back. She would rather sleep on the docks than go with him. *Though how stupid and dangerous would that be, Rachel Dunne?* Such a course of action wouldn't be wise even in Carlow.

Rachel turned her back to him and searched her surroundings again. The lad and the carriage were gone, his passenger collected, she assumed. To make matters worse, another boat had come in, disgorging more new arrivals who crowded the dock with their baggage and bodies, jostling her like she was invisible. If she could, she would hire a cart to take her to Dr. Edmunds's, but she hadn't the funds. At some point, he would have to come for her.

She hoped.

CHAPTER 3

*O*wing to the solid instincts of his mare, James arrived at his street without incident. If reaching his destination had been solely up to him, he might have found himself in Marylebone or Whitechapel, rather than Belgravia. His mind had kept reexamining the sight of a small child in a dying woman's house, had prodded the reflection like a scab that wouldn't heal, drinking in the guilt that accompanied the reflections until his self-reproach made him nauseous.

His mare trotted past the gleaming white-stuccoed terraces, the houses' matched windows and iron railings and porticos so prim and orderly. A thousand secrets might lie behind those sparkling panes of glass, those crisp courses of painted brick. A thousand regrets as corrosive as the one that ate at him.

One day soon he would be reunited with Amelia, would face down that regret. But not today.

James hopped down from his horse, and—characteristic of the smooth operation that had been in place ever since

Mariah had put her indelible mark upon the house—the green front door swung open just as his boots hit the first step leading up to it. His house-maid curtsied as he entered the entry hall, the space with its cut-glass bell lantern, Turkish runners, and polished marble floor just a foretaste of the elegance that lay throughout. More marks left by Mariah. Endless reminders of her. How she had loved this house.

He would not miss it.

"Any patients call while I was out, Molly?" he asked the maid, peeling off his gloves.

"No, sir. But Mrs. Woodbridge is waiting for you in your library. The sweeps are cleaning the drawing-room chimney or else I'd have taken her there, sir."

Sophia. What did she want? "Tell Joe to take my horse around to the mews for me."

A flicker of some emotion—disapproval, James thought—crossed Molly's hazel eyes. "He's not back with Miss Dunne yet, sir."

"Maybe the boat was late arriving." Molly gathered his gloves and hat. "In that case, see that Peg takes my horse around to the mews and bring some tea to the library. I've no doubt my sister-in-law will want some."

He headed up the stairs to the rear first-floor room he'd converted to a library. Seated in the armchair by the fireplace, Sophia's spine was wilting, which meant she had been waiting longer than she liked. Her bombazine skirts imparted a crisp and reprimanding rustle as she shifted to face him.

"To what do I owe the pleasure of a visit, Sophia?" He went to kiss her on the cheek. The muted scent of lavender rose from her clothes. She might be in extended mourning for her husband, gone two and a half years now, but she would never give up her love of sachets and sweet-smelling toilet water. Her only frivolity.

"Can I not simply wish to visit my brother-in-law?"

"Usually not without a good reason."

Ginger-colored eyebrows arched over eyes as dark and piercing as a hawk's. "I believe, James, you have become an unfortunate cynic."

"My apologies for the curt greeting, Sophia. I was assisting a colleague with a case and it's left me in poor humor."

Skirting the mahogany desk dominating the room, James sat in the burgundy leather chair, felt it close around him like a well-worn glove. He let his gaze wander around the library. His *sanctum sanctorum*, as one friend jokingly referred to it. A space for escape, all muted somber tones and funereal quiet. Here he could read by candlelight the books with gilded bindings climbing the walnut bookshelves, smoke the occasional cigar, sit by the fire and think.

Or not think.

Molly returned with the tea and deposited the oval silver tray on the parquetry table at Sophia's knee.

"Everything is well with Amelia, I presume?" he inquired politely, guilt looming but held at bay. "Over her croup?"

"She recovered from that ages ago," Sophia chided. "Surely you remember me telling you."

"Surely."

"She sends her love, by the by," Sophia said, as she always did.

One day he would ask her if Amelia really had. "Send mine in return."

"I shall," Sophia said, dispensing the hot water into the

painted china cups that had been a wedding present to James and Mariah. Endless reminders.

"So Amelia is well and happy?" he asked.

"As ever. Such an obedient and tranquil child. Just like Mariah." She beamed, proud as any mother. Raising Amelia was a solace to Sophia, a surrogate for her lost beloved sister and a replacement for the children Sophia never had on her own. She was a better parent than James could ever hope to be.

More than three years ago, at the side of a deathbed, he had made the right decision. Sophia's contented smile assured him yet again.

Molly quit the room and Sophia brought James a cup of tea. "I did come here on a particular mission. I was sent to invite you to a boating excursion. Miss Castleton has requested your presence."

"Since when did you become Miss Castleton's messenger? I didn't know you were particular friends."

"It's true, we are not." The sniff that emanated from Sophia carried a wealth of meaning he'd long ago learned to interpret—the superiority of her own breeding, disdain for Miss Castleton's, boredom that she had to repeat her opinion one more time. "I do not dislike her, but I can only object to her unladylike persistence. She desperately hopes you will ask to marry her."

James frowned. Louisa Castleton, sister to his good friend Thaddeus, young and pretty and full of schemes, had settled her hopes on him. She would be better served bending her energies toward wishing for the stars or hoping a lord might ask for her hand.

"I'm aware of her goal, Sophia," he said.

"That may be, but have you made it clear to her you cannot possibly be interested?" Her teaspoon clinked irritably against the edge of her cup.

"Thaddeus would love to see us wed." He'd said as much a dozen times or more.

"And what else would your friend, the esteemed Dr. Castleton, think? To be sure, Miss Castleton is a fine, churchgoing woman and not unpleasant to look at. But honestly, James . . ." Here she paused, readying for the volley that always came next. "She would never make a good mother for Amelia. She is not fit to hold a candle to the memory of my dear, dear Mariah."

James clenched his jaw against the bitterness, tired of Sophia's reminders that she—and his father—had thought Mariah the most perfect woman in the world.

Do you love me, James?" Mariah's pleading words echoed in his memory.

"You needn't fear my marrying Miss Castleton, Sophia," he said, working his jaw loose. "I have no intention of taking another wife. I promise you that."

Her smile was small, tight, swift as the dart of a kingfisher plunging. Concerns relieved. "I merely expect that someday you might change your mind. Provide a mother's guiding hand to little Amelia."

"She has you. What more could I want for my daughter?"

"You do truly mean that, don't you? I often wonder . . ."

"Sophia, you stepped in when I needed someone most. You know I'm grateful to you."

"I try my best, for Mariah's sake." Sophia rearranged her skirts around her like a bird fluffing its fine plumage. "So I should tell Miss Castleton that you send your regrets?"

"Even if I wished to go boating, I'm far too busy preparing for our move to Finchingfield. I haven't the time for pleasure excursions."

"Poor creature shall just have to be disappointed," she said. "But we all have our crosses to bear, don't we?"

Knuckles rapped on the library door, and Molly stuck her head through the opening. "Sir, I'm ever so sorry for disturbing you, but there's been a problem with Miss Dunne. It seems, well, it seems Joe couldn't find her at the docks."

James struck a knee against the desk in his haste to stand. A jolt of pain shot through his leg, making him flinch. The day was going from bad to worse. "What do you mean, he couldn't find her?"

Behind Molly, Joe shuffled his feet and twisted his scruffy wool cap in his hands as if he hoped to strangle it. "Sorry, sir, but there weren't an older Irish lady come off the boat. Well, there were one, but she 'ad a ride an' all and didn't 'ave reddish hair. Our Miss Dunne's gone missin'."

"James, what is this?" Sophia's attention perked like a hound on the scent.

"The worst," he replied. "It seems the woman I've hired to assist in packing the library and office has gotten lost."

"You've brought a woman from Ireland to help with your collections?" she asked, her voice rising, latching onto the piece of information that troubled her most. The possibility Miss Dunne had drowned in the Irish Sea or been accosted off the boat didn't concern her.

"I have tried to bring a woman from Ireland to help, yes."

Sophia swept her arm to point at the bookshelves. "But these books are valuable. They're to pass to Amelia, and I've been told some have been in your family for generations. How do you know this Irish creature won't steal some and sell them for profit?"

"It's not as if she is some St. Giles street urchin," he said impatiently, rubbing at his throbbing knee. "She is Miss Harwood's cousin. You remember her, don't you? Mariah's good friend."

"Yes, I remember, James." Sophia huffed. "However, I do not find you hiring a relation of Miss Harwood a comforting thought. The Harwoods may be wealthy and influential, but Claire Harwood herself . . . a reprehensibly immoderate do-gooder."

"Joe, bring the gig out again," he directed, turning away from Sophia's pique. "I'll go back to the docks with you to search for Miss Dunne." Molly lurked near the doorway, a half smile on her face, apparently relishing the clash over the new arrival who hadn't arrived. "And you may return to whatever you were doing, Molly."

They both hustled off. James left the library and started down the stairs toward the back of the house, Sophia on his heels.

"You did not send this Miss Dunne the money for passage, did you?" asked Sophia. "If you did, she's probably made off with it and never got on the boat at all."

Such a typical comment; Sophia always thought the worst of everyone. "I didn't send her money. Miss Dunne paid her own way."

"Even so, she hardly sounds competent. Getting lost when she has just arrived. You should just leave her at the docks. Or suggest to Miss Harwood she go and retrieve her cousin. Isn't that what family is for?"

James gripped the finial at the first-floor landing and propelled himself down the stairs. Sophia's thin-soled shoes slapped against the treads behind.

"I am responsible for her, Sophia, and I won't just leave her at the docks."

"There are plenty of perfectly fine English girls you could have hired."

Abruptly James stopped, Sophia nearly skidding into him. "None with the skills Miss Harwood assures me her cousin possesses. Miss Dunne required a position, and I have one. It was a serendipitous solution for the both of us, and I'll not pass it up."

Her eyes narrowed. "Mariah always said you were too trusting. A strange Irish girl whom her London relatives have foisted upon you. Bah."

"They haven't 'foisted' her. Miss Dunne is only half-Irish, and she isn't a girl. She's an aging spinster. Even more harmless." James turned and marched down the hallway.

"I refuse to be swayed by your arguments. The Irish are dangerous, young and old. I cannot believe you would let her into your house."

They swept through the back door, crossed the garden. He shot a glance at Sophia, struggling to keep up. "Are you intending on accompanying me to the docks to search for Miss Dunne?"

"I rather think not!"

"Then I must say good day to you."

He entered the mews, leaving his sister-in-law to frown after him.

Traffic in the city was as miserable as ever. He might be grateful that the rain promised by the sky all day hadn't come to pass, but James was too distracted to acknowledge that bit of God's benevolence.

After an hour's drive, Joe pulled the gig to a halt at St. Katherine's Docks. James searched the crowd pushing and shoving past the crates of living—and some not-so-living—animals, the barrels of goods, the sweating wharf laborers and porters. What a wretched sea of humanity, many of them looking as if they'd swum to London rather than come on a boat, they were so bedraggled and salt-crusted. To be lost among this horde . . . disquiet buzzed along his nerves like a relentless wasp. Had Miss Dunne failed to get on the packet from Ireland or fallen overboard during the journey? Or had she been lured away when she arrived, another victim of the criminal element that plagued the city?

"Cor, sir, she's still 'ere," said Joe.

"Who? Who's still here?"

Joe jerked his chin to the right. "That a one. In the dingy brown dress snoozin' on the carpetbag. She were 'ere before. But she's no old lady."

He spotted the woman Joe was pointing out. "Shall I ask if she's Miss Dunne, Joe?" he asked, only partly serious.

Joe shrugged. "Can't 'urt, I s'pose."

"No, it can't hurt."

James climbed down and went up to the woman, dozing on the bag she'd sat upon, her back propped against a crate. Young woman, he corrected himself. She couldn't be past twenty years of age. She was pretty, too, with coppery hair that peeked out from the edge of her plain straw bonnet and fine features, even if those features could use a good scrub.

This couldn't possibly be Miss Harwood's relation. He could have sworn she'd said her cousin was older, explaining her extensive experience and utter dependability. She had made Miss Dunne sound so sober he'd expected she would look like his old nurse, wrinkled and smelling of burnt milk. He would never have expected Miss Harwood might mislead him.

Unceremoniously, James prodded the young woman's foot with the toe of his boot. "Miss Dunne?"

She didn't respond.

A squat fellow in wildly colored patched clothing sidled up. "I'd leave that piece alone were I you, guvn'r. She'll bite your head off, sure she will."

"I think I can handle her."

Out of the corner of his eye, James saw that the man had shuffled off. He bent down, nearer Miss Dunne. *Bite his head off, would she, this petite thing?*

"Miss Dunne," he repeated, more loudly.

Her body jerked, and her eyes flew open. Eyes that were the most extraordinary color—blue-green, like deep water—and unafraid of looking him in the face. She scrambled to sit upright.

"Who are you?" she asked suspiciously, pressing her back to the crate. "What do you want?"

"Don't be alarmed. I mean you no harm."

"As you say," she replied, skeptical, caution keeping her pinned to her spot, courage lifting her chin. "But excuse me if I do not believe you."

"You can trust me. Take my hand. I'll help you up."

He clasped her hand, small and fragile within his, and gazed reassuringly into her eyes. Suddenly he felt a connection that was startling in its intensity, utterly unexpected, a flash like a spark being thrown from a fire. He felt a pull like an anchor thrown from a ship, sucking him right down into the watery depths of her eyes.

What in heaven's name was happening?

There was only one explanation.

He had lost his mind.

CHAPTER 4

he man bending over Rachel released her hand so quickly she nearly fell back upon the stack of crates.

"I . . . I . . ." he stuttered, the confusion that flashed across his face turning into a scowl. "I beg your pardon. It was forward of me to clutch your hand so familiarly."

"Then perhaps you should not have done so," Rachel retorted sharply. She didn't care if she was rude. She was angry she had fallen asleep, leaving herself vulnerable. And now some stranger—a gentleman, she corrected, based on the cut of his graphite-colored superfine wool coat and the sound of his voice—had accosted her. "What do you want with me?"

He answered with a question. "You are Miss Dunne, aren't you?"

"Yes, I am. And you have the advantage, because I do not know who you are."

"No, you don't." He frowned deeper, the muscles flexing along his jaw. The expression marred the handsomeness of his face, cast a shadow over his eyes, gray as the stones of the Brownshill Dolmen, and just as hard. "I am your employer."

"Oh." Her cheeks flared. Not precisely the gracious first meeting she might have hoped for. "Of course, I should have thought so straightaway."

"Joe," he glanced over his shoulder, "this is she, it appears."

Just then she noticed the boy standing to one side, the one he called Joe. It was the lad from the gig who'd been at the docks earlier.

Joe whistled between the gap in his front teeth. "Cor, sir, she ain't no agin' spinster lady."

"No, Joe, she isn't. And please don't say 'cor.' Miss Dunne, I am Dr. Edmunds." He offered a perfunctory bow of his head. "This here is Joe."

"Good day to ya, miss," said Joe, a friendly grin tilting his mouth. "Glad to see ya made it safe, after all. We was wonderin' where you'd got to. Didn' figure you 'ad any money to run off, though—"

"That's quite enough, Joe." Dr. Edmunds's gaze made a quick assessment of her carpetbag. "Do you have any other luggage?"

"No, this is all I have," she replied defensively.

"Just as well," he answered, and signaled for the lad to take her pitiful lone bag. "There's not much room in the gig."

He began striding toward the carriage at such a rapid pace that Rachel imagined anyone observing them would conclude he was attempting to evade her.

"If I may, I have a question, Dr. Edmunds," Rachel said, clutching at her skirts as she struggled to keep up. "Your lad there seems to think I was supposed to be an aging spinster. Was there some confusion over my age?"

His eyes grew even stonier, if such a thing were possible. "Yes, there was. I was expecting someone nearer forty, which is why Joe didn't recognize you initially."

"I see." The confusion explained the scowl. "You do not think that my cousin and I intentionally misled you about my age, do you?"

"Should I?"

"Of course not. I would never . . ." *lie to you?* But wouldn't she, when she planned to never admit to him the most critical detail of her life? "I did not ask her to give you the impression I was anything other than twenty years old."

"I'm glad to hear it."

"I trust my youth will not be a problem."

"That depends on you, Miss Dunne," he answered, stopping to look at her as they reached the gig. "If you do good work, then there is no problem at all."

"I will work very hard, Dr. Edmunds." So long as he did not ask her to sit with his patients, as Claire had assured her in the letters she had sent to Mother, all would be well. She could never sit with a sick person again. She had made a vow to herself never to fail again, and attending the ill would only result in failure. "You will have no complaints about me."

"As I expect of any of my staff," he said tersely, conversation concluded, and climbed into the gig.

Joe easily hoisted her carpetbag onto the back of the vehicle. It was pathetically light, holding only another gown, a thin cloak, some undergarments, and a few items to dress her hair. She had left her Bible at home, sitting atop her chest of drawers. If God had forgotten her in her time of crisis, she'd reasoned, there was no need to remember Him.

Once she settled in the gig, Dr. Edmunds grabbed the reins and steered them away from the docks, Joe clinging like a boy-sized spider to the rear of the vehicle. They journeyed up one street and down the next, past warehouses and bustling markets overflowing with vendors. Church towers pierced the sky like so many upraised arms reaching for God. Officious buildings with grand columned entryways fought for space. And all the people—the clamor and the commotion—were stifling, making Rachel long for air and open sky. There would be no more of that here, though, where any glimpse of green seemed unlikely, where any hope for the sound of a warbler's trill would be muffled by the impossible din, and the warm smells of a neighbor's oven would be drowned in the cloying stench of sewer.

She must have shuddered, because Dr. Edmunds glanced her way. "Overwhelmed, Miss Dunne?" He almost sounded sympathetic.

"It is quite different from home."

"But there is some beauty here, beneath the filth. Many magnificent buildings that are the glory of England. Such as that one." He nodded toward a building with a great dome rising. "That is St. Paul's. I've been promising my staff I would take them to services there, but I've not found the time. They've had to make do with our St. Peter's." He peered over at her. "By the way, I would expect you to attend church services with the rest of the staff."

Rachel could not bring herself to nod. God was not a part of her plans. "What are those buildings?" she asked, pointing to the right.

"They're the Old Bailey and Newgate Prison. There's

been a prison on that site since the time of Henry Planta-
genet. I've been told that when those doors close behind a
prisoner, the sound they make is like entering the realms of
hell. A very fearsome place."

Her skin prickled; she knew exactly how fearsome the interior of a prison could be. In considerable detail, she could
describe the smells and the chill and the ungodly noises, the
weeping and wailing. The other sounds people made while
they bade their time and avoided contemplating their fates.
She could tell the good doctor precisely what it was like
to face a bewigged judge, her hands gripping the rubbed-
smooth rail of the defendant's dock, the sounding board
overhead echoing every tremor in her voice as she pleaded to
be believed. Even as she had stopped believing in herself.

Heavy traffic forced the gig to halt, and Rachel felt Dr.
Edmunds watching her. Did he see the guilt on her person, like the mark they used to put upon thieves' hands?
Here sits an accused murderer. Someone he might not want
within a hundred miles of his patients, let alone living in
his very house. The irony . . .

With all the courage she possessed, Rachel returned his
gaze. *Look him in the eye.* He must not suspect she had any
secrets to hide. Her future depended upon him believing
her to be the most upright woman in the world.

"Being inside a prison must be very fearsome," Rachel
replied, grateful the shaking in her voice was just a tiny
echo of the shudder moving through her body, relieved
when the traffic cleared and they began moving again. "The
most dreadful experience imaginable."

The remainder of the trip to Dr. Edmunds's residence passed in awkward silence. Although it might have only been awkward for Rachel. Dr. Edmunds simply seemed irritated, his back as stiff as a hitching post, his grip strangling the reins.

He bounded out of the gig when it stopped in front of a terrace house, the iron railing surrounding its area perfectly black, the steps gleaming white, the brass door knocker shining in the dim sunlight sifting through the clouds. The house of a gentleman.

Joe offered his hand to help her down, giving a wink before handing her carpetbag to her. "Welcome to the 'ouse of the esteemed Dr. James Edmunds. Beware what lies within."

"What do you mean?"

"You'll see, miss."

Two women waited in the entry hall. The younger one, dressed in a black frock topped with a crisp apron, was obviously the maid. The other, imperious in widow's weeds, scrutinized Rachel like she was a blot on the carpet.

"Sophia, I'm surprised you're still here," Dr. Edmunds said to the widow.

"I wished to see your aging Irish spinster, James. Who actually looks to be a young woman. A very dirty young woman. Are you certain you've got the right one?"

Rachel flushed.

Dr. Edmunds cast Rachel a quick glance. She thought she saw an apology in it. "Sophia, this is Miss Dunne. Miss Dunne, this is my sister-in-law, Mrs. Woodbridge."

Rachel bobbed her head. "I am pleased to make your acquaintance, Mrs. Woodbridge."

"Yes," replied his sister-in-law, refusing to return the courtesy to a mere employee.

"Molly, show Miss Dunne to her room," Dr. Edmunds instructed the one Rachel had decided was a maid. "Miss Dunne, I presume you'd like to clean up and have something to eat. Probably rest, also. We'll meet in the morning to discuss your duties here. Seven o'clock sharp in the library. Molly or Peg can tell you where that is."

"Yes, Dr. Edmunds," she said, nodding. Food, rest would be heavenly. Getting away from Mrs. Woodbridge's disapproving stare would be even better.

Rachel followed the maid up the stairs, carpetbag gripped in her hand. Mrs. Woodbridge watched her depart, her gaze boring a hole in Rachel's back.

"You're not going to keep her, are you, James?" Mrs. Woodbridge asked, her voice carrying clearly, making Rachel sound like a stray mongrel Dr. Edmunds had picked up. "Her cousin obviously misled you about her worth. For a reason, I would warrant, that is not to the girl's credit."

Rachel couldn't hear Dr. Edmunds's response, though Molly's concurring harrumph was more than sufficiently loud.

Cheeks flaring, Rachel gripped her carpetbag more firmly and climbed behind the maid. It appeared she would find no friends in this household. Well, she would only be there for a month at most, according to Claire's note. She could make do.

"How long have you been in service to Dr. Edmunds, Molly?" Rachel asked, trying to be friendly.

"Almost three years," Molly answered brusquely, her voice bouncing off the staircase paneling, snowy white as the flowers of a guelder rose. Her tone was just as frosty.

They reached the third-floor landing with its low ceiling. Molly threw open the nearest door. "Here is your room. Next to Peg and me."

The maid stepped aside and Rachel entered. The space was tiny, hardly bigger than a privy, and spare of decoration save an old multicolored carpet cut down to fit the space and a creamware ewer and basin on a stand adjacent a chest of drawers. Beneath a dormer window, a narrow bed clung to the faded pink wall. Rachel dropped her carpetbag next to the door. The room was clean and private. She should not expect anything more.

"Dinner is in a half hour," said Molly. "I guess you're to eat with us tonight. Don't know about what's to happen after. Best not be late. Mrs. Mainprice won't wait for you."

"I will not be late. Thank you, Molly."

Molly tossed her head and strode out, skirts swirling.

Rachel cast a longing look at the bed. How she wanted to drop onto the thin, rose-colored counterpane and rest. She had hardly slept on the cramped ship and weariness ached in her bones. But dinner was only thirty minutes away, and she needed to wash up and brush the stains from her gown. The staff's attitude would not improve if she continued to look like she had been sleeping in a gutter somewhere.

After carefully hanging her straw bonnet on a wall hook and putting her meager things in the chest, she changed into her green-trimmed dress and washed as well as she could. She found the back stairs and started down them. Voices ricocheted up the narrow stairwell and reached her ears. Rachel slowed her steps. They were talking about her.

"You should've seen the master's face when he came back with her. He wasn't happy to have had to go fetch her. I could see his blood was up across the room!" Unmistakably Molly's voice.

"Naw! Say yer foolin'." The voice of another girl. Peg, perhaps. She followed her declaration by a whinnying giggle.

"I say, what do you expect from some Irish girl? They're all the same," Molly declared. "Can't even figure out how to properly arrive at their place of employment."

"Molly, cease your tongue." An older-sounding woman this time, with a deep and commanding voice. "Miss Dunne is not some 'Irish girl.' From what I've heard, her father was a respectable shop owner and her mother is as English as you or I. And her cousins are the Harwoods."

"Her mother might be English, but her hair's as red as any Irishman's!"

"As though that proves something. I've had quite enough of this talk. It is most unchristian of you, and poor Miss Dunne is your better."

"My better?" Molly scoffed. Rachel's heart plummeted. They would be enemies for certain. "She doesn't know her place, I say, Mrs. Mainprice. Didn't even curtsy to Mrs. Woodbridge, like would be proper. And she and Miss Harwood lied about her age. Joe was told he'd be meeting an old spinster lady, not someone barely my age! Even the master didn't know." Molly paused. Maybe she leaned forward. Maybe she shook her finger to emphasize her point. "Why did they lie, I ask you? Trying to pretend she's something she's not, is what I think."

Rachel's pulse raced while she tried to convince her arm

to push open the kitchen door so she could deny that she and Claire had lied about anything.

"I think she's hiding something," Molly continued. "And I think Dr. Edmunds believes so too. I wouldn't be surprised if the master dismisses her at once. Cheeky bit."

"He'll do no such thing," stated Mrs. Mainprice. "We should welcome Miss Dunne and pray for her while she's with us, is what we should be doing. Not gossiping." A bowl or pot thudded onto a hard wood surface. "She'll be down here soon, and I expect you both to be respectful and nice. Dr. Edmunds deserves a peaceful household, not a gaggle of staff members who fight with each other. For shame."

"He shouldn't have brought her, is all I'm saying." Molly wasn't finished arguing. "We could've helped him properly without anyone else's help. Even with Miss Guimond gone, we could've taken care of everything ourselves."

"Aye. I'm with Molly, Mrs. Mainprice," said the girl with the piercing giggle. "For all we know, she's like all the other Irish and'll rob the 'ouse while we sleep."

"Quiet, Peg. Don't be silly."

"Or worse. Mebbe she'll kill us!"

Stillness followed Peg's proclamation, while dread crept numbly along Rachel's arms.

She could run back to her room and hide—and hence, starve—or stride into the kitchen to face them. Inconveniently, her stomach rumbled. She had huddled on the stair long enough.

Rachel pushed through the half-open kitchen door and stepped into the lions' lair.

CHAPTER 5

*D*on' think it's the best news, sir," said Joe, standing in the doorway of James's office.

The tension in James's neck, which had pinched like a vise since Sophia's visit earlier that day, had no apparent chance of easing. He kneaded the knot with his fingertips. "No help from Dr. Harris, then?"

"Dunno for certain, sir. Can't right read," he answered with only the faintest hint of apology for his lack of education and handed over the message.

"I keep forgetting, Joe."

"S'all right, sir. No need for me to read an' all, I s'pose."

James opened the note and held it up to the light of the desk lamp. Not good news. Dr. Harris had no attendant to recommend and certainly couldn't spare his wife to assist. James crushed the letter in his hand. He had heard the same from every colleague he'd queried. He wasn't surprised by their responses, though. It had taken him months to find Miss Guimond, with her special training, and she had come all the way from France.

"You don't happen to know anything about tending to patients, do you?" James asked Joe. "It would only be for a short while."

"Me tendin' patients, sir?" Joe blinked. "No, sir. I mean, I can't even stand the sight of me own blood! One time I was passin' a bloke on the street who'd cu' his foot on a broken bit of pavemen' and I nearly lost me breakfas' right . . . I mean, no sir."

A colorful description that requires no further embellishment, James thought. Frankly, he might be able to do without a medical attendant. Already the number of patients he saw was diminishing. So long as there wasn't some sort of outbreak in town, he could handle the load on his own. It would still be best, though, to have someone to greet those patients who came to the house for consultations, someone with more refinement than Joe. Someone with courage and a calm manner.

Should I do this, Lord?

It seemed imprudent to entrust Miss Dunne with more responsibilities, especially with the welfare of his patients. She might turn out, as Sophia had uncharitably suggested, to be a liar. Or worse. But Miss Harwood had assured him she was well educated, and he could tell by her speech that was true. She also carried herself with a certain grace his patients would find reassuring, enough perhaps to overlook her obvious Irish heritage. Maybe it was time to take a risk or two. After all, she was already here, the proverbial bird in the hand . . .

Joe cleared his throat, reminding James of his presence.

"Joe, tell Miss Dunne I would like to see her in the dining room. In about fifteen minutes."

"Aye, sir," Joe replied, tugging the wayward shock of hair hanging across his forehead before hurrying off.

Rising from his chair, James swept the crumpled letter into the top desk drawer and closed it tight. He needed to dress for dinner. Miss Dunne would be there.

The kitchen was three times larger than the one in Rachel's home, so daunting it stopped her in her tracks. Mouth-watering smells assaulted—thyme and mustard and sizzling meat. Copper pots and pans, polished colanders and shiny utensils shimmered in the light from the massive fireplace. And silence, thick as cold porridge, filled every single corner. Seated at the oak table centered on the flags, Molly's face flared the red of a rowan berry. The gangly armed maidservant at her side—most likely Peg—dropped her fork onto her pewter plate with a clink. Her face, awkwardly narrow, turned just as pink as Molly's.

The lions had lost their roar. Rachel felt only a moment's fleeting victory. She knew she would pay for embarrassing them by barging in like this, catching them at their gossipy worst.

A stout woman bustled around the table when it became obvious no one else would budge. She took Rachel's hands in her own. They were rough but cool and strong. Thick, slate-colored hair was scraped away from her round face and held tight beneath a cap. Her eyes were warmly brown as a spaniel's and just as observant.

"Welcome, Miss Dunne. I am Mrs. Mainprice, the housekeeper and cook." She was the woman with the deep, rich voice. She smiled sincerely as she held onto Rachel's hands.

Rachel liked her immediately. "I am most pleased to meet you," she said to Mrs. Mainprice. "I am sorry if I am late for dinner. I hurried down as quickly as I could."

"You're not late at all. Who could expect you to be any earlier when you've just arrived all the way from Ireland this very afternoon?"

Rachel imagined Molly and Peg expected exactly such a thing.

Mrs. Mainprice patted her hand and guided her to a bench pulled up at the table. "Just sit here across from the girls. You already know Molly. And this is Peg. She helps me in the kitchen and the scullery. Molly is responsible for the rest of the house, though this isn't a grand household and we all do what jobs as are needed."

Rachel greeted the maids. Molly and Peg were forced to politely bob their heads in return.

"You're just in time for prayer." Satisfied that some sort of peace had been achieved, Mrs. Mainprice took a seat at the foot of the table, picked up a Bible, and began to read. "O give thanks unto the LORD, for he is good: for his mercy endureth for ever. Let the redeemed of the LORD say so, whom he hath redeemed from the hand of the enemy; and gathered them out of the lands, from the east, and from the west, from the north, and from the south. They wandered in the wilderness in a solitary way; they found no city to dwell in. Hungry and thirsty, their soul fainted in them. Then they cried unto the LORD in their trouble, and he delivered them out of their distresses."

Rachel stared at her hands, clutched in her lap, while enmity rose off Molly and Peg like waves of heat from simmering coals. Just because Rachel was Irish. Or could they read the trials of her past like printed words on a pamphlet? Clearly, the Lord had not delivered her from her distress.

Mrs. Mainprice set the Bible away. "Eat now, everyone, before the meat gets cold. I didn't spend all afternoon roasting that beef to have you gawp at it. And I have a sauce to prepare for the master's dinner, so no dawdling."

Rachel was certain the roast and the beans and the dense bread were wonderful. It may have been water, for all she could taste any of the food.

"Must 'ave been awful difficult comin' all the way to England and leavin' your family and friends," said Peg between mouthfuls. "Miss Dunne," she added as an afterthought.

Rachel decided she was not trying to be friendly. Nosy, was more like it. "It was."

"Just like it was hard for you to leave Shropshire, Peg," said Mrs. Mainprice.

"That waren't so 'ard, Mrs. M! My pa was a mean one, 'e was. I'm 'appy as a lark to be away from 'im!" She turned her eyes to Rachel. "Was that 'ow it was for you? Runnin' away from yer pa?"

"No. Just in need of work. My family has encountered difficult times, and employment is not easy to come by in Ireland," Rachel replied, holding Peg's gaze, trying not to let the worry for her family show in her eyes. Had Mother's customers begun to return, now that Rachel was gone from Carlow? Would there be meat in the stew pot for the twins and Nathaniel? "There are five of us to feed and clothe, and we hoped I could make more money in England to support everyone."

"So that's how it is, eh?" Peg asked, overbold.

"That's precisely how it is if that's what Miss Dunne says,

Peg," scolded Mrs. Mainprice. "Now finish your dinner. We've work yet to do and precious little time for impolite chitchat."

The talking ended, and the dinner ground to an eventual halt with all the grace of a costermonger's wagon bogging down in deep mud. Dishes were hastily cleared and Mrs. Mainprice turned to the task of finishing the preparation of Dr. Edmunds's meal.

"Might I help?" Rachel asked. Peg and Molly's eyebrows lifted in unison, and they set to whispering.

"There's no need, Miss Dunne," said Mrs. Mainprice. "You're not to do servant's work."

"But I wish to help."

"This is not right, Miss Dunne."

Rachel saw she was making the housekeeper fidget with agitation, but she wanted to prove herself willing and able. "I insist."

Mrs. Mainprice nodded. "Peg, Molly, what are you two doing? Get to your chores."

As instructed by the older woman, Rachel brought out from the pantry the serving ware made of fine china decorated with maroon roses. Her fingers traced the intertwining stems and flowers. She had never seen anything so beautiful in her life.

What a world she'd found herself in, as though she had become a thistle among heather. Although she wouldn't have been comfortable in this house before life had tossed her from her secure place. In Carlow, she had once known where she belonged, what was expected of her, what her future held. Now . . . her finger curled over the smooth edge of the platter. Now she was adrift and scrambling for a toehold.

Rachel felt Peg's gaze on her. Was the girl wondering if

Rachel was planning on pinching a saucer or teacup to sell on a street corner somewhere?

"Peg, if you don't mind the gravy, it'll boil and curdle quick as you can say 'Jack Robinson,'" Mrs. Mainprice reprimanded. "Back at it now."

Onto the good china went the food—a duckling, stewed cucumbers in the gravy Peg had prepared, asparagus soup, currant pudding. It was enough food to serve several people, certainly enough to feed Rachel's family back at home, used to so much less and so much simpler, some fish or stew being their usual fare. Nathaniel would laugh at the cucumbers, limp green discs floating in a sea of caramel-brown. Right before her brother gobbled them down.

Molly balanced the tray and headed for the staircase. "Hey, watch it now, Joe," she called out as the lad bounded into the kitchen.

"Sorry there, Moll. Miss Dunne, the master's asked to see ya."

Peg shot Rachel a quick, knowing look.

After the confusion at the dock and the questions about her age, had Dr. Edmunds already decided to dismiss her? "Where is he?" Rachel asked Joe.

"In the dinin' room. Where else would 'e be at this hour?"

Rachel followed Joe out of the kitchen. "What sort of mood is Dr. Edmunds in?"

Eyes brown like burnt toast turned to stare at her. "'is typical mood."

Whatever mood that was, though it didn't sound promising. Rachel chewed her lip and searched for conversation. "What do you do for the doctor, Joe?"

"I'm the boy."

"What does 'the boy' do?"

Joe looked at her as if she were teasing. A few seconds passed as they ascended the stairs before he appeared to realize her question was genuine. "I do all the stuff the maids don't like to do, like fill the coal scuttles. Take care o' the doctor's 'orse and gig. Sometimes I take 'is physics to 'is patients. Stuff like that."

"What do you think of your master? Do you like him?"

They turned the corner of the ground-floor landing. "Dr. Edmunds? 'e's an all right bloke. A bit 'ard sometimes because of losin' his wife an' all. That were three years ago, I've done been told."

"But he is a fair man."

"D'pends on what yer plannin' on doin'." Joe eyed her. "Though if yer worried about 'im likin' you, you should claim you know everythin' to be known about tendin' patients and whatnot. 'e'd like to hear that, 'e would."

"I know nothing about tending patients." Did she shout that?

"Didn' think ya did. Jus' sayin' it might come in 'andy an' all to pretend you did. Door at the far end," Joe said when they reached their destination, then scampered off.

Rachel entered the dining room. It shimmered golden in the candlelight. The walls were covered in sumptuous yellow silk, coordinating saffron draperies hung at the windows looking out at the street, and the marble fireplace gleamed creamy white. Crystal pendants suspended from the candelabra refracted rainbow light. A corner cabinet displayed chinaware even more delicately lovely than what she had seen in the kitchen.

Molly was laying out the last of the dishes, and at the head of the polished table sat Dr. Edmunds, alone yet dressed for company in evening kit—indigo coat, gray waistcoat, white neckerchief. The master of an empty dining room.

It was utterly, indescribably sad.

He looked over as Rachel approached the table. His expression was impossible to read.

"There you are, Miss Dunne," he said, "Molly, there's no need for you to stay. You may go. I wish a word with Miss Dunne in private."

Molly hustled out of the dining room, a tiny smile on her lips, and shut the door behind her.

"You wished to see me, Dr. Edmunds?" Rachel asked.

"I do, and you're welcome to sit, Miss Dunne." He waited until she pulled out a chair, heavy and beautifully carved. The cushion was thick and extraordinarily comfortable. Or would have been comfortable, if she could relax.

"I trust I did not disturb your dinner," he said.

"I have already taken my meal in the kitchen."

"You're not a servant, Miss Dunne, and don't need to eat in the kitchen. In future, you can ask to have a tray sent up to your room. Or use the Blue Room on the second floor, if you would like."

'In future' meant she had one. "So you've not changed your mind about keeping me on here after the mishap at the dock, the misunderstanding about my age?"

His eyes searched her face. "You assured me there was no intentional deception. That is still the case, correct?"

"Absolutely."

"Then the fault must be mine. Your cousin told me you were highly experienced, and I must have equated that with age."

"I apologize again," she said, relief rushing her words, "for that and for causing you to come down to the docks to search for me. I do not mean to be difficult."

"Good, because I don't have time for difficulties." He steepled his fingers and watched her over their tips. "I called you up here for another reason. I have a proposition for you that I'm hoping you'll accept."

There was no "hoping" in the firm tone of his voice. Dr. Edmunds expected her to accept, and based on what Joe had said, she feared she already knew what he was about to ask. "Yes?"

"My medical attendant, Miss Guimond, was recently forced to return to her home country of France. Some of the tasks she used to perform for me still need to be done until my practice is completely closed. I know you've come to England looking for a better situation . . ." His gaze sharpened, making her skin prickle from its intensity. "But as you're already here in my employ, I thought you could take over her tasks in addition to the other work you'll be doing for me."

"I am afraid, Dr. Edmunds, I would not make a good attendant," Rachel replied, cold dancing down her spine. God let innocents die under her care. "I know nothing of use about medicine. In fact, I've had a very bad experience."

"Did it involve a man who cut his foot on a piece of pavement?" A smile flitted across his lips. Fleeting as it was, the smile transformed him like the wink of candlelight on a gloomy night.

"Pardon me?" she asked, confused. Both by the question and her reaction to his smile.

"Just something Joe said." He shook his head as if apologizing for the question. Or the smile. "Of course, I'm not asking you to diagnose ills or treat any cases. I need someone to wait with patients when they come into the office during my open hours, gather information from them, and comfort them while they wait, if needed. The skills you would acquire would be impressive to any future employer."

"I intend on teaching children, Dr. Edmunds, and such work will not require me to serve as their nurse."

"One never knows about that." He lifted his brows to emphasize his belief. "I'm sure after a good night's sleep, you'll see the sense in my request and realize the benefits behind the opportunity I'm presenting you."

If you knew I was accused of murder, you would retract the offer in a heartbeat. But Rachel could not tell him about the accusation and destroy her prospects. She could only bow her head and agree. "Yes, Dr. Edmunds."

"I'll see you tomorrow morning, then. Seven sharp," he said, indicating she could leave.

Rachel rose and bade him good night.

Seven sharp.

It sounded like an appointment with the executioner.

CHAPTER 6

ary. Mary. Wake up.

She's so cold, so cold. And blue . . . Mary!

"Miss Dunne, what's wrong with her? What's happened?"

She is gone. I gave her the decoction of hawkweed with honey, but it did not save her. God, what did I do wrong?

Mary! Wake up. Just wake up . . . Wake up!

"Miss Dunne. Are you all right?" Mrs. Mainprice's voice was insistent, loud enough to penetrate the wood of the chamber door.

Rachel bolted upright in bed, her skin clammy, heart hammering. She'd had another of her nightmares. Why could they not leave her alone, stay in Ireland where they belonged?

"Miss Dunne!"

"Yes, Mrs. Mainprice. I am coming." Jumping up, Rachel threw on her thin robe and pulled open the door.

"Are you all right, child? I heard you calling out." Worry creased the older woman's face.

"I . . . talk to myself in my sleep. What time is it?"

"Near seven, miss."

"I am going to be late!" Rachel grabbed her brush and began dragging it through the stubborn tendrils of her hair.

"I brought you breakfast." Mrs. Mainprice held out her tray—toast, an egg, and coffee on its lacquered surface. "But you might not have time. Master's in the library already. Waiting."

Not good. "I shall not be late again. I promise."

"No need to promise me, miss," she answered, leaving the tray teetering on the bedside chair.

The clock rang seven as Rachel turned the corner of the first-floor landing. Dr. Edmunds was outside the library, waiting for her as advertised.

"Ah, Miss Dunne, there you are," he said, his voice steady and calm. "Did you sleep well?"

A strand of his dark hair had fallen down over his brow, curled boyishly, so incongruous on that serious face. She noticed anew how handsome he was, possibly the handsomest man she had ever seen, especially when he wasn't frowning at her. Which he wasn't.

Thank heavens.

"I did sleep well, Dr. Edmunds. Apparently too well. I am sorry if I am late. That is not my habit."

"Don't worry. You're just on time. Come along." He shoved the errant strand of hair off his forehead and entered the library, moving across the carpet in long strides. She hurried to keep up. "I've a large collection of books, some of which I inherited from my father, many of which are duplicates of what I previously owned. I need them all logged so I can decide which I should keep and which I should give away."

Large barely described the endless rows upon rows of books, shelves not sufficient to contain them all. Some rested atop a corner table; others were stacked in a neat pile. Could he or his father possibly have read every one? Or did he own them simply because he could, a rich man's habit?

"There are . . . so many." She felt inadequate in the midst of such an obvious show of wealth.

"Do you find the quantity daunting to catalog, Miss Dunne?"

Rachel confidently squared her shoulders; she could ill afford him to think her incompetent. "There are simply more books than I have ever seen, is all. I am up to the task."

He nodded, satisfied. "Let me show you the system I've devised."

Her responsibility was straightforward: classify the books by topic and log them accordingly. Organizing his collection would be tedious but simple, bookkeeping of a sort she understood. She nodded as he spoke. Yes, she could separate the books of poetry from the works of botany and track them separately. Yes, she understood that he wanted common topics merged—all books on travel in England maintained apart from those discussing Europe.

"Not difficult at all, Dr. Edmunds."

His eyes seemed to brighten, as though a smile was captured within them but was unable to escape. She could stand there for some time, looking at those eyes, so harsh and beautiful and captivating at the same time, like the heart of a storm cloud.

"You will also need to assist in packing some of the household things, in addition to the contents of my medical office," he said. "My plan is to close down my practice in a month and leave for Finchingfield, where I've inherited my family's small estate. As a result of the short time remaining and the sudden absence of my attendant, the staff needs your assistance. Which is why I took you on."

"None of the work should be difficult, Dr. Edmunds."

"Excellent." He offered a brisk smile, and Rachel soaked up his approval like a bone-dry cloth soaking up water. *I should like to see him smile more often, and more fully. He would look less stern and forbidding if he did.*

He turned on his heel. "Now for the office. There is a great deal to be done in there."

Swallowing down a burst of nerves, Rachel followed him out of the library. "You need me to pack all of the contents?"

"Yes, but not for me to take along when I move. I'm retiring from the practice of medicine and becoming a gentleman farmer."

Rachel knew surprise had to show on her face. He was too young to retire. "You are no longer going to be a physician in Finchingfield?"

"No, I'm not. A friend of mine who attended medical college with me, Dr. Thaddeus Castleton, is taking over my practice, along with most of the contents of my office. I've already transferred many of my patients to him."

Did Dr. Edmunds sound regretful of his decision? She couldn't tell.

They arrived at the rear ground-floor room he used for his consultations. Dr. Edmunds extracted a key from his waistcoat pocket, turned it in the lock, and went inside. The room was cool, shadowy like much of the house, and smelled of camphor. The aroma bit into her nose and tightened her throat, but it drew her in nonetheless, her curiosity beckoning.

He lit a lamp upon his desk. "I keep the room shuttered against the outside. I've always felt the quiet helps calm my patients."

The room was as neat and tidy as he was. A sturdy oak desk filled most of the space, the forgotten remains of his breakfast fighting with orderly piles of paperwork for space upon its surface. His chair stood behind and another in front, padded with several thick pillows, while a narrow sofa was positioned against the wall with a small drop-leaf table at its side. Shallow bookshelves on the opposite wall bracketed a glass-fronted cabinet. Rachel peered inside and found it contained what any healer would need—powders and pills for the stomach, ointments that would treat rashes or sties of the eye, fever mixture, styptic water. Laudanum. She could smell their aromas without unstoppering a bottle or opening a packet—the acidic bite, the odd sweetness.

She straightened, curiosity satisfied. Those aromas belonged in her failed past.

"I did not expect to find the space so sparsely equipped." She had never been in a physician's office before. Her family could not afford the services of a doctor. Neither could most folks in Carlow, leaving them to the care of the apothecary, or women like her mother and herself.

I tried so hard, Mary. Though none of the Fergusons had believed that.

"I require little more than what you see," he said. "As a physician, I don't need saws or bottles of leeches. And I do not stock more than a minimum of medicines in that cabinet. It's easy enough to obtain preparations from a nearby apothecary. There's no need for me to keep much on hand in the office, aside from simple instruments such as my stethoscope."

Crossing to a table against the far wall, he opened an intricately inlaid walnut case polished to a dizzying sheen. He pulled out three pieces of pale wood tubing, one bell-shaped on its end, and began fitting them together.

"It's a device to aid in listening to the heart and lungs, Miss Dunne," he continued. "I purchased it last year in France. When I hired Miss Guimond, in fact. It's quite simple yet elegant. Would you like to examine it?" Pride lifted his voice.

"No. Thank you, Dr. Edmunds." At one time, she would have been intrigued.

Returning the stethoscope to its case, he pressed his hand gently upon the lid to close it, running his fingertips across the top of the case until they slid off the nearest side. A strange little gesture, bittersweet. Clearly regretful.

"On these shelves and in my desk are where I keep my patient files . . ."

Rachel crossed to his desk to follow his instruction when her gaze settled on a medical text atop it, previously hidden from her view by the stacks of paper. Pages lay open to a small illustration of the inside of a swollen throat.

In a flash, she was back at Mary Ferguson's bedside, her face the oddest shade of blue . . . *Wake up, Mary.* "Oh," she muttered. Every ounce of blood left her head to pool in her feet.

"Miss Dunne, you are unwell." Dr. Edmunds clutched her elbow to keep her from falling. What did he see on her face, in her eyes? A woman who had failed at the one thing she'd long believed herself most competent at—healing? "Why didn't you tell me?"

His hand shifted to feel her pulse, brushing back with his thumb the cuff banding her sleeve. At the gentle touch of his hand, her blood came rushing back, a wall she ran into full force.

"Doctor . . ." She jumped back, jerked her sleeve down over her hand. "I . . . Dr. Edmunds. I assure you I am not ill. I missed breakfast, that is all, and am still weary from my journey. You need not examine me."

He looked almost as startled as she felt. "I didn't mean to upset you. My apologies again for being overly familiar. It seems I cannot help myself. A physician's habit."

"I . . . I need to go outside." What was wrong with her? She was made of sturdier stock than what she was exhibiting. Irish stock. Timelessly strong, weathered but never beaten, the blood of Celtic warriors in her veins.

Too late to wish for her hastily discarded sachet. "I must catch a breath of air."

"Let me escort you. If you faint, you might strike your head and hurt yourself."

His words echoed down the hallway after her, because she had already fled.

※

"Miss Dunne looks unwell, sir." Depositing the morning newspapers on the office desk, Mrs. Mainprice peered at James, the corners of her eyes creasing until her skin looked like the pattern of cracks in a glaze of sugar. "I passed her in the hallway, rushing headfirst for the garden, white as a ghost."

"She nearly fainted in here. Something in my medical text upset her." It lay open to a section on throat diseases. He'd been advising Dr. Calvert on the treatment of a patient suffering from diptheritis, and the picture of swelling and excess membranous tissue, though unpleasant, was far from the worst. Although the illustration had certainly bothered Miss Dunne. "I suppose I should have listened when she told me she'd had a bad experience with illness. Whatever happened, it's made her apprehensive. She hasn't told you anything of her past, has she, Mrs. Mainprice?"

"Very little, sir. Just that times were hard back in Ireland and she came here in search of work. The girls tried to get her to say more, but she's closed tight as a mussel shell. Not a happy past, I'd warrant. She's borne something unpleasant, but 'tis that not true for most of us?"

His housekeeper's eyes, which always reminded him of pure country earth, were filled with sympathy. As much for him as for the newly arrived, and increasingly intriguing, Miss Dunne.

James flipped shut his medical book. "I wonder if Miss Dunne is going to be able to do what I need from her, after all."

"I think Miss Dunne wants to be helpful, and I trust she'll work hard." She swept up his dirty dishes from breakfast, loading them into her arms. "Besides, she's got a good heart."

"How can you possibly know that?"

"There's not much gets past me, sir."

He knew how true that was. Mrs. Mainprice had served his family since James had been a boy, and she'd always been keenly observant. Father had relied on her advice when hiring other servants and James had done likewise, because she could see through the hardest of shells right down to the meaty core of a person. He suspected she was seeing right down to the core of him at that moment too.

"I suppose I should go out to the garden and see how she's faring," he said.

"Miss Dunne might appreciate a kind word, sir."

"Then I dare not dawdle."

Once she departed with the dirty dishes, James headed out through the rear door of the house and into the murky London morning. He averted his eyes from the tattered condition of the flower beds. He hadn't come out here to remember former days.

Miss Dunne heard the crunch of boots upon the gravel walk and looked over. Hastily, she stood. "Dr. Edmunds, I did not mean to spend so long in the garden—"

He halted her with a raised hand. "Take as long as you need."

The color was returning to her cheeks. She was very lovely, fresh and bright in a way so many of the young women of his acquaintance weren't, their faces already dulled by cynicism and self-obsession. Even Louisa Castleton, only nineteen and jaded.

"I am certain you would prefer I got to work in the library," she said. "You are not paying me to enjoy the flowers."

What little was left of them. "I'm not, but I'm also not paying you to endure situations that make you ill. Don't feel badly over what occurred in my office. If you aren't comfortable attending to my patients, I understand. I shall be able to manage them on my own, I'm sure."

"Thank you for your kindness, Dr. Edmunds."

"It isn't kindness to recognize when a member of my staff is unsuited for a particular task. It is an investment toward a well-run household."

"Nonetheless, I do not like to cause a commotion or be a bother."

But she already had caused a commotion, if the surprising way he felt when he touched her hand was any indication. Selfishly—or stupidly—he was looking forward to discovering what further surprises were in store.

"I believe, Miss Dunne, you would never be a bother to me."

CHAPTER 7

"I am truly sorry, Mrs. Mainprice, but I cannot attend services this morning. My head is splitting," Rachel fibbed, padding the horrible untruth with an apologetic smile. She did not have a headache yet, but she would if she had to face God in His house.

"Another bad night's sleep, miss?"

"No, not at all." Thankfully, last night had been free of nightmares. "I simply do not feel well. I must still be adjusting to London and all its noises and whatnot. I hope Dr. Edmunds will not mind."

"If you need a powder, I keep some in the pantry off the kitchen."

"I might just sit in the garden for a while. Sunlight and fresh air should cure it."

"We're off to St. Peter's, then." She bustled out of Rachel's room. Rachel heard the front door closing downstairs. She let a few minutes pass before she headed out to the garden.

The garden was just as quiet—and just as sad-looking—

as it had been yesterday. Weeds intermingled with flowers, many of which were exotic types she did not recognize and certainly would never see in Ireland. The gravel paths needed new rocks and the stone milkmaid fountain standing guard at the center sprouted a growth of black mold along her skirts. Even the bricks in the wall needed fresh mortar. It had to have been beautiful once. If it were her garden, the roses would still be blooming and scenting the air with the rich perfume Mother so loved. Instead the roses grew spindly, dead blossoms choking the ends, their promise of beauty and hope faded and gone.

She and the roses were kindred spirits, Rachel thought as she sank onto one of the iron benches, and why she found the garden strangely consoling. It had certainly settled her mind yesterday, after that disaster in Dr. Edmunds's office. Or had it been his sudden thoughtfulness that had calmed her?

"Eh, there, Miss Dunne." Joe's voice, followed by the slap of the rear door shutting, interrupted her thoughts.

"Oh, Joe. Good morning. I thought you were at church with the others."

"Too many chores today. Don' tell Dr. E." He winked. "You all right, then? Heard your 'ead was botherin' you."

"It is much better, out here in the fresh air."

"I guess it's fresh," he said, pushing back his cap to scratch his head. Joe sniffed the air. "I think it smells like the 'orses out in the mews."

She grinned at his comment. Thank heavens someone in this household could lift her spirits. Someone besides Dr. Edmunds on the rare occasions when he smiled or told her she would never be a bother.

"What are you about this morning?" Rachel asked, nodding at the thin-bladed saw hanging from his hand.

"I've come to trim the branches of the pear tree there. It's 'alf-dead. Though it seems awful late an' all to be trimmin' the trees in 'ere. The garden's gotten so tattered, were it a cloth a rag-picker'd want nothin' to do with it."

"Why was it permitted to go to such ruin?"

Joe shrugged. "Dr. E stopped anyone from tendin' it after 'is wife died. Reminded him of 'er, I s'pose. Was 'er garden, an' all. But it's not like 'e was gonna do the work 'imself. Coulda hired a gardener to keep it trimmed and tidied. I woulda done the work meself," he stated, dropping the saw beneath the sickly tree and wandering off to retrieve a ladder propped against the rear wall.

Dr. Edmunds's wife's garden. Her death must have pained him deeply, for him to have ignored the garden so as not to be reminded of her.

"It is a shame, even for that reason," she said when Joe returned.

"That it is," he replied, setting up the ladder. "I coulda got those lilacs bloomin' again."

"You really would like to be a gardener." She tried to imagine Joe, scrappy and streetwise, hunkered down among pansies and ladies' slipper.

"I grew up in the stews, but I still remember the first time I saw Hyde Park. So green it made your eyes 'urt."

"You would like Ireland, Joe. It is a green like you might never imagine here in London." Here, the colors were muted by the soot and fog, like clothing that had been washed one too many times. "The sky overhead can be soft and blue like ducks' eggs or ruffled with scudding clouds. And when the heather blooms purple, there is nothing sweeter on this earth than to lie down among its scented flowers. My little sisters love to bury their faces in the blossoms and breathe deep . . ." Oh, this was making her heart hurt worse than thoughts of church services. She had to stop.

"So ya see why I like bein' out 'ere. It were pretty, when I first got 'ere, a few months after the missus died. Not anymore." He shook his head and started climbing the ladder.

"Why not go ahead and tend to the garden yourself?" Rachel asked. "I doubt anyone would stop you."

"I'm the boy, Miss Dunne. I know my place and my place knows me. I don' aspire to better than what I got."

"Is it so wrong to aspire to greater? I always wanted . . ." Rachel stopped before she voiced her wants. Any dreams she'd once owned had died in a cramped and filthy room back in Carlow.

"Wanted what, miss?" Joe asked, sawing away at a dead branch.

At one time she'd intended to write a book on everything she had learned about herbs and medicines and nursing. Too many women had to rely on word-of-mouth and unreliable recipes handed down by family members. A straightforward book written in plain words would be helpful to many. But no one would seek to purchase medicinal recipes written by someone accused of killing a patient. Unless they anticipated such a treatise would teach them about poisons.

"Nothing, Joe. I have had to put my lofty dreams away in favor of a more practical reality. I came to England to find a position as a teacher." *I shall be good at it, and teaching will not require nursing skills.* "To me, there is no work more fulfilling than helping children."

"Teacher, eh? That sounds right good, miss. I've never 'ad learnin' meself."

"Maybe I could tutor you a little while I am here."

"Naw. Books an' all scare me." Joe grunted as the saw blade stuck in the branch.

"But a gardener who can read would be very valuable. It would make it easier to reach your dream, Joe." Her dream might be dead, but his needn't be.

"Me mum always said not to give up until God shows us our end an' they're shovelin' dirt on top our coffins." Joe worked the blade back and forth on the branch, trying to free it. He glanced over at Rachel. "But look what good dreamin' done for 'er. Died of the pox." He suddenly groaned and let fly a curse as the blade whipped loose, throwing him off balance. Arms wheeling, he fell from the ladder and thudded to the ground. The saw skidded across the gravel.

"Joe!" Rachel ran over to him, crouched down. His cap had flown off and she felt along the back of his skull, her hands moving with long practice that required no thought.

He winced as her finger found a lump. "It's nothin'."

"Does anything hurt? Your head? Your legs? Back?"

"No. It's nothin'."

He tried to sit up, but Rachel pressed him back onto the ground. "It is not nothing. You have a bump on your head and you cut your arm with the saw. Press your hand to the wound and lie still. Do not move." She gave him a shove on the shoulder to keep him down. If he had broken or strained anything, movement would only aggravate the injury. "I will fetch something for the cut."

The office door was locked tight, and Dr. Edmunds had not

entrusted her with the key. Rachel rushed down to the empty kitchen. Mrs. Mainprice had mentioned she kept headache powders. Maybe she would have other medicines as well.

Rachel located the housekeeper's supplies. After a few moments of searching, Rachel found dried cuttings of the mushroom known as agaric of oak but no sticking plaster. The agaric would quench the bleeding. Her binding would have to seal the wound shut.

Snatching up a clean rag from a pile lying next to the sink, then dipping a mug into the pitcher of fresh water standing nearby, she hurried back out to the garden. Joe had followed her directions and remained stretched out on the ground. However, he looked peevish.

"Ya know what yer doin'?" Joe eyed her as she tore the rag into two halves.

"Lie still. I am going to wash your wound then apply agaric of oak to it. The bleeding should stop. I will have to tie a rag around your arm until sticking plaster can be obtained to keep the wound closed."

She worked quickly, carefully, probing the wound for any gravel or dirt stuck within, picking out what she could and pouring the clean water over the cut. Thankfully, the saw had not penetrated far. A deeper cut would require more serious medicine than what she had brought.

"Mrs. M would say God's watchin' over me, to 'ave you on 'and to patch me up. I coulda been out 'ere screamin' for 'elp till I bled to death. That's what I get for not goin' to services."

God. Him again. "I do not know that my presence in the garden was any blessing at all." Crushing the dried mushroom, she pushed it into the wound and wrapped the cloth around his arm, sealing it shut. "It's my fault the blade slipped and you fell. I distracted you with my silly conversation about aspirations."

"Naw. Don't be blamin' yerself, miss."

But she did. Of course, she did.

Finishing up, Rachel helped Joe lean against the tree trunk. She settled back on her heels. And nearly collapsed onto the rocky path when she realized what she'd just done. Poor Joe. Had she cleaned the wound well enough? The cut might get infected; she had seen shallower wounds fester and blacken, resulting in amputations. Without his arm, Joe would be useless as a servant . . .

Rachel lurched toward the bench and pulled herself onto the seat while she gulped air and fought lightheadedness. *Breathe in. Breathe out. Do not faint.*

Startled, Joe sat up. "The cut's not that bad, is it, miss?"

"I do not believe so."

"Good! Cause as green as you look, I'da thought my arm were gonna fall clean off." His eyes widened. "'ey, wait now. Where'd you learn to doctor like this?"

He'd taken longer than she had expected to ask the question. "I learned bits here and there about herbs and tending. Mostly from my mother. Things any woman might know."

"Not jus' bits an' not jus' any woman, miss."

Standing on legs as wobbly as a newborn colt's, Rachel snatched the damp rag and mug off the ground. She needed to get away before he asked any other questions and she had to come up with more answers. "I need to get back to my work now, Joe. Rest there until you feel stronger."

"But, miss!"

She hurried toward the house. Dr. Edmunds was destined to hear how his new assistant, who had claimed to have no knowledge of medical things, who had nearly fainted in his office, had known how to tend Joe's wound. There would be more questions and more prevarications from her, adding to the stack growing like a refuse pile.

Oh, Rachel, your soul is going to be black as a charred pot bottom before all is said and done.

She suppressed the voice, reached for the rear door latch, and stepped into the cool darkness, away from Joe's quizzical gaze.

On the Monday after Miss Dunne had been too unwell to attend church services, James wandered down the hallway toward the library, a bundle of patient notes he had been consulting tucked in his hand. He needed to discuss with Miss Dunne how he wanted the paperwork handled for this particular patient—a crotchety old gentleman who his father had tended before handing him off to James. He paused before entering the library. How many times precisely had he found an excuse to come up here today? The first occasion, he'd come to check that she had fully recovered from yesterday's headache. The next had been to relay some information on when the packing crates would arrive. Another had been to review her progress on her first full day of working in his library. So that made two . . . no, three times.

Three times? *Surely I'm too busy to keep finding reasons to talk with her.*

After all, he was not the sort of man who was normally intrigued by women he barely knew. Especially those who worked for him.

James peered into the library. Miss Dunne leaned over the ledger spread across his desk, a curling tendril of coppery hair come loose from her chignon to fall along her chin, and chewed her bottom lip as she concentrated on her entries. Who was she really? he wondered. She was well educated, her voice betraying only a trace of her Irish heritage, and she held herself as if she were used to possessing authority and being respected. But her clothes were worn, the material shiny in spots where it had rubbed against surfaces, the hems of her two dresses taken down more than once. Poor and Irish, Sophia would say with a disdainful sneer. Words that went together like *cold* and *winter*. Or *patent medicine* and *unreliable*.

Miss Dunne backed away from the desk, retreating to the far bookshelves, and James inched closer to the doorway not to lose sight of her. She was humming quietly, some Irish country tune perhaps. She must miss home; he suspected she had never been away before.

She brushed back the loose strand of hair, tucking it behind her ear. Her fingers were long and elegant, and she kept them meticulously clean. A habit James had as well, vitally necessary when treating disease every day. An unusual habit for someone in her situation, though.

"Sir?" Molly's voice jerked him back from the doorway. Her eyes narrowed as they glanced between him and what she could see of the library. "Is there something you're needing, sir?"

"I was going to instruct Miss Dunne on a patient's files," he explained, waving the papers as proof even though he didn't have to provide any reason to his house-maid for loitering outside his library.

"Are you wanting me to help with your patients today?" she asked hopefully.

"No. Miss Dunne will help if I need any assistance. You may continue with your chores up here." He nodded at the dirty bed linens bundled in her arms.

Her expression went rigid. "Yes, sir."

Briskly, James turned on his heel and headed for the stairs, his forgotten papers dangling from his hand.

CHAPTER 8

'm feelin' right well, I am, miss," said Joe, sitting atop Dr. Edmunds's desk in the library, scuffing its polished surface with the backside of his woolen breeches. He grinned at Rachel, one of his wide grins that filled his face and showed the gap in his teeth. "Healin' up clean." He tapped his linen sleeve at the spot where he had cut his arm.

Two days had passed since he had fallen from the tree. If the wound had not become infected in that amount of time, the risk that it might had passed.

"I am very glad to hear that, Joe." Books cradled in the crook of her left arm, Rachel retreated down the ladder that ran on a brass rail atop the bookshelf. "You haven't said anything to Dr. Edmunds about cutting your arm, have you?"

"Cor, no! I'd never get to be his 'ead gardener if 'e thought I were clumsy!"

"You are not clumsy. Anyone can have an accident." She

dropped the books onto the desk, slid the ledger nearer, and inked her pen. "I was merely thinking it might be best not to worry him, that's all."

Rachel glanced at Joe. Nothing in his demeanor indicated he guessed Rachel's real concern. If Joe never said anything to Dr. Edmunds about his wound, then Dr. Edmunds would never think to ask Rachel about her readiness to tend it. And she wouldn't have to tell the truth.

"'e's so busy, miss, I doubt 'e'd notice if me arm 'ad been sawn clean off!"

"He is not quite that oblivious, Joe," she said, though his observation seemed apt. Dr. Edmunds had been busy, burying himself in his paperwork and patients. Although she had noticed him in the hallway outside the library more than once of late, and he had been in to see her quite often.

"Some days 'e is obli . . . obluvi . . . em, awful daft," said Joe. "Jus' glad to know I've got someone else to go to if I needs medical 'elp. You're a right good 'ealer."

Rachel shook her head at him as if his compliment was the most ridiculous thing she'd ever heard. "Mrs. Mainprice's skill with a sticking plaster has more to do with your healing than my initial feeble efforts." The housekeeper had tended to Joe's wound after returning from services on Sunday, asking nothing about Rachel's treatment or her knowledge. An ally. Rachel needed one.

"Aw, Miss Dunne, yer always puttin' yerself down," Joe chided.

"Your high regard for me is unwarranted."

"Not at all."

He winked at her the way her brother might do, making

Rachel smile. Making her heart twinge over how much she would miss Joe when he left for Finchingfield.

"You've a visitor," announced Molly from the doorway, casting a pall. She frowned first at Rachel then at Joe, likely thinking how she would have to repolish the desk later. "Miss Harwood."

Her cousin Claire had come at last to meet her. "Please show her in here, Molly."

"I wouldn't make it a habit to have visitors in the master's library, Miss Dunne. Next time, you might want to use the Blue Room."

"I shall keep your suggestion in mind."

Molly lifted an arrow-straight eyebrow, sniffed, and went to retrieve Claire.

Joe hopped down from the desk. "Best be goin' then. Work waits for no man!"

He scampered off, a whistled tune drifting behind him.

Rachel removed her apron and tidied her hair. She wished she had time to make herself presentable. Instead, her first impression would be made in a rehemmed frock with frayed trim, her hair coming free of its pins.

Molly reappeared, leading a slightly built woman dressed in the height of fashion—gray silk sprigged with violet, a cream pelerine and matching wide-brimmed bonnet trimmed in violet lace. Her features were even and might be called pleasant rather than pretty. Eyes the shade of cocoa assessed with intelligence and sympathy, and Rachel realized she knew next to nothing about her cousin. Least of all why she had agreed to help.

Claire waited only a second after Molly had shut the door to rush across the room. "Rachel!" She pulled Rachel into an embrace, hugging her tight. She smelled of rose water and the coal dust of London.

"It is good to see you, Claire."

"And you!" A spray of smallpox scars fanned across her cousin's cheeks, making her appear more careworn than Rachel had expected. "My goodness, but you were only five years old when I saw you last. I remember you as such a precocious child, running all over the grounds of our house outside Weymouth, trying to climb the lime trees."

She motioned toward the settee and took a seat across from it.

"I tried to climb the lime trees?" Rachel asked, surprised. Not by the fact she might have tried to climb the trees, but that she could no longer remember doing so.

"Indeed. Father feared you would break your neck!"

"I seem to have forgotten everything about that trip." Rachel and her mother never spoke about the last time they'd been permitted to visit Uncle Anthony and his family in England, the memories discarded like a broken dish onto a rubbish pile.

"It's just as well. That visit did not end happily," Claire admitted, peeling off her kid gloves. They were dyed the same violet as her bonnet trimmings and whispered of wealth. Mother had given up so much for the love of a charming, and not particularly successful, Irishman.

Rachel looked down at her own gown, noticed the tear she had mended last summer, and felt embarrassment heat her skin.

"I should have asked Molly to bring us tea and biscuits." A wealthy woman like her cousin would expect such courtesies. "Not that she would necessarily oblige me."

"I don't need tea. I've an appointment at Lady Anthistle's after this and she'll fill me to the brim with pekoe, trust me." Claire smiled reassuringly. "Tell me how your family is doing. I must hear everything."

As Claire settled in, Rachel obliged, telling her of Mother and Nathaniel and the twins, who Claire had never met. Stories spilled like water over a weir, streaming from Rachel's too-full heart. Claire smiled and nodded as Rachel talked until she grew hoarse.

"And your position here," Claire asked. "Dr. Edmunds is kind to you?"

"He seems a good man and the position is excellent. I do not know how I can thank you for securing it, especially after all that happened in Carlow. You have taken quite a risk for me."

The expression on Claire's face froze, caught between an interested smile and the growing frown of confusion. "What is 'all that happened in Carlow' that makes you a risk, Rachel?"

Realization came sharp as a knife prick. "Mother did not tell you why I had to leave Ireland."

"I presumed it was due to financial hardship, a disastrous investment, perhaps."

"It was because . . ." Dare she lie to Claire too? She could not. She would not, though the truth pained her. "I was accused of murder."

Claire stilled while the air swirled with the word. *Murder.* The mantel clock chimed inside its glass dome, ticking off the unforgiving passage of time while Rachel waited for Claire's response.

Please do not judge me harshly. I could not bear it.

"But you were not guilty?" Claire asked quietly.

"I would not be here if I had been found guilty."

"Then I do not wish to know more. If you provide me details, then I might have to explain to my family, and it's best they never learn about this. They already disapprove of everything I do." Her long-fingered hands twisted her gloves. "What of Dr. Edmunds . . . how much does he know?"

"Nothing. I was afraid he would toss me on the street without a reference."

"He might, if he knew." Claire leaned forward and gathered Rachel's hands in her own. "I do not care what you did in Carlow, Rachel. All that matters is that you are here now, and I can help you find a new future. God didn't provide me with this opportunity to heal old wounds simply to have me walk away."

What an interesting way to view her troubles, thought Rachel. As an opportunity from God.

"You will not regret helping me, Claire. I promise you."

"I trust not." She squeezed Rachel's fingers, a signal of her resolve, then released her grip. Opening her reticule, Claire extracted a folded slip of paper from within and handed it to Rachel. "I have arranged an appointment for you already, with the mistress of a school near St. Martin's Lane. On Friday morning. It is a place I work at often as a volunteer. You might find a position as a teacher there, though they'll not pay you much. Twenty pounds per annum might be all you could expect to start out, especially without a certificate."

Rachel unfolded the paper and a few coins fell onto the carpet. She picked them up and held them out. "I cannot accept money from you."

"Do you have any funds for an emergency? No, I thought not. It's only a few shillings, anyway." Claire shoved Rachel's hand away. "I'm going to send over a dress for you to wear, if you don't mind. First impressions are critical."

Blushing, Rachel wrapped the note around the coins and tucked the entirety into her pocket. "Thank you for the dress." She wouldn't argue about the necessity for one. "And the money. I pray I do not need it, but I will keep it safe in case I do."

"And I shall keep your secret safe. A woman's future depends upon maintaining the purest of reputations."

"Mine has a rather large blot."

"We'll work hard to erase it. With God's grace, we shall." Claire stood. "This will have to be a short visit, Rachel. I don't want to be late to Lady Anthistle's. She's providing a large sum of money to a foundation I'm thinking of starting."

"Your own foundation . . . how marvelous." More evidence of Claire's charity. Pride bit hard. *How far I have fallen that I've come to need it.*

Rachel escorted her cousin into the hallway.

"I'll come by to fetch you on Friday, Rachel. Send a message to the address on that piece of paper if Dr. Edmunds will not release you to make the appointment." Claire deposited a quick kiss on Rachel's cheek. "I know you'll succeed. I will make certain you succeed."

They exchanged fond farewells, and Rachel closed the door behind her.

As she turned away, she spied a flash of black merino disappearing around the first-floor landing. *Molly,* she thought with a pinch in her chest. The maid had been listening at the door.

"Where is Molly this morning, Joe?" Rachel asked as she held the kitchen door open for him.

Joe struggled through with a small crate piled high with chipped plates, bound for the charity wagon waiting on the curb outside. "She's gone off to the grocer's to stock up for dinner this evenin'. Why d'you ask, miss?"

Rachel trailed him up the staircase, a box of old kitchen linens in her hands. "Oh, just wondering if she's said anything about . . . anything."

Joe glanced over his shoulder at her. "Does she 'ave somethin' in particular to say?"

I hope not. "I was just wondering if she ever talks to you about me."

He rolled his eyes. "If Moll 'ad somethin' to say about you, miss, she'd tell the entire 'ouse, not just me."

They passed Peg on her knees in the hallway, a scrub brush in her hand, a bucket of soapy water at her side.

Joe sidestepped her sprawled skirts. "You missed a spot there, Peg," he teased.

Peg glared as she dragged the brush along the baseboard. "Oh, it's right funny you are, Joe."

Rachel went past without catching the girl's eye. She had already learned life was easier if she avoided conversing with Peg. "Everyone is so busy today."

"Don' you know we've special company comin'?" Joe set down the box in the entry hall. He stretched his neck and pretended to tidy a cravat like the greatest peer of the realm. "Dr. Castleton and 'is esteemed sister, Miss Louisa Castleton. Won't be bringin' 'is missus tonight. 'eard she's off visitin' somewheres. 'e's a right stuffy bloke, 'e is. Goin' to be takin' over the doctor's practice when we go. Don't much like how 'e looks around 'im when 'e comes to visit. Like 'e's taken a fancy to ownin' the place on top of everythin' in it! An' there's 'is sister . . . well, she's a pretty one, and I think she 'as 'er 'eart set on Dr. E, the way she bats those eyelashes at 'im whenever she's 'ere. Not that I've been spyin' on them or anythin'."

"Of course you wouldn't." Rachel waited as he opened the front door, retrieved his box, and stepped through. "And Dr. Edmunds, does he return Miss Castleton's interest?"

Joe cocked his head and grinned. "Why, you soft on 'im too?"

"I hardly know him," she protested, warmth creeping along her neck. "Besides, he is my employer."

"All the more reason to be interested in 'im! Sure didn't stop that Miss Guimond from goin' all big-eyed around 'im. Even though folk like us shouldn't be bothered with pinin' after folk like Dr. E and 'is kind. Too high up an' all."

"Yes, Joe," she agreed. "Far too high for folk like us."

He started down the steps toward the curb. A cart with a banner pasted to its side declaring it belonged to St. William's Benevolence Society waited there.

Joe continued on with his discussion of Miss Castleton without breaking stride, the dishes in the box rattling as he thudded down the steps. "But that Miss Castleton, she's the right sort. Though Dr. E keeps 'is feelin's close as a miser's purse. Miss Castleton oughta try to break an arm or somethin' if she wants to get 'im to notice 'er! But then, 'e's obluvis an' all. Might not work."

"Oblivious, Joe," Rachel said slowly and smiled. "I should not be listening to any more of your gossip, you know."

The man from the Benevolence Society gestured toward the cart. His hand swept past his thick waist, which strained the buttons of his waistcoat. Clearly, he had never lacked for food or suffered need, unlike those he ministered to.

"In the back here," he said. "There is space adjacent the other crates."

"Yeah, we see it. Like we're blind or somethin'," muttered Joe.

Rachel set her small box atop the bed while Joe hoisted his box alongside. A wagon moved aside to avoid colliding with them. Rachel hurried out of the street.

"I jes' wish Mrs. M 'ad picked a better day to be haulin' our old kitchen goods aroun'. I've got work in the dinin' room polishin' the silver."

Joe hopped back toward the house. Another, larger crate waited at the foot of the stairs. He and Rachel had brought it out earlier.

"Jes' think, miss," he said, squatting down to grasp hold of the crate. "Pretty soon ya won' be needin' to 'aul boxes around. Yer cousin found you a teachin' position, 'as she?"

"How did you hear about that?" Rachel asked, taking the other side.

"There's nothin' what 'appens in this 'ouse doesn't get spread around like manure in a cattle shed."

"I've no position as yet. But she hopes I shall soon."

On the count of three, they hoisted the crate in their hands.

Joe shifted its weight and jerked his chin at the handful of neighbors and inquisitive strangers collecting to watch, clotting the pavement with their nosiness. "Wish they'd consider 'elpin' rather than gawkin'."

"I doubt they would even contemplate the idea, Joe."

"Too 'igh and mighty for 'ard work, too, aren't they all? Cor."

A tiny girl toting a monstrous basket of apples for sale was forced to walk in the roadway to get around them, the faded and dirty condition of her dress a glaring contrast to the crisp kerseymeres, nankeens, and cambrics.

Rachel's gaze tracked the girl's wary path, her heart tugging. "Little girl, do be careful," she called out. For a moment, the child looked her way.

"Ho!" the man from the Benevolence Society scolded Rachel. "Watch what you're doing. You've almost trod on my foot."

He gave her an irritated push, and Rachel's boot heel snagged on a jagged cobblestone, the box jolting from her hands.

"No!" she yelled.

The box crashed onto the street, plates and pots spilling out to roll away, crockery smashing. A man steering a two-wheeled carriage swung wide to evade a battered pewter platter cartwheeling across the cobblestones, lurching into the heavy oncoming traffic. He shouted at someone to watch out.

And then Rachel heard a scream and the whinnying recoil of his horse.

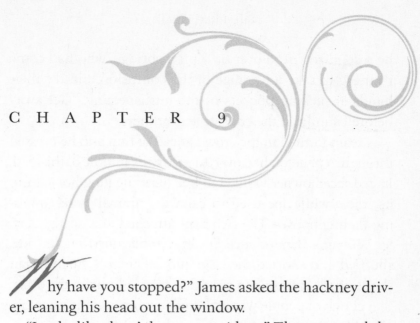

CHAPTER 9

hy have you stopped?" James asked the hackney driver, leaning his head out the window.

"Looks like there's been an accident." The man used the butt of his whip to point. "No one's gettin' through there."

A tangle of horses and wagons and people blocked passage. Someone was trying to back up a cart to turn around and ran into a hitching post at the side of the street. Raised voices rumbled down the roadway, bounced off the sides of the houses, and mixed with the staccato clatter of hooves on cobblestone. A policeman trotted past.

James grabbed his medical bag and unlatched the door. "They might need my help. We're close enough to my house as it is. I'll get out here."

He tossed the driver his fare and headed up the road. The worst of the mess looked to be located outside his front door.

James started jogging.

He heard Mrs. Mainprice's voice before he saw her thundering down his front steps, an old blue blanket in her hands. "Make some room for the lass, will you?"

James shoved aside two scruffy boys, crossing sweepers

he recognized from over on Knightsbridge, who had come running to take advantage of the confusion and try their hands at picking pockets of the unsuspecting. "Get away before I summon the constable over there."

A seam formed in the crowd ahead of him and he pressed through. A phaeton had overturned in the middle of the road. Its red-faced owner worked to free his struggling horse from its traces while Joe tried to calm the animal, barely missing flailing hooves. The two nags attached to a nearby cart, St. William's Benevolence Society emblazoned on its side, shuffled and snorted their agitation. The policeman began shouting for everyone to clear the street, adding to the din.

A clutch of people was gathered just beyond the phaeton. Mrs. Mainprice disappeared into their midst.

"Let me through," James called out, stepping over a broken earthenware pitcher he recognized as once having belonged to him. He thought he saw the top of Miss Dunne's head, the bright blaze of her hair, low to the ground. Was she injured? His heartbeat ratcheted up. "I'm a physician; let me through."

Mrs. Mainprice heard his voice and waved to him. "Oh, sir, thank goodness you're here! You've got to help."

One of his neighbors, the banker's wife with her silverish hair and curiously coordinating day dress, sidestepped to make room, taking her parlor-maid with her.

"It's a girl, Dr. Edmunds. One of those street sellers who are always coming around. She's been run over," she said without any particular compassion.

The last of the crowd parted. Mrs. Mainprice had draped the blue blanket over the huddled pile on the street. The girl's basket lay not far away, apples cascading onto the road, shiny globes of pink lodged in the dung and the filth. Miss Dunne was seated in the disgusting mess, the child's head cradled on her lap, snarled strands of hair the shade of dead grass splayed across her apron. Spots of color rode high on the girl's cheeks—was she more than five years of age?—and she pinched her eyes shut against the pain.

James dropped to his knees next to Miss Dunne. "What happened?"

She glanced over. "I dropped the box. She was in the road when the carriage veered around it. He ran into her. It was my fault."

Impulsively James pressed a hand to her elbow, the thick twill of her gown rough beneath his fingers. "Don't blame yourself. Please."

She looked away from his face, down at the girl quietly moaning in her lap.

James dropped his hand. "Has she been moved at all?"

"No. I made certain she was not seriously injured before letting anyone lift her off the road."

"Very good, Miss Dunne. That was precisely the right thing to do. Poor creature." He brushed the child's hair back from her face, scratched from scraping against the ground, a smear of dirt along her jaw. She whimpered and squirmed. "Shh, little one. Hush now."

His fingertips lingered, shaking as he drew them down the side of her face. Cleaned up, the girl might resemble Amelia, with her daintily pointed chin. He blinked away the image. In truth, she looked nothing like his daughter, but he saw Amelia's face everywhere these days.

James peeled back the blanket. A crosshatching of cuts bled scarlet onto her threadbare dress. Her left arm dangled awkwardly from above the elbow, bending in a direction no arm was meant to go.

"I think only her arm is broken," Miss Dunne said, her voice abruptly gone faint, as if coming from a distance. "I checked her ribs and . . . legs and . . . and . . ."

He looked up from his examination of the girl, saw Miss Dunne go pale, and caught her just before her head hit the ground.

Rachel sputtered awake, the acrid stench of ammonia making her eyes water. Voices buzzed all around her, like a hundred flies circling her head. She blinked up at Dr. Edmunds's face, hovering very close above hers.

He smiled then looked over his shoulder. "As you see, Mrs. Mainprice, quick-lime and muriate of ammonia works every time."

Mrs. Mainprice took the bottle he held out and tucked it into the pocket hidden deep within her voluminous skirts. "Glad to see you awake, miss. Was worried about you for a moment there." She nodded and moved out of Rachel's view.

"What is going on?" Rachel's head felt strange, empty and loose as if she had left a portion of her brain on the cobblestones. She tried to focus on his face.

"You fainted, Miss Dunne."

Oh, yes. The little apple seller and her broken arm . . . A fresh wave of lightheadedness swept over Rachel.

Dr. Edmunds shimmied his arms beneath her legs and her shoulders. "Hang on tight. Unless you want me to drop you."

"I can walk," she protested, though the spinning of her

head made clear there would be no walking in her immediate future.

"I think not."

Rachel tensed her eyes against the dizziness and clasped her hands behind his neck. She felt the strong muscles of his shoulders bunch and then he stood. The smell of his shaving soap—the scent of almonds—wafted off his cheek, his face was so near to hers. Shifting her weight, he ascended the steps.

"But what about the apple seller?" Rachel tried to peer around his arm. "She is still in the street."

Curious onlookers knotted around the girl, forming a wall that prevented Rachel from seeing the child. Mrs. Mainprice's familiar frilled white cap peeked between arms and bodies.

"Mrs. Mainprice will tend to her until a surgeon arrives."

"But the girl needs help now." The child had been shivering and Rachel had sent Mrs. Mainprice to get a blanket to keep her warm. There had been so much blood, and the way her arm dangled . . . Rachel's head reeled and she closed her eyes. "The poor child was run over like a dog in the road."

"I know, Miss Dunne." Weariness edged the doctor's voice. He passed through the open front door, and they entered the cool darkness of the hallway. The sight of the crowd was lost to Rachel. "But I will see that she's properly tended to."

"Will it be enough?" she whispered.

If he heard, he didn't answer, though she thought she felt tension move through his chest, crushed tight against her own.

He carried her down the hallway and into his office. Carefully, he settled her onto the settee.

"Molly, bring a lap rug and some hot tea for Miss Dunne," he ordered the maid, who had followed them into the room.

She missed the comfort of his arms the moment he withdrew them. *Silly Rachel.* "I shall be fine, Dr. Edmunds. You do not need to stay with me."

"Let me decide what you need." He smiled a doctor's comforting smile and pressed his fingertips to the pulse in her throat. "Good. Steady." They swept along the line of her cheek, soft as a feather stroke, before lifting away to leave the feel of them on her skin.

He inhaled a rapid breath and stepped back.

"Is anything the matter?" Rachel asked.

"Not with you." He wiped his hands together as if trying to remove something from his fingers. "I believe I shall send Mrs. Mainprice in here to sit with you until you're feeling better."

❧ ❧

"Can't right sees 'em as yet." Joe swiveled his head the other direction and poked it farther through the open window in Rachel's bedchamber. "Nope. Not comin' that way either."

"It's quite all right, Joe. I should not be so curious." What Miss Castleton looked like was none of her affair, anyway. Besides, Rachel's room was so high up from the street, she'd likely see nothing more than the top of the woman's bonnet.

Joe pulled himself back into the room. "But women are always curious 'bout other women."

"Well, this woman needs not to be."

"Eh." He winked. "If you don' mind me sayin', yer a hundred times prettier than 'er, Miss Dunne."

"A fine compliment, Joe."

"A true one." The bells chimed in the nearest church towers, striking five. "Cor, is that the time now? I'll 'ave me 'ead boxed if I don't get those water glasses shined up afore the company arrives."

He scuttled out of her room.

"Thank you for bringing up my tray," Rachel called after him.

She sighed and pulled shut the window before the temptation to lean out it herself took hold. Her tray of food waited on the chair by her bed. A quiet and simple meal compared to the feast that would be going on downstairs. A very boring one if she didn't occupy her mind with something other than pondering the Castletons.

Rachel headed down the stairs, bound for the library and a borrowed book, just as Dr. Edmunds appeared in the second-floor hallway.

"Miss Dunne, I'd just been coming to check on you." He was dressed in evening clothes, his fingers fumbling with his cravat. He was gloriously handsome, the sharp points of his collar emphasizing the line of his jaw, the deep indigo of his tailcoat turning his eyes the shimmering blue-gray of rain-misted pebbles.

All for Miss Castleton.

Rachel bobbed her head, pulling her gaze off his face before he realized she was staring. "I was heading down to the library to borrow a book to read. If you do not mind."

"Certainly not. You are recovered, then?"

"I am, and I regret causing you any trouble today. As my father would say, repentance will not cure mischief, though."

He smiled, a hasty movement of his lips, and she was

caught up in the sight of it. "You've nothing to repent. You've caused no mischief, and the girl will be fine. In fact, without your calm handling of the situation, she might have come to a great deal more harm."

"Do not compliment me for being weak and faint-hearted."

He dropped his hands then, a portion of his cravat coming unraveled as he did so. "I do not think of you as being weak, Miss Dunne. Not in the least."

She blushed. "Dr. Edmunds, your neck cloth needs re-tying. Let me try," Rachel offered, though it had been years since she'd tied a cravat. Anything to change the direction of his words or her thoughts.

"Molly is not the most efficient valet," he said. Rachel stepped up to him, her fingers deft on the heavy white silk, so close to his cleanly shaven chin. The scent of tangy cologne rose off his clothes. She tried not to notice how near her hand was to his face, or that the tips of her sturdy and scuffed half boots were within inches of his polished black shoes. Or that an errant strand of hair curled over his forehead, requiring only the merest lift of her hand to sweep it back into place.

"Regarding the apple girl," he said, his steady gaze on Rachel's face, "if you wish to see how she's progressing, we can go to her home in a day or so. You were very concerned about her."

"I was." Even though she was not Rachel's patient and therefore not her responsibility. But when did that sort of recognition stop her heart from squeezing at the thought of the child's injuries? "I would like that. So long as the visit is not an inconvenience to you, Dr. Edmunds."

"None whatsoever. I usually check up on all my patients. I have to make sure the surgeon's done a proper job."

"They can be so—" Rachel stopped. She had nearly admitted her opinion of surgeons, especially those who treated impoverished children, and the knot slipped in her shaking fingers. "I am not good at tying a cravat at all."

"I trust you'll succeed. Try again," he encouraged.

She picked up the ends of the strip of cloth and began tying it again. What was fashionable? A simple loose knot with the ends tucked into the waistcoat would be best. And all she could manage, with her nerves jangling as they were.

Knot finished, her fingertips brushed against the thick linen of his shirt as she hastily tucked the neck cloth. "There you are. I hope it is passable."

"Very passable, and now I won't be late for dinner."

"Your friends have yet to arrive, I believe. Not that I have been attempting to watch for your dinner companions, Dr. Edmunds . . ." Her cheeks warmed. How she wished she could keep from blushing at the least provocation.

He seemed amused. It was hard to tell, when amusement sat so uncomfortably on his face. "Dr. Castleton would be flattered to know of your interest, Miss Dunne."

Thankfully he had misunderstood who it was she'd been hoping to spot. "I heard that Dr. Castleton and his sister were coming for dinner. He is the physician taking over your practice, correct?"

"The same. A very skilled physician and good friend." He glanced down at what he could see of his cravat. "That looks excellent."

Actually, the knot looked lopsided. "My father would be appalled if I had fixed up his neck cloth so poorly. He was very particular."

"Would your father have another saying for this situation?" he asked.

"Perhaps something along the lines of taking the ax out of the carpenter's hands, because I am certain there is someone in this household more competent at tying cravats than myself."

"I would not be so sure." He paused as if he'd had a sudden thought. "You know, Miss Dunne, Dr. Castleton is very interested in Ireland and would certainly enjoy hearing your father's sayings. Perhaps you could join us after dinner this evening, talk with him about Ireland. Tell all of us about your homeland. I've never been. I would like to hear about it."

Join them? Rachel knew his offer was merely polite generosity, because joining them was impossible for a woman like her. Though a piece, a tiny piece low in her heart, wished desperately that it were possible, and not just so she could satisfy her curiosity about Miss Castleton. She would love to belong in his company, be an equal, be valued as such rather than looked upon as a poor Irish woman in need of charity.

Oh, Rachel, you may as well wish for a storybook hero to come and rescue you.

"I would greatly enjoy visiting with your friends, but obviously I cannot. I doubt Dr. Castleton would be much diverted by my conversation, anyway."

"He would likely be very diverted, especially by a woman as intelligent and capable and sensible as you are."

Sensible. Perhaps not the trait she wished he would see in her.

CHAPTER 10

"Will you be leaving your excellent cook behind, James?" asked Thaddeus, his thick, dark sideburns shifting as he grinned. "My wife would love to have her."

"I'm afraid, Thaddeus, Mrs. Mainprice goes with me," replied James, signaling Molly to clear the remainder of the dessert from the dining room.

Thaddeus leaned back and patted his mouth one last time with the napkin. Molly whisked it away before it barely had time to rest on the tablecloth. "The boiled capon, the turbot, the *haricot verts almondine* . . . most impressive."

"And the marvelous raspberry-and-currant tart. Do not forget that, Thaddeus," said Miss Castleton, seated beside her brother. Blonde and fine-boned, deceptively fragile-looking, she shimmered like dew upon fields of spring grass in her gown of layered lime-green muslin. A beautiful display. And though she had complimented the meal, she'd hardly touched any of it. James knew her thoughts lay elsewhere. On marriage.

To him.

God, show me the way out of this without offending a friend.

"I'm glad you both enjoyed the meal," James said. "I will relay your compliments to Mrs. Mainprice."

"If you change your mind about taking her to Finchingfield with you, just let me know." Thaddeus shook his head. "Ah, James, every time I think about you leaving, I still refuse to believe it. And in less than a month. Though I should have been expecting you might finally decide to go. Your father did want you to take over the property."

"He did." *Though I've been far from ready.* As much as the doctoring had worn him down, the responsibilities . . . the duties he would face in Finchingfield were even more wearying.

James smiled at Thaddeus and his sister, who did not need to know the conflict churning in his head, nor would likely care. "If all goes well, my departure will be sooner than a month. My assistant is rapidly cataloging the library and the contents of my office, my father's property in Finchingfield is being repaired and repainted, and my patients have all been informed—"

"And I can hear them now: 'How dare that Dr. Edmunds leave us to the likes of Dr. Castleton! He has no bedside manner and will likely kill us all off within a fortnight.'"

"None of them have protested as yet."

"Furthermore, there's Finchingfield itself," Thaddeus continued, warming to his subject. Miss Castleton sipped quietly from a glass of lemonade and tried to look disinterested, though James knew she hung on every word. "A lovely area, no doubt at all. And your family's house is grand, if a bit tumbled-down. But you'll be bored in a month's time, maybe a week's time, pottering around in the garden, ambling down country lanes occupied by nothing more than farmers' wagons and country wives on their way to market, counting the hours to your next meal or the days to a visit by the local parson."

An itch developed along James's torso, an itch of irritation. He had heard this commentary repeatedly from Thaddeus since he'd told his friend about his decision to leave London and his thriving practice.

"I shall enjoy the clean air and quiet," James insisted. "And I will finally have time to actually read all the books I've amassed in my library."

"All you need to complete the picture is a dog at your feet, cozy by the fire. Well, that shall be thrilling. Don't you agree, Louisa?"

"Actually, Thaddeus, country air does sound like a most pleasing change from the air of London." She smiled prettily at James, willing him to see how eager she was to join him there.

James gave her a noncommittal nod, sipped from his glass of seltzer, and stayed quiet. The countryside would never suit her. Louisa Castleton was born to the city like a bird was meant to fly.

"Louisa, I do believe you've grown bored with London," said her brother, lifting his brows but not looking truly surprised at her comment. "I never thought that would be possible."

"Indeed. It's become rather tedious. The countryside would be most charming. Of course, I would wish to come to town every so often. As you are here, Thaddeus." She sounded as if she'd rehearsed her plans for some time. "But I know nothing of Finchingfield. You've been there, but I never have. Perhaps Dr. Edmunds will be so kind as to invite me someday."

She turned her gaze on James, and he saw the desperation in her eyes. James's grip on his glass tightened. He blamed Thaddeus for letting his sister cling to the hope they would wed. Blamed himself for not rectifying the mistake earlier. He refused to marry out of obligation. He had done that before . . . and failed miserably.

"Molly," he called out, bringing the maid back into the dining room. "Dr. Castleton and I are ready for our cigars. Also, could you send for Miss Dunne? I would like her to escort Miss Castleton to the drawing room and keep her company until Dr. Castleton and I are finished."

He felt, rather than noticed, Miss Castleton brighten. *She must be thinking that the awaited time has come.*

"Yes, sir," Molly replied, placing the inlaid wood cigar box at his side and hurrying off.

"Who is Miss Dunne?" asked Thaddeus. "The name sounds Irish."

"She's the assistant I hired. Very intelligent, disciplined young woman." Who had weighed next-to-nothing when he'd carried her in his arms, tucked against his chest. He had held her closer than he'd needed to. James swallowed some seltzer. "She is a cousin of an old friend of Mariah's. She was in need of a job for a short while, until she becomes established in London. She plans on teaching, I believe."

"Sounds as though she has quite won you over, this Irish teacher," stated Miss Castleton, voice taut, her face maintaining a polite smile while her eyes hardened.

"If by 'won me over' you mean I've come to appreciate

how competent she is, then yes, Miss Castleton, she has won me over. And I'm happy to have helped her. Her family has encountered financial difficulties, forcing her to seek employment here."

Thaddeus clicked his tongue against his teeth. "Like so many of them. The Irish are coming by the droves off steamers. There must be hundreds of them settling around St. Giles. Turning the place into a stinking hole, if you ask me. They show up at my front door during my one hour of seeing charity patients with their grimy children or drunk husbands and think I can cure them." He scoffed. "What they fail to realize is if they would live in clean surroundings, not packed cheek-by-jowl like herring in a jar, and abstained from their drink and their other foul habits, they might not contract every known disease."

His sister was nodding in agreement.

"I doubt they enjoy the surroundings they find themselves in, Thaddeus," James said, seeking to defend a people he had paid little attention to in the past. Miss Dunne's people. "We must help them where we can, even if all we do is offer treatment and advice. If they wish to improve their condition, the best will manage."

"I do wonder if they know how to work hard enough to do so. Soon they'll overrun the city, and then what will the rest of us do? They bring disease along with increased crime. I've heard from several colleagues that the cholera has returned among the immigrants and poor on the East Side. Soon it will be in the slums of St. Giles, mark my word. And that is coming too close for comfort."

"I didn't realize the cholera had returned," James said, gleaning the one piece of significant news buried within

Thaddeus's diatribe. "I have been so preoccupied recently, I hadn't heard."

"A case here or there." He looked over at his sister. "There is no need to worry, Louisa. It's a disease that prefers the poor, as you know. You will be perfectly safe, so long as you stay away from St. Giles."

"Oh, Thaddeus, I pray it stays there!" she said, her cheeks paling. "Do you recall that my lady's maid lost her sister to the cholera in March? And so quickly. She died in less than twelve hours. Horrid, wretched disease. I shall insist upon leaving London if it spreads."

"If you truly feel the need, Louisa, I shall make certain you do."

A knock sounded on the doorframe and Miss Dunne entered. She wore her usual drab frock, but her hair blazed in the light of the chandelier, rich as flames, attracting the eye. James wondered if she knew how she demanded attention. Even Thaddeus was staring at her.

Courteously, James stood, catching Miss Castleton by surprise that he felt the need to do so. Catching himself by surprise as well. *Miss Dunne has won me over.* "This is Miss Dunne. Might I introduce Dr. Castleton and his sister, Miss Louisa Castleton?"

Miss Dunne's gaze flicked over Miss Castleton. He would pay money to know what those eyes saw, what that mind thought.

She gave a quick curtsy. "I am pleased to make your acquaintance. What did you wish, Dr. Edmunds?"

"Could you show Miss Castleton to the drawing room and make sure that refreshments are brought up? Coffee and whatever else Mrs. Mainprice believes appropriate. Dr. Castleton and I shall be joining her there shortly."

Thaddeus pulled back his sister's chair and she rose, imperious. What she thought of Miss Dunne was evident in every rigid line of her face. "Take as long as you need, gentlemen," she said. "I shall be perfectly all right in the company of this . . . charming young woman."

"Please come with me, Miss Castleton," said Miss Dunne. She was better at keeping her opinions concealed.

"A lovely young woman," said Thaddeus, once they left the dining room. "For a creature of her class."

How easily Thaddeus had placed Miss Dunne, assigned her the compartment all the newly arrived Irish occupied whether they belonged in it or not. James found it far more difficult to classify her, though. Was she the draw of an undertow? The soft murmur of twill skirts brushing across leather boots? The faintest scent of some wild Irish flower he had smelled on her hair when he'd carried her away from the injured apple girl?

Or something else entirely?

"Cigar?" Opening the cigar box, James withdrew one and held the box out to Thaddeus.

Thaddeus grinned at his cigar. "Ah, I shall miss these. Tell me that after you've married Louisa, you'll let me come to Finchingfield House to smoke your excellent Havanas."

"We need to talk about that, Thaddeus." James lit his cigar off a chandelier candle and pulled in a long hot breath of smoke. The taste, which he usually enjoyed, was sour in his mouth. "I have no intention of asking Louisa to marry me. I don't intend on asking anyone to marry me, ever. I am sorry. Tell her I'm sorry."

"A widower for the rest of your life . . . what an idiotic plan."

"The reality, Thaddeus, is that marrying again would be the wrong thing for me to do. I don't need another wife."

"You do need a wife, like any sane man does. Even I finally gave in. Louisa would make the perfect mistress of your household. She is lovely, accomplished, well spoken. Knows not to mind what sort of hours you'd keep. I don't understand why you are so unwilling to have her."

"Because I do not love her." A voice from his past haunted: *Do you love me, James?*

He wasn't sure he could love anyone.

"Is love a requirement for marriage?" Thaddeus asked, far too coolly. His wife was quiet and proper, an excellent hostess and calm companion, admired but not adored. Like most wives James knew.

"It is a requirement for me." James flicked ash off his cigar onto a plate taken from the sideboard. Ash showered across the plate, off the edge, and onto the table.

"And what of Amelia? If you remarry, you could finally remove her from your sister-in-law's care and bring her home. I know Mrs. Woodbridge has done a marvelous job, a task many a woman has done for a deceased sister, but Amelia needs both a mother and a father."

The earlier itch along James's spine returned. "Sophia will be moving to Finchingfield House with Amelia, once the house is ready for them. She will have the both of us then."

Behind a thin curtain of cigar smoke, Thaddeus's eyes took on a pitying look. "I'm sure Mrs. Woodbridge is more than delighted with that arrangement. She shall never have to leave Amelia's side."

"Sophia loves Amelia like a mother. The child is all she has, since her husband died. I can't just force the girl away from her, and Amelia wouldn't ever want to leave Sophia."

Thaddeus groaned. "I don't like any of this. The decision to quit your practice, flee London, and take up puttering in the countryside because your father requested on his deathbed that Amelia be raised there . . . Don't mistake me, I respect your father's dying wish, but none of this feels right. I had hoped when you didn't rush up to Finchingfield immediately that you agreed with me. But farming . . . It isn't what I ever thought you would do with your life. What happened to the James I used to know? The one who used to be ambitious, confident. The most promising physician I had ever met."

He died three years ago, Thaddeus. "You should be pleased I'm leaving London. You'll profit handsomely from taking over my practice."

"I'm hardly pleased. Just do me a favor . . . make certain you know what you're doing."

"I am retiring to the countryside. The last time I checked, that is not a criminal offense." James stubbed out his cigar, barely smoked, and tugged hard on his waistcoat. "Let's join the ladies before I regret having you take over my practice. Those patients of mine just might be right about worrying that you'll become their physician."

Rachel smiled nervously at Miss Castleton, perched on a sofa placed at an angle to the large drawing room window. She could hear Dr. Edmunds's voice, loud in the dining room just below them, his words but not his tone muffled by the thickness of the wood between. She imagined Miss Castleton could hear him as well, though her expression was a calm and unruffled flatness as if she were deaf to the world. Sipping her coffee with practiced elegance, Miss Castleton looked around the room, though Rachel suspected she had been there before.

Unease stretched between them, pulled tight as the warp on a loom, until Rachel feared her nerves would snap. *What am I doing here?* She wished she could leave, her curiosity about Miss Castleton well sated, but leaving would be unpardonably rude.

Downstairs, the voices stopped. Certainly Miss Castleton had noticed, for the sudden silence below caused her shoulders to visibly relax.

"Would you care for more coffee, Miss Castleton?" asked Rachel, looking to fill the void with something resembling polite conversation. Miss Castleton hadn't said a word to her other than "yes" or "no" since they had been alone together. To expect she might say more was unrealistic. A woman who was the sister of a gentleman, who aspired to be the wife of a gentleman, would not readily converse with someone she viewed as her inferior. Although Rachel evidently intrigued her. Miss Castleton had watched her closely when Rachel had poured the coffee for them both. "Or perhaps a bite of seedcake?"

"More coffee would be pleasant." Miss Castleton stared

down the length of her fine nose while Rachel refilled her cup. "Can you remind me what your position is in this household, Miss Dunne?"

"I am Dr. Edmunds's assistant." *And right now I feel as insignificant as a bug . . .*

"I thought he already had an assistant. Miss Guimond."

"She is no longer with Dr. Edmunds, but I have not replaced her. I am cataloging the contents of his library and helping pack his office. A temporary position until I find a place in a school as a teacher."

Miss Castleton's eyes, a gorgeous violet fringed by fair eyelashes, peered at her. Rachel decided they were her best feature and made her quite amazingly lovely. "So you're not to go with the rest of the household to Finchingfield."

"No."

"Yes, I remember that is what James . . . oh, I mean, Dr. Edmunds, told us." She attempted to look embarrassed at having so familiarly dropped Dr. Edmunds's Christian name, though Rachel suspected it was no accident. "It must be hard to find respectable employment, coming as you are from Ireland."

The barb found its mark, but Rachel ignored the temptation to react to its sting. It was likely Miss Castleton meant to be spiteful; it was just as likely she was merely speaking the awful truth as she knew it. "I am fortunate that my cousin, Miss Harwood, will assist me. She knows of several charity schools where I might find a position."

"Ah, a charity school. Of course, that would be perfect for you, Miss Dunne. I've visited many of them myself, when I've been able, and the children are so pitiable." A moue of compassion attempted to fix itself upon her mouth. "Perhaps I can assist in founding such a place in Finchingfield, if there is a need."

The stupid pinch of jealousy returned. "You are also moving to Finchingfield?"

"Oh, I should not have stated it so plainly, but I believe I shall be." She began to whisper conspiratorially, "Between us, Miss Dunne, I do expect that Dr. Edmunds is about to ask for my hand in marriage. If he has not already broached the subject with my brother, who acts as my guardian in place of our father, long deceased."

"You must be very excited by the prospect of such a marriage," replied Rachel, vividly aware that she did not want to be party to Miss Castleton's expectations. She would prefer to know absolutely nothing about Miss Castleton and Dr. Edmunds's matrimonial plans. "Dr. Edmunds is a fine man."

"Indeed, I am thrilled," said Miss Castleton, dreamily. "I have always longed to live in the countryside."

Rachel bit back a hasty rejoinder. *You should be thrilled to be with him.* That sentiment should be Miss Castleton's uppermost thought. How could Dr. Edmunds wish to marry Miss Castleton? They were as opposite as the poles of a magnet. He was serious and she decidedly frivolous. He needed someone who could understand him. Who knew what it meant to be drawn to an injured child in a road. Miss Castleton seemed more likely to stride away, eyes averted from the street urchin, than to bend down to offer aid.

"Congratulations, Miss Castleton." Rachel scraped together all the goodwill she could gather and found sufficient to truly mean her words. "I wish you great joy."

Miss Castleton's eyes widened, taken aback that Rachel—a

poor Irish girl—could be gracious enough, well bred enough, to extend sincere felicitations. "Why, thank you."

The men entered the drawing room. Dr. Edmunds's gaze sought out Rachel before looking anywhere else. Before drifting to the woman who intended on moving to Finchingfield with him. Drift to Miss Castleton, though, they eventually did.

Rachel stood. "It was very agreeable to speak with you, Miss Castleton. Good evening to you."

"Good evening, Miss Dunne. I wish you success with your endeavors."

Dr. Castleton went to join his sister on the sofa. Rachel attempted to slip by Dr. Edmunds, still waiting just inside the doorway. He lifted a hand to stop her. "Please stay, Miss Dunne. It's early yet."

"I cannot, Dr. Edmunds. Because of my unfortunate fainting spell earlier, I still have work to attend in the library and must leave you to your guests."

"If you insist."

"I do."

"Always sensible, Miss Dunne."

"That I am." *For I know where I do not belong.*

"Dr. Edmunds," called out Miss Castleton possessively, "please join us. Thaddeus has started to tell an amusing story about a hot potato seller he encountered today, and you must hear it."

Dr. Edmunds bowed his head and ceased attempting to convince Rachel to stay, strolling away to take a seat across from Miss Castleton. He made a remark to her that was out of Rachel's hearing and she smiled. The sight constricted Rachel's chest for no particular reason she could name. Miss

Castleton was of Dr. Edmunds's world. Maybe she would make him happy. She obviously enjoyed his company and wanted to be his wife. They would have beautiful children and be blessed by God.

Rachel turned slowly on her heel and closed the door behind her.

CHAPTER 11

*M*orning didn't bring an announcement of an impending wedding. In fact, the day was progressing much as the past few days had, with Joe bustling around the house or out by the outbuildings, Mrs. Mainprice in the kitchen, Peg and Molly cleaning and washing and tidying. And Rachel at work in the library, with nothing to disturb her save the twirling of her thoughts, fast as the feet of a dancer.

Had Dr. Edmunds not asked Miss Castleton to marry him, after all? Was that what he and Dr. Castleton had been discussing after dinner?

"Miss Dunne, you've a letter."

The voice at the library doorway—Molly's—jolted her, and Rachel plucked the end of the dip pen out of her mouth. She had been chewing it absentmindedly while she'd fretted over matters irrelevant to her.

Molly stood in the library doorway, a folded bit of paper in her outstretched fingers.

"A letter?" Rachel asked, setting the pen aside and taking the note from the maid. She glanced at the outside and recognized the handwriting—her mother's. Rachel tucked the letter into her apron pocket to send the clear signal she was not about to read it while Molly stood there. "Thank you for delivering it."

"Do you have the postage, or do I have to ask Dr. Edmunds for the money?" Rachel paused long enough to generate a sneer on Molly's face. "That's what I thought."

Molly briskly strode out. Rachel hurried over to the window, retrieved the note from her pocket, and broke the red wafer seal. It was filled with the expected greetings and words of love, news of the twins and Nathaniel, even the cat, making Rachel's chest ache from nostalgia. She could hear her mother's voice reciting everyone's antics, her words light and happy. Did Sarah and Ruth not notice that their older sister was gone? Was Nathaniel so occupied with being the eldest child of the household that he didn't miss Rachel? Or was Mother masking the reality to keep Rachel from fretting?

Rachel rotated the note to follow the twists and turns of Mother's message, her cramped handwriting making the most of the single sheet of paper to economize. She nearly skimmed right over the most critical lines, the reality that couldn't be masked:

I don't wish to distress you, but Mr. Ferguson is still angry. He is claiming to all who'll listen—which is a greater number than ought be—that the trial was a sham and justice wasn't served. Do not worry for us. We can weather it. Thankfully, by the time you receive this letter you should be safe and settled in London.

My deepest love,
Mother

Heart in her throat, Rachel pressed the note to her face, fancying it carried the soft scents of home—bundled herbs, stew in the pot, heather. All she loved and missed was in jeopardy, placed there by a vengeful man. She had to get her family away from Carlow immediately, before Mr. Ferguson destroyed what was left of the Dunnes' reputation.

Or did worse.

The Harwoods' London home stood in a part of town that spoke of gentility in hushed and ancient tones, echoing disdain for the new neighborhoods with their boring symmetry and stubby fresh-planted trees, disdain that Rachel could hear among the tall maples crowding the square and the decorous clip-clop of horses' hooves on cobblestones. Even the street sellers' banter was subdued, as if afraid to disturb the perfect order.

Rachel hurried down the pavement, her rough twill skirts slapping against her half boots, drawing the condemning glare of a neighbor descending from her carriage. How could Claire tolerate the constant scrutiny? Claire, however, would pass inspection, Rachel reminded herself.

A pert maid in a crisp black uniform answered Rachel's knock, reluctantly taking Rachel's message before leaving her to idle outside on the steps.

At last, Claire arrived at the door, shutting it behind her. Hastily, she brushed a kiss across Rachel's cheek. "Rachel, how unexpected."

"I would not have disturbed you, except I have received a letter from home that has me very worried."

"I see." Claire guided Rachel down to the pavement. "I would invite you in, but . . ." Her cousin glanced up at a first-floor window. "It's easier for us to talk out here."

Claire led her across the street to the gated park filling the neighborhood square. The trees and clipped hedges would shield them from the view of whoever it was Claire seemed so anxious to evade back at the house. Probably Aunt Harriet. She disliked Dunnes as much as Uncle Anthony had.

Releasing the park's gate, Claire ushered Rachel inside. She looked about her, as if the park might be concealing spies. A nursemaid wheeling her charge past did not even look their way.

Satisfied they would not be overheard, Claire reached for Rachel's hand and dragged her down onto a bench. "Tell me what has happened."

"A relative of the person I was accused of harming is still very angry. He is claiming that I should not have been let free. Mother did not say what he has done beyond complain to everyone he can think of, but I am afraid he might harm them. He drinks heavily, at times, and . . ." So clearly, Rachel could remember how Mr. Ferguson had looked at her trial, his eyes rheumy and vacant. An irresponsible and vindictive drunk.

"I must get my family away from Carlow sooner than I had planned, Claire, but for that I need money. At least four pounds for passage."

Claire frowned. "I don't have that amount. A few shillings are all I'm ever allowed. My brother pays all my expenses. If I go to a shop, he receives the bill and attends to it. I only ever have enough just to pay for an ice or some flowers or to offer coins to a beggar."

"I cannot ask Dr. Edmunds for the money." An employer never lent money to his staff. "Perhaps you could ask your brother. I would pay him back, with interest."

"Ask Gregory?" Claire scoffed. "He would never agree."

"Then I must find some way to get the money. I suppose I could sell my other dress and a pair of stockings."

"And maybe get a half crown for the both, if you're lucky." Claire looked down at Rachel's hands, clasped within her own. Rachel eyed the pearl ring set in gold that gleamed on her cousin's finger. It was pretty and had to be valuable, an elegant token of Harwood wealth. Rachel had no idea what it was worth, however, because she'd never owned a piece of jewelry so fine.

Claire's eyes met Rachel's; she had caught Rachel staring.

"The ring was a gift from Father on my eighteenth birthday. When he'd still been pleased with me." She rolled the ring's band beneath the pad of her thumb. The opalescence of the pearl trapped the dim sunlight filtering through the leaves overhead. "It must be worth far more than four pounds. But if Gregory notices the ring gone from my hand, he'll be unmercifully furious with me."

"I cannot ask you to sell it," Rachel said, though she was too desperate to absolutely refuse Claire's suggestion.

"I'm going to pawn it, not sell it." Clasping Rachel's hand, she dragged her upright. "Come. Let's do this before I lose my nerve."

⁂

"Eight pounds," the pawnbroker declared, his sharp eyes concealing any genuine interest in Claire's pearl ring.

"Eight pounds!" Claire exclaimed. Beyond the pawnbroker, out in the body of the main shop, a customer in shabby tweeds looked over from his perusal of silver watches and gaudy snuffboxes. Claire slunk back into the shadows of the tiny cubicle, a row of which lined the rear of the shop and offered some privacy to those unwilling to march in directly off the street to pawn their bits and pieces.

"Truly, you do not need to do this," Rachel whispered, tugging on Claire's sleeve. "I will find another way."

"I do need to do this," she answered, her tone unyielding. She stared at the pawnbroker, her shoulders back, head high. Brave. "The gold band itself has to be worth more than eight pounds."

"Might be so, miss, but I run a business here, not a charity," he said, his expression flat, almost bored.

Resting his arm on the counter separating them, the pawnbroker held out the ring, the band pinched between his fleshy thumb and forefinger, daring Claire to take it back. Rachel recognized the game, having observed other pawnbrokers in other pawnshops act precisely the same. If a woman like Claire, clearly well-off, was desperate enough to come to this grimy back alley shop, she wouldn't leave without some money.

"I'll not accept less than ten," Claire insisted, but she made no move to reclaim the ring.

"Eight," the pawnbroker repeated, scratching his ear.

"Nine. I must have nine."

He sniffed, his rather large nostrils flaring, and turned to the counter behind him. He fiddled with a locked money box and withdrew coins.

"Eight and six, and that is my final offer. Because the

both of you are such lovely ladies." He scribbled the information about the exchange on a scrap of a card, pressed the paper into a box of sand to set the ink, and handed it over. "Here's your ticket. That'll be one pound per month interest. If you're so inclined to fetch the ring back, that is. If not, I sell it at year's end."

Nine pounds six due by the end of the month? Ten and six by the month after that? Rachel stared at her cousin, aghast. If she didn't have the money to lend Rachel four pounds, she would not have the funds to pay off the pawnbroker's loan. The ring was as good as gone. And Gregory Harwood would be unmercifully furious.

"Are you certain you want to pawn the ring?" Rachel asked.

"It's done," said Claire firmly. "Good day to you, sir."

Grabbing the money and the ticket, Claire deposited them into her reticule. Rachel pushed open the cubicle door and together they hurried down the hallway, exited the side door, and burst into the courtyard. Claire took the lead, more anxious than Rachel to flee the pawnshop, running past a gin shop and women hawking rotten vegetables, a knot of boys throwing stones in a game of gully who shouted lewd remarks at the both of them.

Passing beneath the courtyard's archway, Claire kept up a rapid pace until she reached the street and her family's carriage, waiting on the road.

"You all right, miss?" The Harwood coachman hustled to the door and threw it open.

"I am quite all right, Benjamin." She took his hand and let him help her up the steps. Rachel followed and dropped onto the carriage seat next to her.

"Don't you dare breathe a word to my brother that you brought me here," Claire ordered the coachman.

"Never, miss." Gravely, he shook his head and clicked shut the carriage door. "Now to Belgrave Square?"

"Yes. Dr. Edmunds's house."

Once they were underway, Claire burst into a fit of giggles. "Good heavens, Rachel, what have we done?"

"You have pawned a ring Uncle Anthony gave to you, which will likely bring you untold problems, I am certain." Rachel shook her head. "How can I ever thank you?"

"By spending the money well and making certain my most favorite aunt and the cousins I've never met come safely to England." Sobering, Claire retrieved the coins from her reticule and spilled them into Rachel's palm, a tiny waterfall of silver and gold. "I'm glad I never gave that ring away, even though I've wanted to more often than I could count. Obviously, God had plans for it."

⁂

Rachel and Claire plotted and planned the rest of the way back to Dr. Edmunds's house, and when she climbed down from the carriage and waved good-bye, Rachel's mood was more buoyant, more hope-filled than it had been in ages. Soon, she and her family would be together again. Sooner than they had planned, actually. The thought made her smile.

She rushed down the area steps and hastened through the kitchen, stripping off her bonnet and shawl as she offered a quick greeting to Mrs. Mainprice, carrying supplies from the pantry. The moment she rounded the ground-floor landing, she spotted Dr. Edmunds.

"Miss Dunne," he called out. "I'm glad to see you back."

Beyond him in the entry hall, Molly glared at her for a reason Rachel could not fathom.

Rachel looked away from her. "Did you need me, Dr. Edmunds?" she asked. "I am sorry I was gone longer than I told you I would be." Almost two hours instead of the half hour she'd requested.

"It's quite all right." He frowned as he interwove his fingers to ensure his gloves were on tight. "I need you to accompany me on a visit to a patient, Miss Dunne. I'm sorry, but the fellow is going to require that someone attend to him for several hours, and I have an important appointment this afternoon with a baroness I had best not miss. If you think you can manage, Miss Dunne."

"I . . . I . . ." she stuttered, while Molly's face pinched with resentment. Did the maid despise Rachel because she wanted to help the doctor with his patients, take on the superior role of acting as attendant to a physician? *I should let her do it, because heaven knows I do not want to.*

But the doctor was waiting, his shoulders beginning to droop in anticipation of Rachel's refusal. She did not want to disappoint him. Or, she thought pettishly, to let Molly win.

"Indeed, I am willing to help you, Dr. Edmunds. I shall endeavor to keep my head this time."

Molly's face fell.

"Thank you, Miss Dunne. I greatly appreciate your assistance."

A smile flitted across the doctor's lips. Rachel might agree to walk on hot coals to see his smile. Or tend a patient, even.

So much for vows.

CHAPTER 12

*M*r. Fenton-Smith looked shrunken beneath the white dimity sheets. The last time James had seen the fellow he'd been robust and ruddy-cheeked, thick-bellied and as bellicose as ever. This creature with hollow cheeks and blue veins popping along his neck was not the same man. The change was sudden and startling. He was far gone. There was almost nothing James could do.

Miss Dunne hovered off to his left, clutching a damp cloth in her hand. She was pale but still standing upright, a triumph when being here was nearly as bad as confronting a girl with a broken arm.

"He's been so very ill, Dr. Edmunds," said the man's wife, her graying hair tightly wound beneath a white lace cap, the wrinkles of her face deepening from concern. "I cannot keep up with all the . . . all the . . ." Her gaze flicked to the chamber pot, stinking at the bedside, then her husband's face, then away.

"You've been giving him laudanum to quiet his stomach?"

"Yes, and it has worked briefly, but he seems to be ebbing." Tears quavered at the edge of her small eyes. "And he's grown so warm to the touch."

"Cool cloths may help his fever. For now." He gestured for Rachel to bring a fresh one over. She gently draped it over the man's forehead. The cream-colored woven cotton was almost the same shade as his flesh. "He won't come to harm if we open the window a bit and let in some air. I will leave you a recommendation for another tonic that may aid in settling his stomach."

Mrs. Fenton-Smith pressed her lips together until white lined their edges. "Is it the cholera?"

James stared down at her husband. He feared it was, but nothing could be gained by proclaiming his fears prematurely. "Don't worry yourself about that, Mrs. Fenton-Smith."

"But I have heard it has returned, Dr. Edmunds."

"Not in this part of town, madam. Miss Dunne will stay and watch for some time to see how your husband fares today, see if the fever turns or worsens or if his other symptoms change. Then we'll know for certain." *And be just as helpless as we are now.*

"Shall we pray together, doctor? Beg God's mercy?" asked Mrs. Fenton-Smith, her face tight with desperation, her eyes imploring him to reassure her that prayer would work.

"Prayer is always welcome," he replied.

Nodding, she bowed her head and he began the Lord's Prayer. Normally, the words rolled off his tongue unattended, rote-spoken from years of habit. Now each one seemed to echo in his brain. *Forgive us our trespasses.* His were too many.

And lead us not into temptation . . .

James glanced up. At the other side of the bed, Miss

Dunne's lips moved silently as they finished the prayer, her eyes pinched closed as though willing everything away. Last night, as she'd stood close tying his cravat, the scent of her hair surrounding him, he had longed to trace a fingertip along the line of her cheek. He had been wondering for too long if her face was as soft as it appeared.

God, save me from the temptation to take when I have nothing to give back in return.

"The Lord is my rock and my salvation," proclaimed Mrs. Fenton-Smith. She bent toward her husband, insensible to their prayers. "Oh, how ill he looks." A sob bubbled up from deep in her throat.

He drew his gaze away from Miss Dunne and sucked in a long breath that only succeeded in reminding him how fetid the air in the bedchamber was. "Mrs. Fenton-Smith, I'm sure you could use some time away from the sickroom. Please send for your maid to tidy up in here while I instruct my assistant on her duties before I depart."

Mrs. Fenton-Smith needed little encouragement, rushing out in a swirl of heavy dark skirts. Almost immediately a maid hurried in to empty the chamber pot.

James strode to the window, pulled wide the heavy curtains, and flung open the sash. Air, not exactly fresh but sweeter smelling than the contents of the room, blew in.

"I am sorry for being so little assistance to you." Miss Dunne's voice shook. "I was hoping to be stronger than I was with the young apple seller, but I am just as useless this afternoon."

"You are hardly useless." He faced her. In the brighter light, he could see the misgiving in her eyes. "And you are strong. You haven't fainted," he pointed out.

She smiled a little. "That is progress, I suppose."

James walked over and took her hand in his. It was cold to the touch. "All you need to do is sit by the bedside, dab Mr. Fenton-Smith's head with damp cloths, and observe if his fever seems to be worsening. Or if he begins to stir violently, suggesting he is in pain. That is it. Nothing further. I will return from my appointment with Lady Haverton as soon as possible to relieve you."

"You should have brought Molly instead of me to tend him, Dr. Edmunds."

I didn't want her with me. I wanted you.

He closed his other hand around her one, until it was cradled within his palms. "Mr. Fenton-Smith and his wife need your sort of calmness and quiet. Molly, for all she is willing, can't provide that."

"I have not been calm."

"Yes, you have."

Her eyes held his and he felt their pull, again. She drew him to her, whether she realized it or not.

"I shall try my best, Dr. Edmunds, but please do not take long."

"Have courage. I'll be back as quickly as I'm able."

Her fingers trembled. If he could will strength into her, he would.

But he had little enough of his own to spare.

A medical education from an esteemed college was not required to understand that Mr. Fenton-Smith was worsening. Rachel's own experience gave her the ability to see.

She stood up and went to the window, breathing in the

scent of coal smoke and someone's dinner already cooking. Her dress collar choked her and her knees threatened
to buckle whenever she walked across the blue-and-white
carpeted room. On the street beneath her, though, life pro-
ceeded as normal. Carriages and carts rattled down the
cobblestones. A nursemaid hurried by with her charge in
hand. Toting a large metal tray hung on straps wrapped
around his neck, a pie-man paraded through the intersec-
tion of the streets, calling out his price. All this going on
while Rachel fervently wished for Dr. Edmunds to reappear
so she could escape.

Pressing her back against the sill, Rachel stared at Dr.
Edmunds's patient, muttering to himself in his laudanum-
induced sleep. The man was dying. Bathing his head, dos-
ing him repeatedly, was only delaying the inevitable. And
all the purging . . .

Her stomach churned as bile rose. *God, why are You doing this to me?* The thought that she might be in this room
when Mr. Fenton-Smith breathed his last—when another
family member would stare at Rachel with sorrow and disbelief and accusation—choked off her breath. *You let him
die. It is Your fault.*

"*You killed her . . .*"

The room spun and Rachel clutched at the windowsill,
resolved to keep from fainting. If only she could gather her
wits to think what to do, what her mother might do. Did
he need more fluids or less? A tonic, broth fortified with
wine? A cold bath or a hot bath? Blankets, fresh air, windows closed, leeches? She knew she should feel reassured—
instead of lost and helpless—that Dr. Edmunds seemed to
be no more certain of how to help the man.

A noise out on the street caught her attention. A hackney had arrived and was depositing a man onto the pavement. Dr. Edmunds was back. She grabbed up her bonnet and fled the room. She was down the stairs almost as quickly as it took a maid to appear to open the door to him.

He stepped back, startled. "Miss Dunne!"

"Mr. Fenton-Smith is sinking, Dr. Edmunds. It is well you have returned. Now I must hurry to catch your hackney before it departs." She brushed past him, hurtling headlong through the doorway.

"But will you be all right?" he asked as she leaped into the carriage.

Rachel slammed the door behind her. "Dr. Edmunds, truly, I wish I knew."

She rapped on the roof, signaling the driver to depart, leaving Dr. Edmunds to stare worriedly after her.

Moonlight crept along the floor and the sounds of the house dwindled until all Rachel could hear was the noise of carriages returning neighbors from suppers and fetes. Dr. Edmunds had yet to return from the Fenton-Smiths'. The staff had given up waiting and gone to bed—even Joe, who tended to scurry about in the wee hours, attending last-minute tasks. Sleep eluding her, Rachel stared up at the bedchamber ceiling until she memorized every dip and crack in the plaster. She feared the nightmares about Mary would return as soon as she closed her eyes. Maybe they would even include Mr. Fenton-Smith. The sight of him squirming on his bed, his face beading with sweat and then going dry as chalk while he moaned and heaved, kept swimming in her brain. She should probably just get up and do some work in the library.

Sighing, Rachel threw back the top sheet and counter-pane, dropped her feet to the floor, and shimmied them into her slippers. After lighting a candle, she fetched her robe and slipped out into the hallway. She was just passing Dr. Edmunds's office at the rear of the house when she heard a key in the back door lock. She froze, uncertain whether to flee or scream the household awake. Before she could decide, the door eased open on well-oiled hinges and Molly stepped through.

"Molly! You frightened me!"

Startled, Molly dropped the key onto the tiled floor with a clatter. "Bloo . . . what're you doing up?" She bent to retrieve the key and held still, listening to hear if the rest of the household had awakened to the noise.

"I came down to fetch some water before doing some work. I could not sleep."

Molly closed the door behind her and threw the bolt. "Well, get some water then."

"I did not realize you were out. Is everything all right? It must be past eleven."

She tossed her head flippantly, the action making her wobble as if she was having difficulty maintaining her equilibrium. "It's none of your business what I've been doing."

"You should be thankful it was me rather than Dr. Edmunds coming through the hallway. He would not be pleased to find you out at such an hour."

The maid crept close. Her eyes were watery and slightly unfocused. Rachel could smell the sweet aroma of gin on her breath. "Are you planning on telling him?"

"I would not do that, Molly, even though it is not right for you to break the rules."

"You're a fine one to lecture me on breaking rules."

A frisson of apprehension shimmied along Rachel's arm. "You have been out drinking. I can smell it on you."

"I know your secret, so don't be trying to scare me." Molly inched even closer, and the stench of alcohol stung Rachel's nose, making her choke. "I know about your trial. Oh yes, Miss hoity Dunne, come to help the master as a special assistant, has a criminal past. Wouldn't the good doctor be shocked to hear about that? I'm thinking of telling him too."

She had listened at the library door during Claire's interview and . . . *the letter*. Rachel had left it in the pocket of her apron, tossed hastily onto her bed when she'd gone to Claire's house. She hadn't retrieved the apron until after she had returned from Mr. Fenton-Smith's. Had Molly been prying in her room and found the note?

Rachel hoped her expression concealed her mounting alarm. "I do not have a criminal past, so there is nothing for you to tell Dr. Edmunds except lies. And what if I told him that I encountered you creeping about in the dead of night, returning from an assignation, stinking of cheap gin? He would not be happy with you either, Molly."

Rachel could see Molly calculating the possibility she might inform Dr. Edmunds, though in truth she never would.

The maid retreated and lifted her chin. "I've decided I won't say anything to Dr. Edmunds for now. I'd rather you worry awhile about when I might. Yeah. I think I rather like that idea."

Molly smirked, gathered her cloak around her, and barged past. Pulse hammering, Rachel waited until the girl was out of sight to hurry up to her room. Slapping the candlestick onto the chest, Rachel grabbed her apron off the hook where she'd hung it that evening. She examined each pocket—twice, foolishly enough. No letter. Molly must have found it. Its contents would be serious evidence against Rachel. She grabbed up the candle, swept it before her. She had to hold onto hope the letter might still be somewhere in the room.

But there was nothing. Not beneath the chest of drawers. Not beneath the narrow bed. Not slipped under the rug.

Rachel's heart sank. The letter was gone.

CHAPTER 13

wo days later, Rachel sighed at her reflection in her bed-chamber's mirror. She'd had another sleepless night, and no matter how much she pinched color into her cheeks, nothing would mask the dark circles beneath her eyes. Nothing would banish the apprehension in them either. Even the beautiful dress Claire had sent for Rachel to wear to her interview today was failing to make her feel better, feel confident.

Rachel fastened the last hook-and-eye on the gown. It was cut to the latest fashion, with a high bodice, belling sleeves closed at the wrist, and a wide ribbon of patterned cream at the waist. Its soft calico material was printed with a pale copper and red flower motif that echoed the shading of Rachel's hair. The last time she had owned anything as handsome was when she'd turned twelve and Mother had presented her a lovely violet dress for her birthday, sewn by her own hands. Rachel had worn that dress on every occasion until the lace had frayed and the hem mended to where it had become far too short.

If Molly destroyed her reputation, though, and Rachel didn't obtain the teaching position at the school, this dress might not ever have the opportunity to fray from too much use.

Stop it, Rachel. You are worrying over matters you cannot control. Be strong.

Squaring her shoulders and snapping taut her bonnet ribbons, Rachel descended the rear stairs just as the hall clock chimed eleven. Out on the street, Claire waited in her carriage. Perfectly prompt.

Her brown eyes lit when she spotted Rachel.

"I see you received my gift," Claire said as her driver handed Rachel into the carriage.

"I did, and thank you, Claire." Rachel ran her hands over the printed cotton, smooth beneath her fingers. "It is quite fine."

As the carriage pulled away from the curb, Rachel stared back at the house. At the face she fancied she spotted peeping through the drawing room curtains.

Claire shifted to get a better look at Rachel. "What's the matter? Are you not happy with the dress? Or perhaps you're nervous about the interview. Is that it?"

"Of course I am happy with the dress!" Rachel assured her. The last thing she wanted was for Claire to think her ungrateful or spineless. "And I am a trifle nervous about the interview, but that's not what is bothering me. It's one of the maids. Molly. She found my letter from home and now she knows about the trial."

"Oh, dear."

"Indeed." Rachel shuddered, as much from exhaustion as worry. She relayed to Claire her encounter with Molly as the carriage rumbled toward the center of town. "I have not been able to sleep, petrified Molly will show the doctor my letter. And for the past two days I have crept about like a frightened rabbit, certain I would be called to Dr. Edmunds's office and told to leave his employ."

"She won't dare show him the letter." Claire sounded convinced. "The fact you saw her coming in late, smelling of alcohol, is just as damaging to her as the little she's learned about you. She would risk losing her position without a reference. Her threat to show Dr. Edmunds the letter is just that—an empty threat."

"I hope you are right."

Claire patted Rachel's knee. "I am right. I know servants."

Rachel leaned back against the carriage seat and rested her hands—encased in their new gloves, another gift from Claire—at the waist of the gown. "You have been too kind to me, Claire."

"For listening to your concerns about Molly? Or for giving you that dress?"

"For everything you've done."

Claire waved off Rachel's thanks. "Think nothing of the gown. It used to be one of mine. I instructed my maid to remake it from an old day dress, had her add a few trimmings, and now it's perfect for you to wear to the interview. Mrs. Chapman will be impressed."

"By a dress?" Rachel asked skeptically, though her mother had often told her a good cut of material, a row of mother-of-pearl buttons, and a neckline edged with a modest amount of guipure lace could transform a woman.

"By the woman in the dress."

"I will do my best, Claire."

"I know you will." Claire glanced out the window as the carriage slowed. "Here we are." She reached across the narrow gap between the facing benches and gripped Rachel's fingers. "Erase that look of terror from your face. These women know nothing about you, other than you are my cousin, but they'll scent nervousness like a hound on the trail of a fox. Believe you are the answer to their prayers, and they shall believe it too."

Rachel breathed deeply and nodded her head. She would forget about Molly, think only of what she needed to accomplish today. Her future depended upon her poise and self-assurance. So she placed a confident smile on her face and climbed out of the carriage behind Claire.

The school was a narrow three-story building leaning against its neighbor like a drunk in need of support. Broad windows filled the expanse of the first two floors, though Rachel doubted they let in much light, given the dirt crusting their panes. However, the front steps were clean and the sign declaring it to be The School for Needy Boys and Girls was freshly painted in bright blue letters.

Claire told her coachman, Benjamin, to wait for them and marched up to the door on the right marked Girls. Within a few moments, a young girl of about ten, dressed in a faded woolen gown that reached no further than the tops of her ankles, answered Claire's knock. She curtsied politely and showed them up the uncarpeted stairs. The aroma of cooking meat drifted up from a distant kitchen to intermingle with the smells of vinegar and lye that seemed to permeate the very walls. Voices swelled and receded. Somewhere, an adult shouted for attention.

"Watch your step here, miss. Tread's loose," the girl alerted them, heading ever upward. Each time she took a step, a hole in the bottom of her shoe revealed itself.

"Can we wait a moment?" Rachel asked. They reached a landing and Rachel spotted, across a hallway, an open door to one of the classrooms. "I would like to go see."

"Ma'am doesn't like to be kept waitin', miss," the girl called to Rachel's back.

The classroom was a large area that had been divided into at least two spaces by a partition at the far end, probably to separate boys from girls. On a raised platform, a teacher and her student assistant were instructing a small clutch of girls in their sums. Another group read Bibles, the hum of their voices like a hive of bees, while another sat sewing, and another copied lines of text onto slates. They looked studious, or at least skilled at feigning interest. One dared to flick a glance at Rachel, standing in the doorway. The girl did not smile but looked bored, as if she were used to women coming to stare at them like animals on display.

Rachel looked away from her, scanning the remainder. Young, so many were young, not a one over ten, maybe eleven at the most. Clean, for the most part, though their dresses did not fit well and their stockings, where they peeped beneath skirts, were worn and much darned. One child coughed quietly into her hand, thick and raspy, and Rachel wondered if anyone tended to their ills or cared precisely how well they were fed. Did they have someplace warm to sleep at night? Did their parents resent or welcome the time spent at school, time not spent earning pence to help the family? Was the girl nearest her bruised along her chin, as if she'd been hit hard? Surely not by any of the teachers. Maybe by a father, or a mother . . .

An accustomed compulsion spread through Rachel's chest.

She had to do something to help them. That desire was undimmed, no matter how she had failed Mary Ferguson.

"Miss, you have to come along." Their young escort plucked Rachel's sleeve. "Ma'am will be angry that I've taken so long to bring you up."

"I did not mean to delay." Rachel turned away, caught Claire watching.

"They are pitiful, aren't they?" Claire asked, resuming her place at Rachel's side as they continued up the staircase. "The ragged schools are so much worse. The children there do not even have shoes or mended clothes. At least here, there's hope."

"Do they treat you well in this school?" Rachel asked the girl leading them ever upward.

"As well as can be expected, miss."

Claire tutted quietly at Rachel's side. They arrived at the second floor and paused before a closed door. The girl knocked and a muffled voice told them to enter.

The office was small, carved out of a bigger space, the makeshift walls not even reaching the ceiling. Hushed tones of women tending to young children trickled over. From behind a table being utilized as a desk, a woman in a starched white bodice and a rusty-red twill skirt stood. She was of middle age, her hair feathered with gray, her features unremarkable except for the intensity that radiated from her eyes, piercing as a magistrate's.

She gestured for the girl to depart. "Miss Harwood, it is a pleasure to see you again."

"Mrs. Chapman, may I present my cousin, Miss Rachel Dunne." Claire's firmly applied fingertips pushed Rachel forward.

Rachel swallowed, her throat suddenly so parched she expected her tongue to stick to the roof of her mouth. "Mrs. Chapman, I am most grateful you have agreed to speak with me about a position as a teacher."

The headmistress indicated she and Claire could take a seat. "You did not tell me she was Irish, Miss Harwood."

"My cousin is very well educated, Mrs. Chapman," Claire responded, her voice cool. "I believed that to be all that was of consequence."

"If by well educated you mean she does not have a significant accent, I can hear that."

"Which is no small indication of her schooling, you must agree."

Rachel shifted on the hard chair, the legs rocking on the uneven floor. "I can read, having had access to numerous volumes of literature, and write with a good hand, Mrs. Chapman. My mother was a rector's daughter and a very strict instructor. I kept the books for my father's business, so I can easily teach the fundamentals of arithmetic. I also can execute decent needlework and . . ." Carelessly, she had almost admitted her knowledge of herbs and physics. "And other skills necessary for young girls to know."

"This is all well and good, Miss Dunne, but you have no certificate. You have never managed a classroom or learned the art of instruction of children."

"However you will find me more than willing to work hard, and I am well used to being around children. I believe I know how to handle them." So long as they were not seriously ill and in need of nursing, she would have no difficulty whatsoever.

"The girls might not be problematic for you, Miss Dunne. They respond quickly to correction. However, some of the boys are of rough temperament, having spent many years in the streets before we took them in. I think you might not be so ready to 'handle them' as you believe. We have had other teachers flee in terror."

"I shall learn how to manage them." Rachel leaned forward, eager to impress upon this woman the sincerity of her desire to work hard. To help. *I must help, some way, somehow. It is all I know to do.* "I am not afraid of rough boys. I have a teenage brother. I will do whatever you require."

"Do you have a reference as to your character?" Mrs. Chapman's glance encompassed both Claire and Rachel. "Your cousin has vouched for you, of course, but you must understand that I require recommendations from people who are not relations."

Her hand, with its cording of veins and sinews, extended above the papers on her desk, waiting to be supplied that which Rachel lacked.

Claire's shoulder moved forward as if to shield Rachel from the woman's grasp. "Her current employer, Dr. James Edmunds of Belgravia, will supply a recommendation at the end of her service."

"I will not consider your cousin, Miss Harwood, without such an item. There are several teachers here who will not welcome a non-English girl, and I cannot begin to contemplate hiring her without a reference of highest quality." Mrs. Chapman's hand withdrew. "As it is, Miss Dunne, you will only be brought in as an assistant teacher. Until you have the ability to attend school and obtain a certificate, you will never be offered greater."

"I do not presume I would receive greater, Mrs. Chapman."

Rachel's pronouncement eased the headmistress's tight frown of displeasure. "When might you begin?"

"In two weeks." A time that sounded like forever, and certainly long enough to permit Molly to decide to reveal all and send Rachel's growing house of cards tumbling.

"I will speak to you then, Miss Dunne. But only if you have that recommendation in hand."

Claire slid her chair back, a rapid scrape across oak flooring, said their good-byes, and departed with haste.

"This is excellent, Rachel. Perfect," she whispered, leading Rachel back the way they came.

"Molly could so easily ruin this chance for me, Claire."

"We must trust that our cause is just and that God will lead you safely through these trials."

"How can you be so trusting, Claire?" Rachel asked, aware that Claire could hear the frustration and doubt in her voice.

"I've had to learn to be, Rachel." The planes of Claire's face flattened. "It's all that gets me through."

"Did all go well with your appointment, Miss Dunne?" Mrs. Mainprice, streaks of flour powdering her chin, looked up from the dough spread across the table in a circle of yeasty ivory. Her shoulders heaved as she worked the pastry.

"My cousin reassures me that I was marvelous. Now for the headmistress to agree with her." Rachel yanked off her bonnet, a curl of hair unwinding. "I hope Molly and Peg were not forced to do more work because of my absence."

"*Wheesht*, why are you fretting over the two of them when your interview is so much more important? Truth be told, Molly's been so unwell she couldn't budge from her chamber if King William commanded." Mrs. Mainprice stopped just shy of sharply clucking her tongue. "Her stomach's been ailing her, and my linseed tea doesn't seem to be helping much."

Which might explain why Molly hadn't said anything to Dr. Edmunds as yet.

"I wonder if a tonic my mother used to make for stomach ailments would work for her." The words were out before Rachel could stop them. A *banaltradh* to her core.

Mrs. Mainprice straightened and brushed loose flour off her hands. "Joe mentioned you knew a bit about the herbs when you fixed him up."

"Only what I have learned here and there," Rachel equivocated, her hands beginning to tremble. To busy them, she extracted a hairpin and worked the loose strand back into the bun at the nape of her neck. "The recipe is simple enough. An infusion of dill and parsley in cinnamon water with a tiny quantity of diluted syrup of poppy. It always helped me when I felt ill."

"There's dill and parsley in the kitchen garden. I don't know if I have any syrup of poppy. Ah, the memory fails at times, Miss Dunne. You're welcome to check the storeroom to see, however." She beamed at Rachel, adding to her feelings of guilt. "You are a kind soul to offer to help the girl. Her sickness comes at an awful time. I worry that no matter how well your tonic works, though, she will still be too ill to accompany us when the doctor leaves for Finchingfield in three days."

"I was not aware he was leaving for Finchingfield."

"He needs to check on progress there, miss. Before the household moves, you know. But as I was saying, now Molly won't be able to go and do the tasks he'd assigned her." Mrs. Mainprice brushed a dusty knuckle across her jaw. "Well, now, I've just had a thought. What if you came with us in Molly's place?"

Rachel jabbed the pin into her scalp. "Me? To Finching-field?"

"Why not?" The housekeeper shrugged. "Take a break from London. Help me inventory the kitchen stores, what Molly was going to help me do."

"I have only been here a week. Surely not sufficiently long to warrant a break." But the countryside . . . fresh air, clear skies, grass and trees and maybe flowers even. Such a temptation. A temptation made even greater by the prospect of being away from Molly.

"A week 'twas long enough for me when I first arrived! This trip would be a fine chance for you to see the country-side, which I'm sure you miss," the housekeeper replied as if she could read Rachel's thoughts. "'Twill only be for a day and a half."

Rachel shoved the hairpin home. "Thank you for think-ing of me, but I imagine Dr. Edmunds would prefer I stay here and continue to make progress in the library."

The housekeeper's dark eyes twinkled, and her smile widened. "Now I don't know if he prefers that at all."

CHAPTER 14

James paced the library. The heels of his shoes rapped on the bare floor, the carpet rolled against the wall, twine cording its length like a sausage ready for the boil. Signs of progress toward his departure, but no sign of Miss Dunne. He knew she had returned from her interview. He'd seen Miss Harwood's carriage on the curb.

He tapped the volume of poetry against his thigh in rhythm to his steps. With each passing minute, he was feeling more and more idiotic. He glanced down at the book. A gift for an employee and it wasn't even Boxing Day. What was he thinking?

Thrusting the book beneath his elbow, he headed for the hallway. Miss Dunne, a flurry of copper-colored hair and billowing skirts, rushed into the room before he reached the doorway. She was wearing a new dress, one he'd never seen before, and it made her look like . . . a lady. A very pretty and very appealing young lady.

"Sir! Peg just told me you were waiting up here." A strand

of hair unraveled behind her ear. "I seem to be always late or away from my tasks. It is not my usual habit, I assure you."

"Don't worry." Her eyes flicked to the book tucked under his arm, and he pulled it out. "I . . . Here. I was waiting to give you this."

"A book?" Miss Dunne's gaze moved from James's out-stretched hand to his face and back again. "For me?"

Had no one ever given her a gift before? Or was she simply reluctant because it was a gift from him? *What am I thinking by doing this?*

"A token of appreciation for being so brave with Mr. Fenton-Smith." Good heavens, he was actually nervous she might refuse it. "And, if I'm completely honest, a token to ease my guilt over forcing you to sit with the man when you warned me you had no stomach for nursing."

"I cannot accept such generosity. A book is too valuable."

"It's a duplicate of another I already own, and it will be donated elsewhere if you don't take it," he said, book still extended, her hands still clasped at her waist. Well, he could be just as stubborn as she was proving to be. "This gift comes with no obligations or expectations, Miss Dunne, if that's what you're worried about."

"Dr. Edmunds, I insist—"

"And so do I. Stop refusing, Miss Dunne." He waved the book at her. "Take it."

"All right, then," she conceded and slipped the volume of poetry from his grasp. She traced the gold-embossed tooling on the cover, a loving caress, a smile lighting her face. "I do love poetry. My mother brought a few volumes with her when she left . . . when she moved to Ireland."

"See if there is a poem within you particularly like."

She glanced up. The color of the new dress shaded her eyes more green than blue. "I used to read Mary Herbert's psalms."

"She is in there. Read your favorite to me." James pulled up a chair, flipped the tails of his coat over his legs, and sat. "Please."

Her smile faltered. "Surely you are too busy to listen to me recite poetry."

He was busy, but he didn't care. He'd gotten her to accept the book, and he wanted to steal a few moments with her and forget the pile of work waiting on his office desk.

"It's another hour before I'm expecting a patient. Plenty of time."

"In that case . . ." She flipped through the pages and found the poem. "Here is one. 'Psalm 139.'"

Miss Dunne cleared her throat and began to read aloud:

O LORD, O Lord, in me there lieth naught
But to thy search revealed lies,
For when I sit
Thou markest it;
No less thou notest when I rise;
Yea, closest closet of my thought
Hath open windows to thine eyes.

Thou walkest with me when I walk;
When to my bed for rest I go,
I find thee there,
And everywhere:
Not youngest thought in me doth grow,
No, not one word I cast to talk
But yet unuttered thou dost know . . .

Her voice stuttered to a halt. "I have had a busy day already and my eyes are tired. I can read no further."

"It was very lovely. And inspiring." He had pushed her too hard. "Thank you."

She shut the book. "The poem was one of my mother's favorites."

"You miss her very much, don't you?" Before Miss Dunne had arrived, he'd never thought to ask one of his staff if they missed family and home. For all he knew, Mrs. Mainprice pined for her more northerly climes, and Molly was planning for the day she could return to the Hampshire town she'd left as a young girl, squirreling away funds to make it happen.

Miss Dunne's eyebrows scrunched together. She must think his question callous. If she knew how distant, how unreachable his own mother had been, she might think otherwise.

"I miss my family a great deal. How could I not?" Her eyes glistened. "My mother is the strongest and most intelligent woman I know. My sisters are but four and sweet as fresh honey. And my brother will soon be a man."

James pressed his legs into the chair before he stood and gathered her into his arms, thinking he—of all people—might comfort her. "Perhaps in the future, when you're less tired, you can read me another selection. Another one your mother enjoyed."

She tucked the volume of poetry under her arm. "There shall not be time for that, Dr. Edmunds."

"No," he agreed, regretfully. "I expect there won't."

Reverently, Rachel set the volume of poetry atop the bed-chamber's chest of drawers. Her fingers lingered on the embossed leather cover. She had felt Dr. Edmunds's gaze on her as she'd read, his mouth touched with a ghost of a smile. But of all the poems she might have selected, she had chosen that one. The one that spoke of the ever-observant God, aware of her every move. Her every sheltered thought.

Thoughts she dare not share with the enigmatic Dr. Edmunds.

With a sigh, Rachel slid open the top drawer of the chest to put away the book. Claire's money winked up at her. Rachel rimmed the nearest shilling with the tip of her fingernail, circling around and around. Joe had promised that, as soon as he could get free of his duties, he would help her post the money to her family in Ireland. Soon, they would all be together again.

Hope glimmered dangerously. Could it be that the brighter future she had hoped for since she'd stepped foot onto the steamer bound for London was within reach? A pessimistic voice in her head niggled. That bright future was only possible if Molly didn't ruin everything. In a heartbeat, the maid could snuff out the light of appreciation that had shone in Dr. Edmunds's eyes as Rachel had read the poem. She wanted him to admire her. Wanted him to ask her to go to Finchingfield, where the sky would be blue and glorious and full of promise. Like the tomorrows struggling to take form out of a shattered past.

She wanted to be near him out in an open meadow, just the two of them, the scent of grass and earth running in her veins, the sun burnishing his hair. Just a man and a woman with no secrets between them. Thank goodness Molly had yet to tell him the truth.

Rachel secreted the coins and the book far in the back of the drawer where they would hopefully stay safe.

She wished her worries had someplace equally safe to hide.

"The message boy wants to know if there's a message back, sir."

James lifted his gaze from the note in his hand, looked up at Joe. "A message?"

"For Mrs. Fenton-Smith."

"Ah, yes. Of course." He released the note, let it drift to the top of the desk like a dead leaf. "Just my sympathy. My deepest sympathy for her loss. Also let her know that we are all praying for her and the repose of her husband's soul."

What James had feared had finally come to pass, though it had taken much longer for the cholera to do its work than he had expected. He let out a deep sigh. His father had never grieved over the loss of a patient like James did. "If it was the Lord's will to take the poor souls, then who am I to stand in the way?" Father would say.

I do not understand why You give me the heart to care, God, the mind to learn the skills, but not the stomach to live with the results.

Mrs. Mainprice had anticipated how shaken he would be. Just that morning, she'd extolled to James the virtues of the countryside on rousing the spirits. His spirits in particular, repeatedly sinking like a man trapped in quicksand and struggling to get out, the moments when he felt he might escape coming too seldom and too far apart. Moments like the one he had experienced in the library yesterday. How lovely Miss Dunne had been in her new gown, her face fixed with concentration as she'd read to him, lifting him out of his quicksand. But not for long.

"I'll tell the messenger what you said, sir, an' get back to the packin'. Dinin' room's almost done," Joe offered when the silence grew too long.

James looked up from his unfocused perusal of his desktop. Joe was watching him quizzically. "You've all made remarkable progress on packing the house, if the dining room is almost done already."

"With Miss Dunne's 'elp, sir," Joe said, quick with praise.

"I expect we'll be in Finchingfield a week before I had originally planned."

"'spect so, sir."

James awaited a rush of enthusiasm at the prospect. None came. Why? Why did he not feel a surge of happiness to be gone from London and his medical practice? In Finchingfield, there would be no more praying for God's intercession, only to have no miracle happen. No more Mr. Fenton-Smiths, wasting away no matter what he did.

He crushed the note Joe had delivered. He needed an escape. To find courage. Trust in God. Know that this was His intended pathway and be happy to be on it.

Joe fidgeted and peered anxiously at James, probably wondering if his employer's mind had wandered off and he'd finally gone dotty. "I'll be 'appy to be outta 'ere, if you don' mind my sayin'."

"You dislike London so much?"

"Me, sir?" He snorted. "Too many awful memories in

this 'ere town. Always good to get away from 'em, don' you think, sir? Start fresh."

James tossed the note into the empty fireplace. "Yes, Joe. Always good to start fresh."

Joe grinned, happy the master had agreed. "Better 'n wallowin' in the past any day."

I must be every bit a fool.

Sighing, Rachel looked down at the basket of herbs dangling from her arm. The warm, lemony scent of dill, the tang of fresh-cut parsley rose up to tingle in her nose. Ingredients she needed for the tonic she had promised, even though she suspected Molly would not be grateful for Rachel's assistance.

Rachel set the basket on the kitchen table and went to search the storeroom for syrup of poppy. A swirl of scents greeted her, the aromas of home and her mother's stillroom, bringing with them homesickness and memories. Drawing Mother near. *Through my hands let Your good works come, O Lord.* Her mother's most fervent prayer. Rachel sighed. Would that she had the blind faith to pray it anymore and believe God listened to the words.

Tucking her skirts between her knees, Rachel knelt to poke through the lower shelves. A tiny container of syrup of poppy, dusty from lack of use, was stuffed in the back. Just enough for her needs. Next, she discovered an empty brown bottle that could serve to contain the tonic and was rising to stand when the kitchen door swung open. She turned to smile a greeting, expecting Mrs. Mainprice. Instead, Molly entered.

"Molly!" The bottle skittered from Rachel's grasp. She caught it before it crashed to the tiles.

Molly's eyes were red and puffy as fresh pastry. She had been crying. "Mrs. Mainprice told me to come look for you. She said I'm to take some potion you've made."

"I have yet to gather all the ingredients." Rachel was clutching the bottle so tightly, she feared it might shatter in her hands. Carefully, she set it on the table. "And it is a tonic, not a potion."

"Tonic, then." Molly glanced curiously at the empty bottle and the contents of the basket. "It cures the dyspepsia?"

"It might help you."

"You only want to help me because you're scared I'll show your letter to Dr. Edmunds."

"You should return the letter, Molly. It is mine. You should not have taken it."

"I don't think I'll be returning your precious letter just yet." Molly's eyes narrowed. "A trial, eh? Whose, yours?"

"You do not understand." Thank heavens Mother's letter hadn't mentioned the specifics of the trial, but Rachel was not naive enough to think that any sensible person wouldn't surmise the worst from what she had written. "It is not what you think."

"The doctor might believe exactly what I think, though, and you know it. The chance he will is the only reason you'd help me."

"That is not true. I want to help you because . . ." *it is the right thing to do. Because the urge to cure is in my bones.* She fought to keep her voice calm and confident. "I want to help because it is what I can do, not because I am guilty of anything."

"Humph." Molly's lips pinched into a thin pink line as she frowned at Rachel. "What other medicines can you make up?"

"I know several recipes for poultices, tisanes, and infusions," Rachel answered, trying to follow the new direction of the conversation.

"Do you have one to help womanly complaints?" Molly asked, lowering her voice though they were completely alone in the kitchen.

Rachel followed suit. "Is that what is bothering you? Are your monthlies so painful they are making you ill?"

"It's not pain." Molly rubbed the palm of her hand over the back of the other in an irritated, sawing motion. "You know. I need help with them."

"I don't follow you . . ."

Just then, the servants' bell from Dr. Edmunds's office sounded a harsh, insistent clang. Molly huffed her annoyance. "You're awfully thick, then. I'll go find help elsewhere. I should've figured you'd be no use."

"Molly, I am not trying to be difficult. I honestly am willing to provide whatever assistance you need. The tonic, anything."

"Your tonic won't cure what's wrong with me." She spun on her heel and rushed off, black skirts slapping against a broom propped up near the door, knocking it over.

Rachel sighed with frustration and went to straighten the broom. Her hand paused on the handle as realization struck. Heavens, she was dense. The vague stomach illness, the talk about her monthly courses . . . Molly's troubles were indeed more than her mother's tonic would cure.

The girl was pregnant.

CHAPTER 15

"James!" Sophia's voice boomed down the hallway, followed by the crisp rustle of her heavy skirts drawing near the office. Flustered, Peg scrambled to get ahead of her so that she could be properly announced. "I must speak with you immediately."

James stuffed his pen back into its holder and rose, tugging his waistcoat flat. It was not a good sign that Sophia was in such a rush she was willingly ignoring customary manners.

He waved off the maid. "To what do I owe the pleasure of a visit, Sophia? I would offer you dinner, but I have a previously arranged engagement with Dr. Calvert in an hour and can't—"

"I am not here to be fed, James." With a huff, she dropped onto the settee tucked against the wall. "Miss Castleton came to visit me. She informed me that she is leaving town. Not that I care to know her whereabouts, frankly, but she was rather distressed. It seems her brother has told her there are fresh cases of the cholera, near St. George's," said Sophia, naming a church a few short blocks from her house.

Her hands clenched at the waist of her dress. She sounded as calm as a minister reassuring his faithful, but her fingers told another story. "She has insisted on leaving London, even though he advised her there was no need."

Thaddeus hadn't sent James the news about these latest cases. He must have deemed them irrelevant, even if Miss Castleton did not.

"I'm sure there's no reason to be alarmed, Sophia. They must be isolated cases. I will look into them in the morning. I'll stop in at the hospital and see what's happening, if it would reduce your anxiety."

"It would." The sort of smile one gives to feign valor lifted the corners of her lips but did nothing to soften the anxious lines fanning out from her mouth like patterns of frost along a window. "However, I confess to being a trifle upset with Agnes, in light of this news. Yesterday, she came back from a walk with Amelia claiming to feel rather fatigued. She sent Amelia to bed early and retired shortly after. I have already had the doctor in, and he says it's just exhaustion."

"Symptoms?"

"Agnes felt vaguely unwell, she claimed, and frightfully tired. Her condition worries me because, just a few days ago, she'd gone to see her sister who lives near Soho Square. Not the best part of town anymore." Sophia's knuckles looked white against the black of her skirts. "She took Amelia, too, without informing me first."

James pulled his gaze off her hands. He wouldn't let her agitation affect him. "Agnes must have overexerted herself. It's been very warm lately. She simply needs rest."

"So you do not think . . .?"

"No," he reassured, understanding what she was asking.

It couldn't be the cholera. "I don't think that at all. Agnes is getting on in years and tires easily. By the time you return home, you'll find her up and good as new."

"You are undoubtedly right, but I very much dislike hearing that the cholera is moving closer to my house."

"Isolated cases, as I said before. However, if you're concerned about contracting the cholera, stay out of the city and keep the household from going as well. Especially Amelia."

Especially her.

James had a sudden memory of Amelia's tiny, round face peering back at him from the comfort of Agnes's bony arms as the nurse carried the baby away from the house, off to Sophia's, where she was to be cosseted, tended by a loving aunt who had replaced the mother she'd lost, always safe.

"I would propose we leave London," Sophia was saying, "except we've nowhere to go. Other than Finchingfield House," she added, hopefully.

James shook his head. "The house isn't ready to be occupied. I am heading there in two days, but from what I understand, it's in terrible condition. There is water damage to the north rooms from a leak in the roof and most of the bedchambers on that end need repair. I intended to stay there no more than a day myself, this trip."

"Then Amelia and I have to stay in town."

"If you stay within the neighborhoods of Mayfair or Belgravia, you won't come to any harm, Sophia. Trust me. Everything will be all right."

He didn't blame her for the skeptical look she shot him. He didn't feel much more optimistic himself.

Through the drawing-room blinds, Rachel peered at the top of Mrs. Woodbridge's head, the gray feathers of her bonnet fluttering as she ducked to enter the hired carriage, Dr. Edmunds's hand at her elbow. Had Rachel heard correctly? She had been heading for his office to consult with the doctor on what to do with a duplicate travel memoir she'd found in the library when the sound of his sister-in-law's voice had stopped her. Rachel had no desire to face Mrs. Woodbridge. The woman clearly despised her. Rachel had begun to turn away when she heard the word which had stopped her in her tracks—*cholera*. She had only eavesdropped in the hallway for a few moments before hurrying off, but it had been long enough.

Letting the slat fall, Rachel retreated from the window. The cholera was spreading in London, alarming Mrs. Woodbridge, her voice so taut with anxiety it had affected Rachel. She shuddered and rubbed her hands over her arms. Mrs. Woodbridge should be alarmed. They should all be alarmed. The cholera was a disease to be feared. Rachel could think of a dozen possible cures, but would any of them work against such a rapidly wasting illness? Chalk and laudanum, linseed tea or maybe beef broth, or both. Perhaps her mother's tonic. She didn't want to have to discover what worked, though. If she contracted the disease and succumbed, who would help Mother and the rest? Should they even come to London if the cholera was spreading through town?

There was always the possibility, however, that Mrs. Woodbridge was mistaken. She seemed the sort of woman who might panic. There was only one way to be certain. Mrs. Mainprice would know.

She found the housekeeper out in the garden, clipping chives for the evening dinner.

Mrs. Mainprice straightened from her task, kneading the small of her back. "*Och*, Miss Dunne. This is a sad excuse for a kitchen garden."

"The garden will be better at Finchingfield House, I expect."

"Indeed, it will." She bundled her clippings and stepped onto the gravel path. "You'll be able to see for yourself, miss. Glad to hear you're coming with us."

"So am I." Not that she could have refused Dr. Edmunds's somewhat brisk request.

Mrs. Mainprice handed Rachel the chives, green as fresh lichen and spicy smelling, and descended the stairs leading into the kitchen. Rachel followed her into the dim recesses of the kitchen, hot and sticky from the laundry hanging suspended before the fire. In Ireland, the linens would be hung to dry outside on a day as fair as today. In Ireland, the air wouldn't turn freshly cleaned bedsheets black from soot and smuts in a half hour, however.

"So what were you needing, child?" the housekeeper asked, peering at Rachel as she took the bundle of herbs and spread them on the table.

"I wanted to know if something were true."

"If what were true?" Mrs. Mainprice slid a knife from its block and began chopping the chives.

"That the cholera is spreading through town." Rachel crossed to the other side of the table so she could see the housekeeper's face. "I have heard that the Castletons are leaving London out of worry. Mrs. Woodbridge came to talk to Dr. Edmunds about it."

"*Och*." The knife flashed in her hands. "I've heard the

disease is bad in St. Giles parish, miss. And that's none too far from where Mrs. Woodbridge lives. She should be worried. Poor lass."

Lass? Sophia Woodbridge? "But do you think it will spread further?"

Mrs. Mainprice's attention stayed fixed on the herbs, rapidly being reduced to a pile of chopped green. "There's those who claim 'tis just a matter of time. Heard from the housekeeper down at Mr. Pratt's that the newspapers one day claim it's the Lord's vengeance, then the next they're tamping down any rumors that we've got ourselves another epidemic." She swept up the herbs and dropped them into the iron pot suspended over the fire. "You'll be safe while you're in Finchingfield, Miss Dunne."

"I shall only be there for a day."

The housekeeper glanced over her shoulder. "You could ask the master if there is a position in the house and stay with us. Until the disease passes. Or longer if you'd like, and he'd agree."

And be a servant forever, Peg glaring, Molly hateful . . . Dr. Edmunds close but ever out of reach? Her only true choice was to stay in London and hope for the best. "My family is depending on me. I will make more money as a teacher here in London, helping children as I have always intended."

Mrs. Mainprice clucked her tongue and nodded. "I will pray for you every day, Miss Dunne. Know that I will."

Rachel rolled her lips between her teeth. She would need those prayers.

"So you've had no cases of the cholera, Peterson," James repeated.

The man at his side, robustly officious in his doctor's dark coat and trousers, jiggled a thick chin in affirmation. "As I've said, Edmunds, I had heard of the case near St. George's, but that fellow had, shall we say, unclean habits. An older gentleman who was a bit of a drinker, and you know how that weakens the system."

"Nothing here, though." James took in the length of the hospital ward, the lines of spindly-legged beds on each side, the ward mistress moving among her charges like a dog overseeing the flock, a medical student accompanying her, notes in hand. A man groaned in his laudanum-induced sleep. Another was losing a battle with pleurisy, the burbling wheeze of his breath a telltale marker. The smell of vinegar, rising off the floorboards, failed to escape through any open windows, stagnated in the close air, and burned James's nose.

"Not a single case. A fellow at the end down there," the doctor paused to gesture with his head, "has acute diarrhea, but it's not the Asiatic cholera. I know the difference."

How could he sound so positive? Had any of them seen enough of this new breed of disease to be able to tell?

"I had a patient, a Mr. Fenton-Smith, die from what I believe was the cholera, but that must have been an isolated case as well. He has offices along Holborn. Always a little questionable over there."

"Which makes me ever grateful to have a practice located near Hyde Park," said Peterson smugly.

A patient at James's right cried out, a twisting scream of agony, and he clutched his abdomen. The ward mistress hurried over to calm the man.

Peterson's quick glance dismissed the fellow. "Kidney inflammation from the stones. Screams like that every ten minutes."

He stopped and stared at James. "You're not really bothered about this cholera nonsense, are you? A sporadic outbreak is to be expected, but we're not dealing with an epidemic."

"I would be more at ease if I had a clue how to cure it."

"As I tell my students here, chalk mixture and opium ought to take care of the cholera. Simple enough." He patted James's arm. "I've got to be off—shouldn't even be here on a Sunday. The wife is furious, but what's to be done? Disease doesn't respect the Lord's Sabbath. You know, Edmunds, if flare-ups of the cholera bother you, be thankful you're not a physician on the East Side. Take comfort in your little corner of lovely Belgravia. Speaking of which, if you change your mind about giving your practice over to Dr. Castleton, I would always be interested."

Not likely to ever happen . . . "I shall keep that in mind."

The other man winked. "See you out?"

Slapping his hat atop his head, James accompanied Peterson out of the hospital. He sucked in the outside air to clear his lungs of the smell of disease. He had learned what he'd come to find out—the cholera hadn't reached the western parts of London, so far spreading only to those who had been exposed through poor habits or poor choices. There was nothing to worry about, just as he'd told Sophia.

"Fine day." Peterson glanced around at the passing traffic. "See? Everyone looking healthy, life proceeding as normal among the upright and the strong. Not logical to be concerned about the cholera. Not logical at all."

"I know it isn't logical." James frowned. "But now to convince my gut."

CHAPTER 16

*R*achel was packing the doctor's collection of botanical books when he strode into the library.

"Miss Dunne. Working on a Sunday?" He had just come in from outside, his hat and gloves clutched in his right hand. He ran his fingers through his hair to tame a few wayward locks. Which never worked for long. "It's a day of rest for you."

"I have taken too much time away from my tasks of late, Dr. Edmunds." Rachel tidied the topmost books and forced herself not to stare at him, notice how handsome he looked in his deep green coat and buff trousers, his shoes polished to a gleam. "And since we leave for Finchingfield in the morning, I thought it best to finish this set of shelves and not have to worry over it while we are gone."

His gaze scanned the bookshelves. Most of them were empty, dust tracing the outlines of departed books. "You've accomplished quite a lot. It seems to me you can take an hour away from your chores and visit the apple girl. If you still want to go, that is."

"I do." Truthfully, her mind had not been much on her work. Between worrying about Molly and the threat from the cholera, Rachel hadn't been able to concentrate on Milne's *Botanical Dictionary* or Dr. Stokes's *Botanical Materia Medica*. She might not have even logged them properly.

"I do indeed wish to see how she is doing," Rachel answered firmly.

"Good." Dr. Edmunds slapped his hat against his thigh. "I'll have Joe get the gig ready, and I'll meet you out at the mews."

Once he left, Rachel untied her apron and hurried to fetch her bonnet and shawl. She paused in front of the hallway mirror just long enough to check the condition of her hair.

He waited for her at the door in the garden wall that led into the mews-house.

"I've heard from the surgeon that her arm is setting well." Dr. Edmunds ushered Rachel inside, the pungent sweet-musty odor of straw and oats and horse greeting her nose. They passed into the open mews beyond, where Joe waited with the gig. The mare nickered upon catching sight of the doctor, and Joe steadied her as Dr. Edmunds grasped Rachel's elbow and helped her up.

The doctor climbed alongside and took the reins from Joe, led them down the mews alleyway, through the arch and then onto the streets. "The girl lives near the river south of here, in Chelsea. Too far to walk."

They set off at a steady pace, the traffic thinning rapidly as the lovely boulevards and gleaming white terraced houses of Belgravia turned into more utilitarian roads and less grand buildings. They passed gardens and a hospital grounds. Smokestacks from distilleries and manufactories punched the hazy skyline.

"They're down this lane," Dr. Edmunds said.

A hodgepodge of houses—crooked timbered buildings from a prior century, multistoried brick apartments thrown up with only a modicum of concern, a squat home with peeling stucco—jumbled together. Dr. Edmunds slowed the mare and hopped down, avoiding the overflowing gutter that ran down the middle of the street. The stench of sewage and the sulfurous gasses from the lead works by the river settled over the neighborhood, making Rachel press a fist to her nose. The smell had to be poisonous, and Rachel searched the people passing in the street to see any indication of disease on their faces.

The apple girl's father opened the ground-floor door, his brawny arms swinging wide as he led them down a narrow hallway to a set of two connecting rooms at the rear. The entirety of their home. His family, which appeared to include four other children ranging in age from an infant to a ten-year-old boy with a twisted foot, were huddled over a lunch of boiled potatoes. The little apple seller was stretched out on the cleanest mattress they owned, her arm swathed tight in bandages, two narrow wood boards securing it straight.

"We did not mean to interrupt your lunch." Dr. Edmunds's eyes made a quick circuit of the space, noting the cots lined up along the walls and the stains on the floor covering. They showed no repugnance or condescending pity. Either he excelled at hiding his feelings, or he'd seen such poverty and want so many times before that it no longer shocked him. Certainly Rachel had, every day back in Carlow.

"Not an int'ruption at all, sir." The man moved his children aside with his foot to clear a path. They were clean-faced and bright-eyed, at least, and appeared reasonably well fed and curious about their visitors. The oldest stared, open-mouthed, at the gold watch fob dangling from Dr. Edmunds's waistcoat pocket.

"Janey, the doctor's a-come to see you."

Dr. Edmunds's crouched at Janey's bedside. "How are you, Janey? Healing up?"

The girl nodded.

"Good." He pointed out Rachel. "This is the lady who first came to your assistance, Miss Janey. Her name is Miss Dunne."

Big eyes dark as damp earth fixed on Rachel's face. Rachel clutched her shawl around her shoulders and stared back. She did not look like Mary Ferguson or any of the others. She did not . . .

"Say thankee, Janey girl," her father prompted.

"Thankee, Miss Dunne." Her voice was faint as a fledgling's peep.

"You are most welcome. For what little I did," Rachel answered.

The doctor peeled off his gloves and rested soft fingers on the girl's tiny forehead. "No fever. Excellent." He examined the girl's unbroken arm, resting atop a paper-thin blanket, gingerly probing around her badly scraped elbow. "Skin isn't hot. No apparent infection. In spite of all the blood the other day, her cuts were mostly superficial."

How many times had Rachel seen her mother's hands move with the same fluid motion, at once reassuring and assessing? Mother would look up at Rachel, observing carefully, and their gazes would connect in common understanding.

Just as Dr. Edmunds's gaze did now. His eyes locked and held hers, their gray depths fathomless. *Yes, Dr. Edmunds. I see that her skin is a healthy pink and dry, her eyes clear and attentive. Yes, I see that I managed to cause her no harm.*

"Did the surgeon apply a poultice of common comfrey to set the bone?" As soon as the words were out of her mouth, Rachel wished them back.

Dr. Edmunds's eyebrows lifted. "How many herbal treatments have you studied, Miss Dunne? I have heard about your mother's miraculous tonic. Are you keeping more secrets from me?"

He was teasing, but nonetheless, Rachel's fingers tightened nervously on her shawl. "I . . . my brother broke his wrist once and the apothecary made up a poultice to heal the break. The bones knit perfectly clean. I merely recalled the treatment, doctor."

Her answer satisfied him. "I suspect the surgeon didn't use a poultice, Miss Dunne, but a correctly applied splint has never failed." Dr. Edmunds stood and faced the father. "You are keeping her absolutely still, as the surgeon ordered? It's critical that the bones in that arm are not jarred."

"We've been a-tryin'. But Janey 'ere 'as to get back to peddlin' soon, sir." The man jerked a thumb in the direction of his children. "We've mouths to feed and the missus's job at the lace works don' bring in much. Not that I'm complainin'. 'Tis a good job an' all."

"If Janey goes back to her work prematurely, her arm might be permanently disfigured."

The man fixed Dr. Edmunds with a hard look. "Then she'll make a good beggar, won' she?"

"I know you don't mean that." Dr. Edmunds fished

around in his coat pocket and pulled out a half crown. He dropped it into the fellow's hand. "Another two weeks at least before you let Janey get up."

"Thankee, guv." The man pocketed the coin. "Well, Janey me girl, you've a 'oliday, it seems."

"Yes, Da." She sighed wearily, seemingly unhappy with the prospect of being a burden. Or being forced to lie about in a hot, damp room where the air stank of mold and factory smoke. Plying the streets of Belgravia must seem like heaven to Janey. She might be just as eager to return to her peddling as her father.

Rachel and the doctor left soon after. Dr. Edmunds stopped on the curb, halting to pull on his gloves. "Do you really believe a comfrey poultice heals bones?"

"Our apothecary has always claimed so."

"Well, I've been wrong about such things before," he said, a shadow of a memory darkening his expression. He shook it off. "I give five days before Janey is up and toting that basket of apples around again."

"Three is more likely, Dr. Edmunds." Rachel refastened her bonnet ribbons and climbed into the gig.

He looked up at her, his hand resting on the toe board as he leaned close. "So you see why I must give up my practice. It's futile to keep trying when your patients won't even do what's right for them."

"They are too poor to ponder the option of right versus harmful, sir."

"Then why do I bother?"

His eyes filled with frustration and pain, the sight twisting emotions deep in her heart. He bothered because he felt as she did, felt the compulsion to help like the instinct to catch a falling bit of crockery or to jump back from a thrown spark. Even though responding to the impulse too often brought only pain and disappointment.

"Because someone must?" she replied, aware of the ache the answer caused in her own chest.

"Not me, Miss Dunne." With a snap of his wrist, Dr. Edmunds released the reins from the pole he had tied them to. "I've vowed to become the most successful gentleman farmer in Essex. And I shall, even if it kills me."

"I've instructed Joe to send Janey's surgeon a note, Miss Dunne, telling him about using a comfrey poultice." A twitch endeavored to turn into a smile at the corners of Dr. Edmunds's mouth.

Rachel paused on the pavement while Mrs. Mainprice and Peg climbed into the hired carriage that would take them to Finchingfield. "You have?"

"Indeed."

How surprising. "I just hope she gives it long enough to work."

"We both expect otherwise though, don't we?"

Lightly touching her elbow, he guided her into the carriage and shut the door, tipped his hat, and strode off.

Mrs. Mainprice watched their interchange with interest. "The master surely enjoys talking with you, miss. More than he ever did with Miss Guimond, 'tis certain."

Rachel blushed. "He is just very kind."

"Aye. That he is, and wise of you to notice."

How could I not?

Rachel settled onto the seat next to Peg, already attempting to doze. Dr. Edmunds climbed onto his mare and gave last-minute instructions to the coachman. Joe watched from the curb; he'd promised that today he would post Claire's money to Ireland. Rachel had included a note telling them to wait until she could be certain the threat of cholera had passed, delaying their reunion. A necessity, she supposed. Molly, who had roused herself, joined Joe on the pavement. Together, they waved off the carriage before the sun had done more than paint the sky a purple dark as the heart of a fresh bloom of hound's-tongue.

They set off as fast as traffic—heavy even at this early hour—would permit. For many minutes, they traveled along the long, green expanse of a great park—Hyde Park, Mrs. Mainprice informed her—then veered away from it. Almost immediately, the jam of townhouses and shops gave way to gardens and orchards and spacious lawns surrounding tidy houses. A hill rose to their north, the former regent's park to their south, and the sky stretched into the distance. Another flurry of development came and went, with its poorhouse and small factories, then suddenly they were in countryside and open air. Rachel sighed deeply, the past days' tension exhaling with her breath, easing from her neck and shoulders. And all it took was the sight of some green . . .

"Ah," she sighed again. Peg grumbled at her to raise the window and close the shade so they could sleep, which made Mrs. Mainprice tut at them both.

Dr. Edmunds rode up alongside. The rising sun cast a golden glow over his features, burnishing them. "Miss Dunne, you might wish to get some rest. It's a long and tiring journey."

"Told ya," Peg muttered, quiet enough that only the occupants of the carriage could hear, and huddled into her shawl.

Rachel ignored her. "I am interested in seeing the sights, Dr. Edmunds. I doubt I could rest if I tried."

"Pleased to be away from London?" he asked, guessing at her true feelings.

She smiled. "I am."

"I thought you might be. Which is why I instructed the driver to skirt the city to the north rather than pass through it. A less direct route to Essex, but a more pleasant one."

"Thank you, Dr. Edmunds."

"My pleasure, Miss Dunne." Tapping fingertips to his hat, he pressed his heels against his mare's flanks and set her trotting. Rachel poked her head through the window and watched the set of his shoulders, his fluid movement of his torso as he rode ahead of them. *He was thinking of me, of what I might enjoy . . .*

"Can ya shut the window?" Peg snapped.

Rachel jerked her head back in, slid the window up, and caught sight of Mrs. Mainprice's contented smile before she snuffed it out.

CHAPTER 17

*S*ix long hours later, which included a stop for luncheon, they approached Finchingfield and Dr. Edmunds's family estate. The place where he would make his mark as a gentleman farmer. The most successful gentleman farmer if it killed him, Rachel recalled with a wry smile.

Kneading the cramp in the small of her back, she raised the window shade all the way. Finchingfield town stood on a small rise, a collection of snow-white houses with thatched roofs marching up the gentle slope, the square stone tower of an old church rising above them, and a windmill turning slowly. They pulled off the main road before reaching the town, venturing down a short lane to a large reddish brick house. Acreage rolling beyond the house lay like an emerald patchwork blanket upon gentle hills.

"Oh my," Rachel murmured. "It is quite lovely."

Mrs. Mainprice stretched wearily and leaned over for a view. "That there would be the old master's house."

The house was simpler and smaller than Rachel expected, only five windows across and lacking a grand entrance, instead making do with a bottle-green door and plain arched light above it. Its very simplicity was elegant. She decided she could not see Miss Castleton being mistress of such a house. She needed bow windows and magnificent iron railings.

It was equally clear that a discredited Irish healer who empathized with a penniless apple seller and blurted out poultice recommendations would not make an appropriate mistress either.

"The house is quite pretty," Rachel observed, the comment inadequate.

"I've always liked it. A home meant for a family. You can't see from here, but it has a lovely fenced garden at the back and a stream where those trees are in the distance. The master used to fish there as a boy and go swimming when it was hot." Mrs. Mainprice smiled, her eyes crinkling at the corners. "Oh, those were good days, they were. 'Twas here that Dr. Edmunds first realized how much he wanted to be a physician. I remember a time when he brought home an injured bird he'd found and tried to convince the old master to fix its wings. When the old Dr. Edmunds refused because he was busy, then the young master went and took care of the bird himself. So proud he was. Ah yes, good days indeed."

Rachel gazed at the trees, the house with its large windows. She breathed in the smell of grass and good soil. If Dr. Edmunds married again, he would do well to raise his children here. Inexplicably, Rachel's throat tightened, and she had to look away.

Wheels crunching gravel, the carriage rattled on to the front door and pulled to a halt. Dr. Edmunds pulled his horse alongside and hopped down. Tying the reins to an iron loop dangling from a post, he came over to the carriage, the tails of his greatcoat flapping against his boots.

"There doesn't appear to be anyone here right now, Mrs. Mainprice," he said. "The steward said he opened the house and aired it out, had one of his girls take up all the furniture covers and sweep out the worst of the cobwebs. I expect there's much left to be done, however, such as examining the water damage upstairs."

"I'm sure Mr. Jackson and his girls did the best they could. We'll manage the rest, sir. Leave the work to us," she said confidently, giving a groan as she squeezed her way through the narrow carriage door. Peg slipped out behind.

"I trust the remainder of your trip was comfortable, Miss Dunne?" he asked as Rachel descended the unfolded carriage steps, his fingertips brushing her elbow in assistance.

Her heart lifted on the crisp air filling her lungs, air that didn't stink of coal smoke or sewers. "Very comfortable, Dr. Edmunds, and much better than steerage on a steamer."

"Do you like the house?" he asked, sounding eager for her response.

"I do. It seems an honest place."

"*Honest* is an unusual word to use."

"However the description feels suitable. The house is so perfect and simple. Such a building would not permit the occupant to be anything but upright and straightforward, like the courses of the bricks themselves."

"My father was a very upright man. A good man."

"As surely are you."

He looked down at her. They stood together, too close to be proper, the air warming from his proximity.

"I appreciate the compliment, Miss Dunne. However, I do not deserve it," he said, his gaze gone solemn, regretful. What could a man like him possibly regret? What memory tortured him so?

Peg called to him from the side of the house, stopping him before he could say more. "Dr. Edmunds, sir, the back door's been left open for us."

"I will speak with you later." He pulled his gaze off Rachel and stepped away from her.

Mrs. Mainprice was waiting for Rachel at the corner of the house. She accompanied the housekeeper to the kitchen door, casting one last glance at where Dr. Edmunds stood in conversation with Peg.

"We've much work to accomplish, Miss Dunne, if you want some time to see the grounds," said Mrs. Mainprice, stepping over the high stone threshold.

Just before Rachel did the same, she noticed Dr. Edmunds return her glance and hold it. Long enough that the contact felt like an invisible caress.

Guard your heart, Rachel.

But it was too late.

Odd to be in his father's house without the old man.

James moved from one room to the next, delaying meeting with Miss Dunne. He needed to do this, prod the wounds, to observe if they were healing clean or infected still. He already knew what to expect he would discover.

He pushed open the dining room door. Mr. Jackson's daughter had forgotten to remove the cover from the walnut dining table. It hung mute and still and white as a winding sheet. James could picture his father at the head of the table, lecturing on botany or the phases of the moon or the discovery of nitrous oxide and its possible uses. Quoting from the Bible as easily as he could recite passages from William Buchan's massive medical text. Mother, when she'd been well enough to join them, wearing her wan, passive smile. And James, not learning his role until too late, daring to argue, turning his father's face crimson.

James retreated from the space and wandered down to the library. Here the memories would be the strongest. Easing open the door, he entered the hushed room. Curtains drawn, it was nearly as dark as James's library back in London. He could pull aside the draperies here, however. Beyond these windows didn't stand a garden of recrimination. James opened the curtains and surveyed the room. So far as he could tell, nothing had been touched since the day his father had taken ill and had been ushered off to a bedchamber that, according to his housekeeper, he had never left again. James should have been there for those final moments, wished his father's soul well on its eternal journey, but he hadn't been. His father had not sent for him.

James sank into the russet leather chair, ran a hand across the surface of the desk, breaking a trail through the coating of fine dust that had accumulated since the Holland cloth cover had been removed in the past few days. It felt wrong, sacrilegious, to be sitting here in his father's chair. He felt as if any second the old man would stride through the door and give the look that silenced all, restored everyone to their proper place.

His father would not be striding through that door, though. Thirteen months ago, James had seen his casket lowered into the muddy churchyard, had thrown the first handful of dirt onto the carved wood surface in the role of son and heir. His father was gone and with the Lord. This house, these grounds, all of it was now his. His and Amelia's, as his father had wished. The message he had left behind was short, frank, utterly clear—bring Amelia to Finchingfield. Even from the grave, his father could control James's life. He had delayed the reunion as long as possible, until his distaste for practicing medicine had grown too strong and he had conceded in the end. Letting his father win again.

Sighing, he closed his eyes, breathed in the familiar smells—musty books, pipe smoke, lemon wax. The aroma of disappointment and disapproval. James's chest constricted. The sooner he claimed the house, the sooner he could banish the old man's ghost from it.

The sooner he could lay to rest all the expectations of a man who had been more judge than father.

"The view from up here is amazing." Rachel pushed the heavy brocade curtains aside. The countryside rolled and dipped, cows and sheep scattered like buff and ivory dots across the hillsides, and not far away stood the rooftops of the town, the giant vanes of the mill twirling in the wind. A world like Ireland and yet not like Ireland. Heather wouldn't turn those hills purple in the late summer, and the dusky smoke from turf fires wouldn't billow from those chimneys in the winter. But the scene was more pleasing than any view of London and made her homesick.

"It reminds me of home."

"Humph," Peg grumbled frostily, not acting in the least appreciative Rachel had volunteered to help her.

Rachel dragged her gaze off the scenery and unhooked the curtain rings from the panels, letting the first one drop to the floor in a cloud of dust. Mrs. Mainprice had chided her for wanting to do servant's work, but the doctor had yet to meet with her about her tasks here and Rachel had thought cleaning out the bedchamber better than idling . . . and letting her thoughts wander where they didn't belong.

"You are very fortunate to be coming to live here, Peg," Rachel said, the charm of the countryside making her feel pleasantly disposed toward everyone, even Peg.

"Work's work. Don't much matter where it takes place." Peg grunted as she shifted the mattress off the bedstead. "Miss Dunne," she appended without a hint of respect.

"But it is much better for your health to work out in the countryside, away from the filth and grime of London. Don't you think?"

The girl cocked a narrow eyebrow. "I haven't a choice one way or 'tuther, have I?"

Rachel blinked back at her. "I suppose not."

"Are you thinkin' you'd a-like to live here, miss?"

"I haven't a choice, Peg," she echoed. "I intend to find work in London, since Dr. Edmunds does not need an assistant here."

"No, he doesn't now, does he?" Peg heaved the bed away

from the wall, the legs of the frame scraping across the boards. "Doesn't need you at all."

Rachel lifted her chin. She should have stayed in the kitchen with Mrs. Mainprice, where she wouldn't be treated like an interloping pariah. "Mrs. Mainprice suggested I ask the doctor if he has a position in the household for me."

"As a servant, miss?"

"What else, Peg?"

Peg's lips quirked. "I dunno."

Rachel did not mistake the implication behind Peg's words, and her cheeks flared with heat. Peg believed she had designs on Dr. Edmunds. Hadn't even Joe thought as much? Did everyone believe that had been Rachel's true reason for coming to Finchingfield House today, to stay near the doctor?

To be near him out in an open meadow, just the two of them, the scent of grass and earth running in her veins, the sun burnishing his hair . . . She flushed anew at the memory of her own thoughts.

Well, Rachel Dunne, it is a wonder the entirety of London hasn't discovered all of your secrets, because you are as transparent as good glass.

Throwing the final panels onto the pile, Rachel jumped off the chair she stood upon. She bundled the brocade in her arms and glared at Peg, who returned the look with an expression so sour it seemed she'd bitten into a handful of lemons. "I believe I am finished up here."

"Yes, miss. I think you might be."

Without another look at the girl, Rachel marched out of the room and down the stairs.

Straight into James Edmunds's arms.

CHAPTER 18

"Miss Dunne!" James retrieved the dusty curtain that she'd dropped. Rachel had plunged headfirst through the kitchen entry and right into his arms. The weight and warmth of her body didn't stay there for long. She had squirmed in his grasp and, reluctantly, he'd had to let her go. "I was just looking for you."

Pink blushed her cheeks. This close, he could spy the freckles peppering the bridge of her nose like flecks of cinnamon atop a sugared cake.

"Our meeting in your father's library." She shifted the weight of the curtains to better balance them. "I was busy upstairs, but I hadn't forgotten."

He took the curtains from her arm, surprising her. She was so petite, she looked as though they would swamp her beneath their weight. He knew, though, she was strong. Enviably, admirably, strong. "The roof leak ruined the chambers up there, didn't it?"

"Not too badly. The plaster has fallen in spots, and some

of the furnishings got wet, but these curtains have only a small stain along the top. Easily fixed by a quick brushing with hot water."

"Now that's a pity. They're so ugly I hoped for an excuse to burn them."

His teasing brought out a smile. He liked her smiles.

James glanced around the kitchen, quite bare but for a few stray pots hanging over the cold fireplace. Cavernous in its emptiness.

"You know, Miss Dunne, I haven't been in this kitchen since I was a lad." So very long ago, when the house hummed with activity and life was still full of promise.

"You haven't?" she asked.

"Father was insistent that the family keep separate from our staff," he explained. "Only my mother would occasionally come down to check on the stores or confer over the menu, but I was such a favorite of Mrs. Mainprice, I often visited. When I used to sneak down here to get away from my lessons, she would fill me up with treats, samples of the evening's dessert or Tonbridge biscuits she would make just for me."

"Have you ever had barmbrack, Dr. Edmunds?" Miss Dunne asked.

"No. What is it?"

"The best treat I know of. Sweetened flour cakes studded with raisins or currants." Her fine eyes shimmered happily. "My little sisters love them as much as I."

"They sound wonderful."

"Not as wonderful as a good tart made with butter and fresh fruit, I would guess, but wonderful enough for us." She snatched the curtains from his arms. "Here, let me take these back to the scullery. No need for you to dirty your clothes with them."

With ease, she moved through the kitchen as if she belonged there. Comfortable in a way James's mother had never been, drifting from room to room in the house, the murmur of her skirts never more than a ghost's whisper. Whereas Miss Dunne . . . just the sight of her bright hair set a spark to the space, eye-catching among the whitewashed kitchen walls and massive plate shelves.

He would miss that spark. Miss her.

Miss Dunne returned, wiping her hands across the yellowing apron she had tied around her waist. "Those are taken care of, and I am ready to examine your father's library now."

James led the way. This time when he entered, the scent of pipe smoke was less noticeable. As if Miss Dunne had not only the power to brighten a room but banish joyless memories as well.

Miss Dunne released a long breath as she strode the length of the library and back. "And I thought you had a great deal of books back in London, Dr. Edmunds." The wall of glass-covered bookcases dwarfed her.

"My father and I shared a love of the written word."

She looked over at him. "You must have had a great deal in common."

"No. Not at all, really. Other than medicine." The key ring jangled as he pulled it from his coat pocket. "Let me get these cases unlocked so you can start measuring the shelves and see if there's any space. I think it'll take an act of God to merge the two collections."

"You will find a way."

"Are you always so certain, Miss Dunne?"

Her gaze met his. "No. Not at all, really," she said, an ironic smile touching her lips.

She joined him, her shape imperfectly reflected in the wavy glass door fronts, standing far enough away that there wasn't any risk that sleeve would touch sleeve or hands would share warmth.

Reach out and grab her, fool, and let her pull you free.

Of course, he didn't.

Mrs. Mainprice was in the kitchen, recording the contents of the pantry and storeroom, making note of needed supplies.

"I have finished in the library, and I thought I would take a stroll around the grounds, Mrs. Mainprice." Rachel fetched her bonnet from the hook where it hung. "If you do not need my help in here, that is."

"Nay, not a bit of it." She waved her hand. "You get away with you. 'Tis a lovely day out there and fast fading. Get in a walk, and when you're back you can help me pull together a bit of dinner."

"I shall not be long."

Rachel stepped out into the sunshine and strolled across the weedy kitchen garden and onto the lawn, the brilliant green grass crushing beneath her half boots, releasing its scent. She inhaled the warm bright air, the sweet scent of some yellow-blooming plant, fresh hay thrown to a cow standing in a distant shed. She let the aromas ease through her.

A shepherd doffed his cap as he passed on his way to

tend his flock, his black-and-white dog dancing circles around his legs. "Good day to ya, miss."

His deferential treatment, the sound of his country-rough voice, the happy bark of his dog, made her smile. "I am in search of a walk that can give me a view of Finchingfield's property. Do you know the best way to go?"

"Yer headed in the right direction, miss."

After thanking the fellow, she continued on, up a gentle slope. She found the view. And, as fate would have it, Dr. Edmunds as well.

One hip resting on a crumbling stone wall, he was looking over his fields. From somewhere he had unearthed a simple straw hat with a broad brim, and he had stripped down to his shirtsleeves, the thin linen revealing in detail the width of his shoulders, the breadth of his chest.

She dawdled overlong, and he noticed her standing there. Maybe she had intended him to.

Hastily, he stood. "Miss Dunne."

"I did not mean to intrude on your solitude."

"You're hardly intruding." He opened then closed his mouth and cleared his throat. "I take it you're finished in the library."

"I have accomplished what was needed, Dr. Edmunds, and have drawn up a plan for how you might accommodate your collection."

"Then would you care to see the property?"

With him alone, out in an open meadow, the sun burnishing his hair . . . She could refuse, turn back now, claim she had only sought a breath of fresh air and scamper off to the refuge of the kitchen. Not be accused of wanting more.

Never know what it would feel like to be near him.

The time together might come to nothing, but at the moment, Rachel did not care.

"If it is no trouble, I would love to be shown around," she answered.

He smiled, the rarest gift he had to offer, the one she always craved. "It's been so long since I've been here, I need a tour myself."

They started out at a crisp pace, back toward the house. He squired her past the barn and the milk shed, over to an old dovecote and the yard where they had kept chickens when he was young. They moved across the lawn, skirted a pond hidden from the house behind a small knoll. They reached the stream Mrs. Mainprice had mentioned, its waters burbling over rocks. Dr. Edmunds's private place, a willow licking the surface, the flow moving too quickly to skip a stone across.

Using a rickety bridge constructed of flimsy beams, Dr. Edmunds took her elbow to help her across. Though he withdrew his hand quickly, his touch lingered while they found the path that led to the fields of hops and summer wheat.

"I'm told we had a good rye crop earlier in the year," he said, pausing at another low wall that separated his property from his neighbor's.

"Your estate is very impressive," she said, clasping her bonnet to her head against a sudden stiff breeze, the wind rippling the young wheat in long, rolling waves. "And very beautiful."

"Does the land remind you of Ireland?" He had taken off his hat to keep it from blowing away, and strands of his dark hair fell forward over his face. She was reminded of the first time she'd seen him like this, his hair tousled. This time, she had no wish to straighten it. The slightly unkempt Dr. James Edmunds belonged among the stalks of wheat and hedgerows and purple flowering thistle. And yes, the sun did burnish his hair, bringing out golden strands among the dark, colors she would never see beneath a smoky London sky.

"It is like Ireland in that the sky is overhead and the earth is underfoot," she answered. "But the green there is a vibrant shade, soft and deep, rich as an emerald. The hills rise rocky and are shrouded in violet, and the sky overhead is the gray-blue of misty mornings . . ." Her voice cracked.

"I shouldn't have asked." His gaze brought warmth to her cheeks. "We should talk of less unhappy things. Such as my plans for raising sheep."

"Sheep?"

He let out a low, self-deprecating laugh. "I'm trying to learn everything I can about this farming business, and apparently part of my holdings involves a flock of sheep. My steward, Mr. Jackson, thinks cattle would be more appropriate. He's an excellent man, good at what he does. I suppose I should listen to him."

"My father once had a partner he relied upon like a strong staff. A wise man to provide counsel is hard to find." Words Father often said . . . until he and his partner had squabbled and parted ways. The business and their lives in Carlow began to unravel then, a slow unwinding of the thread of their security and happiness.

Rachel sighed and stared out across the fields.

"A true sentiment, Miss Dunne." Dr. Edmunds followed

her gaze. "I'm fortunate to have someone like Mr. Jackson to rely upon as my steward. My father was unwell the past few years, and he didn't oversee the maintenance required. For instance, the few laborers I have need new housing. Some of them have been living in cottages built over fifty years ago. The roofs leak and there are dirt floors. Wretched conditions."

"At least the air is clear. Unlike London's."

He turned to face her. "Would you like to live here?" he asked, eagerness lifting his voice.

Her pulse sped. "What do you mean?"

"Would you like to come live in Finchingfield?"

"As your . . . as your . . ." As what?

"I'm sure we could find a position for you in the house. I'm certain we can."

Her heart plummeted to her feet. What had she thought he'd been asking? "I thought you did not consider me a servant, Dr. Edmunds."

The mistake he had made registered on his face. "That wasn't what I had in mind."

"I do not know what else you could have had in mind." She squared her shoulders to staunch the humiliation spreading from head to toe. "I am committed to becoming a teacher back in London, Dr. Edmunds. But thank you for your offer."

Rachel pushed away from the wall, but he grabbed her hand to keep her from fleeing. "My only thought was that I know you don't like London. I simply hoped to make you happy."

"Why?"

"Ah, Miss Dunne." How softly he said her name, gentle as the sigh of a breeze tickling a stand of reeds. "Because I have come to care about you."

His words stopped her. He lifted a finger to her cheek, brushed away a strand of hair captured against her lips, tossed there by the wind. Tenderly, he traced the outline of her face. She shivered beneath his touch.

He closed the gap between them. His hand dropped to her elbow and grasped it, pulled her nearer. "You are like a brilliant star, Rachel. Impossible to resist."

He was going to kiss her. She could see the intent in his eyes. She must not let it happen. A kiss would mean something, promise something, that would never come to pass.

Rachel pulled free of his grip and ran back to the house, sprinting along the rocky narrow path between the fields. He called after her but she pushed on. If she stopped she might let him kiss her. Because she wanted him to. Wanted to feel that connection, that binding. *You are a fool, girl. A stupid fool.* Tears stung, distorting her vision. They fell in a hot, salty stream as she stumbled along, her skirt snagging on a stand of thistle taken hold along the path.

Distracted, she failed to notice a tree root arcing across the path in time to evade it. Her foot caught and she hurtled to the ground.

"Rachel!" shouted Dr. Edmunds.

Her hands bled from where she'd scraped them along stones and scattered branches. Quickly brushing off the gravel stuck to her palms, she pushed herself up onto her knees and tried to scramble to her feet.

"Wait, don't get up," Dr. Edmunds commanded, throwing down his hat and dropping next to her, taking hold of her shoulders to keep her from rising. "You might have hurt yourself."

"I am fine. You can release me."

"You will stay here until I've determined that you can get up."

She shimmied free of his hands and planted her feet on the ground, intent upon rising. Her left ankle protested with a razor-sharp twinge of pain.

He noted her grimace. "If you attempt to walk on that ankle, Miss Dunne, you'll only injure it more." He reached beneath her skirts and examined her ankle through her half boot.

Rachel slapped off his hand and flicked her skirts back into place. "My ankle is fine."

"Don't be stubborn."

She had every intention to be stubborn. "Is the ankle swollen, Dr. Edmunds?"

"Not yet."

"Then I can walk." She pressed her palm against a near-by stump and stood. The ankle throbbed and she bit her lip. She would not wince and she would not rely on him to help her back to the house, let him put his arm around her waist or the crook of her elbow. Not when the simple brush of his fingertips made her crave more than he could ever give.

"At least lean against me so I may guide you back," he said.

"I shall make my own way."

"Rachel, really—"

"My name is Miss Dunne. In case you have forgotten that I am not a servant."

He frowned. "If you insist."

"I do."

She lifted her chin and turned away, headed for the house. With every step, her ankle throbbed. It was worth enduring, she told herself, though she had to clench her teeth to keep from crying out in pain. The ache was the price she would simply have to pay for salvaging her pride.

***

"She's a right pretty one, sir. I'd 've chased after 'er."

James turned to face the voice. A shepherd with a battered tricorn hat crooked an eyebrow, the corner of his mouth rising with it. His dog, flopped at his feet, looked up at James with the same amused, expectant expression.

A local and his dog were smirking at him. How appropriate. "Do you work for the steward of Finchingfield House?"

"No. Fair View, sir."

"Good thing for you."

Undeterred, the shepherd jerked his head in the direction of Miss Dunne's limping form, now past the edge of the fields and halfway across the lawn. "She's not got too far. You could catch 'er yet."

And do what? Apologize for wanting to hold her close, feel her tucked against his chest, her lips on his? Or apologize for knowing he had nothing more to offer her than a hasty embrace and a kiss?

"I believe you have sheep to tend to," said James, his frown deepening.

"That I do."

The man doffed his hat and whistled for his dog to follow, his shoulders shaking with laughter as he strolled away.

James slapped his hat against his thighs, scrubbed a hand across his eyes, and started back toward the house. Even impulsive fools like him still had responsibilities to attend to. Apologies, however, would have to wait until he figured out exactly for what he was repenting.

CHAPTER 19

*J*ames evaded Miss Dunne until she and Mrs. Mainprice left for London. His conscience, however, was far more difficult to evade. There was only one thing for him to do—humbly ask Miss Dunne's forgiveness and tell her she could leave his employ early, if she wished. He would pay her the totality of the salary he had promised, help her find suitable lodging, and understand if she left immediately.

The prospect sat heavy as a lump of sour cheese in his stomach.

James went through the motions of preparing for his own return to London. Peg was left behind to help ready the house. James mounted his horse and turned it down the lane for town. London approached quickly—more rapidly than he desired—the city swallowing the countryside in small bites until the fields and hedgerows were totally consumed and there was nothing to see but houses and shopfronts and traffic. Nothing left to face but his impending duty to an innocent young Irish woman.

Joe sat on the house steps, teasing a neighborhood cat with a piece of twine he had found somewhere. Spotting James, he tucked the twine in a pocket and jumped up to hold the horse's reins while James dismounted.

"Good mornin', sir. 'ave a good trip home, did you?"

"Good enough. I made it home and in one piece." *Did I pay a sliver of attention?* He could have been robbed and not even noticed. "Did the others return safely?"

"Mrs. M and Miss Dunne got back las' night 'bout ten, I'd say. Also in one piece. Or two pieces, I s'pose." Joe barked a laugh at his joke, then muffled it when he realized James wasn't laughing along.

"Where is Miss Dunne at the moment?"

"In the library. With 'er ankle wrapped." Joe uttered the last words reproachfully, as if he blamed James for Miss Dunne's injury.

Good heavens, had the entire household already heard about what had happened between them?

"She twisted it while out walking," James explained tersely. "Take my things up to my chamber. If anyone is looking for me, I'll be in the library discussing the packing of the books with Miss Dunne."

He pounded up the stairs, Joe making a speedy decision to drop the horse's reins to yank open the front door before the master reached it.

Miss Dunne stood in front of the center of the bookcases, staring at a closed book in her hand as if trying to decide what to do with it. She didn't hear him as he entered the room; she continued staring, her head cocked to one side, like a marionette waiting for the puppeteer to twitch her strings and move her to action.

"Miss Dunne, I must speak with you."

The book thudded to the floor as she spun around. She winced at the hastiness of her motion. "You startled me, Dr. Edmunds."

James came no closer to her. It would be better for the both of them if he maintained some physical distance. He shut the door behind him.

"I am not going to repeat my despicable actions, Miss Dunne," he reassured. "I've closed the door because I thought you might appreciate this conversation being kept private."

Eyes averted, she nodded. The tension clung like the damp of a humid summer day. She shifted her stance, the sway of her skirts revealing a strip of cloth binding her ankle. So far as he could tell, her leg readily supported her weight; her fall hadn't badly injured her.

Does that make me feel better, though? Less guilty?

James cleared his throat, the apology heavy on his tongue. "You know what I came in here to say. I need to apologize for attempting to kiss you."

Miss Dunne rolled her lips between her teeth.

"You are a decent and honorable young woman whom I admire," he continued, sweat gathering, "and I owe you nothing less than my utmost respect. You surely don't deserve to be pawed like some common girl. I made a horrible mistake, and I am sorry. Forgive me."

The next words he'd practiced, the ones that were most important of all, never left his mouth. He could not tell her to leave his employ early, if that was what she wished to do. Selfishly, he couldn't bear to have her withdraw from his life one second sooner than she would be forced to. *God, I most need forgiveness from You.*

Miss Dunne blanched. Maybe she was considering not forgiving him. Maybe she contemplated how to best skewer him like a roasting pig with words of righteous indignation. He deserved every bit of her condemnation.

"I accept your apology for wanting to kiss me, Dr. Edmunds," she replied at last, her voice unwavering and rich with calm dignity.

The composure she displayed lanced his heart more than any angry rejoinder could have done, reminded him just how extraordinary she was.

"I apologized for *trying* to kiss you, not for wanting to kiss you," he clarified. "I find I cannot apologize for that. God save me, I know I should, but I cannot and never shall."

Her gaze jumped to his, those incredible eyes, the color and depth of a pool of tranquil water, searching his face. He had yet to learn how to read the thoughts contained within them. Maybe God was at last being merciful by sparing James the ability.

"Do not let me disturb you any further," he said, and turned to go.

Rachel stared at the closed library door for what seemed an eternity, but must have only been mere minutes. She should walk away right now, pack her carpetbag and leave. Not that she had anywhere to go. She had returned from Finchingfield to a note from Claire saying her brother had discovered she'd pawned her ring and was so angry he'd banished her to the family estate in Weymouth. Rachel had no one to turn to now and only a few shillings to her name, Joe having sent

Claire's money to Ireland as he'd promised. She could hardly leave without receiving the salary Dr. Edmunds owed her . . . and would never pay if she abruptly quit. But heavens, how she wished she could march out the front door and never have to face him again. Cease to feel the yearning that stretched her taut as a fiddle string. He wanted to kiss her.

She wanted him to fall in love with her.

Rachel picked up the book she had dropped and placed it upon the desk just as Joe scampered into the library.

"Eh, miss, the blokes from the movin' agency 'ave just come with the crates . . ." Joe cocked his head to peer at her. "Aw, don' go lookin' all glum about that. I'll 'elp you wiv 'em."

"It's not the crates, Joe," she answered. "I am just a little sad that I shall be leaving you all soon."

"You knows we'll all miss you terrible too. 'cept Moll, I s'pose," he added honestly, with a wicked grin. "An' mebbe Peg."

Rachel smiled; it was better than crying. "I will recover from my melancholy."

"I'm glad to 'ear that. 'ate to see you sad. 'specially with Molly still green an' the master stalkin' around, ready to bite off someone's 'ead like 'e's mad at the world—"

"Yes, well, send the man from the moving agency up, will you, Joe?" She interrupted Joe to avoid hearing about Dr. Edmunds's foul mood, even if she felt some satisfaction in the knowledge he might be sad too.

"I've had another patient die from the cholera, James," said Thaddeus, sawing away at a perfectly fine cut of beef like it was a chewy, overcooked shank of mutton. He stabbed the freed piece with his fork. "That makes three for me. Much worse than the outbreak in spring."

"Two of my charity cases have succumbed as well," James replied. He'd had one recover and live, though he was at a loss to explain why. The timely use of Miss Dunne's mysterious tonic, the one her mother claimed cured every stomach ill, might have been the reason. He would like to talk to her about the tonic and his patients, but they had avoided each other these past few days. Life in the house had been easier, but not pleasant. He only had himself to blame.

"The disease is moving fast in this heat," James said, ignoring his own food turning cold on his plate. "I hear they're scattering lime in the streets in St. Giles."

"Maybe that will stop the disease from moving farther west. You'd never know there was an outbreak in town, watching these fellows." Thaddeus waved his fork in the general direction of the chophouse crowd, neither ranks nor vigor visibly diminished by the disease. Waiters in white aprons hurried between tables, arms laden with plates. Associates called to each other across the room, smoked cigars, and hunkered over papers while they ate. At a nearby table, a newspaper headline tallied the latest fatalities. The press had begun to change their tune.

"They all know there's not much to be done to prevent the spread," said James, the familiar press of helplessness weighing heavily. "They may as well go on about their lives as normal."

"It's the poor Irish and their filthy slums. The miasma lifting off their hovels will strike us all down, I fear."

A lump hard as a fist jammed in James's throat. "I've heard it proposed it's coming from the Thames."

"Little does it matter. The cholera won't pass until winter sets in. I'm just glad Louisa convinced me to send her to Bath. You should probably send Amelia and Mrs. Wood-bridge away too. Just to be safe." Thaddeus paused to chew his bite of food. "Louisa sends her greetings, by the way."

"Send her mine in return, when next you write."

"Nothing further?" Thaddeus asked, still sounding hopeful.

"Nothing further, Castleton."

"If you insist." Thaddeus frowned and washed down the beef with a drink of soda water. "Hey, what the . . ."

Thaddeus's glass halted in midair. James heard the ruckus that had captured his friend's attention. He craned his neck to see over a man blocking his view.

"Can't a man eat a meal in peace anymore?" grumbled Thaddeus, shifting in his seat to catch a look. "We have to have waiters scuffling with patrons now?"

Then James heard it, the whisper leaping like fleas scattering before a fumigant of burning sulfur. "Cholera," it chattered. *Cholera.*

James jumped up, threw his napkin on the table, and pushed his way through to the front. Thaddeus was close on his heels.

"What's going on?" James asked of the waiter who'd locked arms with the man.

The waiter was a burly fellow and easily subdued the other. "It's nothing, sir. You can go back to eating. This fellow's just a mite upset over something he saw out on the street."

The man, a tradesman by the look of his breeches and heavy dark coat, was sweating. His eyes were wide as a copper penny. "There's a woman outside on the pavement. She's perished from the cholera. Right before my eyes, she did!"

"I'm a physician. Show me where she is."

The waiter relinquished his grasp, and the fellow sprung free. "Out here, doctor." He shoved back out through the door and pointed down the street a short way. A crowd huddled nearby, hands over noses and mouths, staring aghast. Someone had thought to send for a policeman, for a man in the familiar blue uniform and helmet was running their direction.

Thaddeus joined James as he crouched next to the woman. She was someone's servant or charwoman, dressed in a simple dark gown, hair graying beneath her mobcap. The items she had been carrying in a basket were scattered on the ground nearby. A skein of twine. A shattered bottle of oily boot blacking.

James felt for a pulse along her neck, the skin already gone blue. "There's no heartbeat." The front of her gown was soiled from where she had vomited, the stench sour and pervasive.

Thaddeus finished his own quick assessment as the policeman arrived to drive back the onlookers and send for an ambulance. "I say, it just might be the cholera," he whispered. "Blessed Lord in heaven, they're dropping in the streets now."

James rocked back on his heels. "Dreadful business." He cocked his head and looked at the woman's face, twisted in agony. She looked familiar, but he couldn't place her. Why would he know this woman? He was probably mistaken.

He pulled out his handkerchief and draped it over her face, heard the distant clang of the ambulance wagon's bell as it came to take the woman's lifeless body away.

"Cor, miss, what a mess in here!" Joe complained, picking his way through the library, past the crates and stacks of books waiting to be packed.

The house was buzzing with activity, every room swarming like ants on a hill. Soon the household would be moving to Finchingfield.

"The packing is taking longer than I expected," Rachel answered. "Will you be able to help me today?"

"I can 'elp once I'm done dancin' like a cat on 'ot coals." He gave an apologetic grimace. "I'm havin' to clear out the stable, then I 'ave to 'elp Mrs. M down in the kitchen. And Moll thinks I'm 'er messenger boy, sendin' me up 'ere to tell you she wants a talk."

Rachel's throat knotted. She had not only avoided Dr. Edmunds these past few days, but she hadn't crossed paths with Molly either. She could have predicted her good fortune would not last forever. "Did she say what she needed to talk to me about?"

"'Course not, miss. Moll don' care to share that sor' of information with me."

"Where is she then?" Rachel asked, stripping off her apron.

"Out in the garden."

Rachel found the girl staring at the green-tinged pool of water surrounding the unused fountain. She glanced at Molly's middle. The maid's frock hung loose enough to conceal any increase in girth. She might not be far enough along to obviously show she was with child.

Molly heard the crunch of Rachel's approaching foot-steps and looked over. "You have to help me. I need a potion. To start my monthlies again."

Abrupt and clear, leaving no doubt as to her condition.

Rachel's heart pounded hard, her feet begging to flee back to the house. "I cannot help you in that way."

Even while she denied Molly, ingredients whispered in Rachel's head.

"I cannot," she repeated.

Eyes wild, Molly rushed up to her and grabbed hold of her arm. Her fingers pinched. "You have to! I can't have a baby!"

"Molly, I will not help you get rid of your baby."

"He was going to marry me, he was! The liar! Says he never promised me anything." A sob hiccupped out of her, and tears as fat as chandelier prisms rolled on her cheeks. "I bought a tonic from the apothecary. He said it would work. All it did was make me sick and twopence poorer. Men, they're all liars."

"Do not try to harm the child. It is wrong." Dreadfully, horribly sinful. "Besides, most of those tonics will not work, other than to make you severely ill, perhaps fatally ill."

"Ha! Telling me not to make myself ill." Molly threw down Rachel's arm. "As if you care about me. If you cared, you'd help! Well, I know what to do about that. You're going to help me or I'm going to show Dr. Edmunds the letter. I'll tell him what I think you're all about."

Molly spun away, black skirts belling, and hurried to-ward the house.

Rachel rushed after her. "Molly, wait! Do not do this! You will ruin both our lives. Stop, please. We can think of some-thing else to do to help you."

Molly pulled open the rear door, Rachel on her heels. "What, are you afraid now, Miss hoity Dunne? Well, wait until Dr. Edmunds hears everything I know about you! Then you'll be sorry."

"What is it you know, Molly?" asked a man's voice from down the hallway.

Rachel's heart stopped. Dr. Edmunds was waiting for an answer.

CHAPTER 20

What is it you know, Molly?" James repeated.

Silence permeated the hallway like a mist rising off damp cobblestones.

Molly's eyes jerked to where Miss Dunne stood rooted to the ground, her face turned an unearthly shade of white. "She's been lying to you, sir. All this time she's been working for you, she's fooled you into believing that she's of good character. Well, she isn't, Dr. Edmunds. There was a trial in Ireland, and she was the accused."

"You must be mistaken, Molly," he said dismissively. "You have misunderstood the situation, I'm sure."

Molly's face flushed an ugly shade of red. "I have not. I've a letter that proves what I'm saying."

"What do you have to say for yourself, Miss Dunne?" He waited for her to deny Molly's ridiculous assertion, waited for her to throw back the accusation. Waited for denial that did not come.

"Molly is telling the truth," she answered, her soft lilting voice steady. Unbelievably calm.

"You were accused of a crime?" It wasn't possible. "What could you have done? Something desperate, like taking a loaf of bread to feed hungry family members, perhaps," he said, grasping for a palatable explanation, one he might comprehend. "Tell me it was something like that."

"I cannot, Dr. Edmunds." Her gaze was unwavering. "I was accused of murder."

His blood ran cold through his veins. Funny, when he was young he had always believed that expression to be just a saying, but indeed it was truth. "Impossible."

"I assure you, it is not."

Molly started laughing, a feral sound emanating from low in her throat. "Murder! What a rotten hypocrite you are, saying you won't help me."

What an odd comment, James thought, his eyes never leaving Rachel's beautiful face. He stared at her as though she were a stranger, an unfamiliar woman he might pass in the street and wonder about. *Who is she? What is her past?* He thought he had known, at least enough. He'd just learned he had not known her at all.

"I did not murder Mary," Rachel said to Molly, so smoothly it sounded as though she were saying nothing more startling than she did not wish to have jam with her toast. His physician's mind analyzed; he'd had patients so shaken by their injuries they acted with utter calm, as if the wound were happening to another person. He witnessed the same response here. "I was accused, but not convicted. The jury acquitted me."

"But you obviously did something that made the officials think you might have been a murderer! Constables don't go accusing folk for no good reason!" Molly shrieked.

"Quiet down, Molly," he ordered. Mrs. Mainprice would hear; the men from the moving agency scraping furniture across the floor even now would hear; his neighbors would hear. Miss Dunne had barely flinched.

"She died while in my care," she answered Molly's hysterics. "While I was asleep. I do not even know what happened, why . . . But I did not murder Mary Ferguson. That I swear."

"Mr. Ferguson doesn't think you're innocent, does he?" Molly spat, her gaze venomous. "That's what it says in the letter."

"Molly, enough!" James said. "I'll deal with Miss Dunne. This is none of your concern. Please leave us."

"Make sure, sir, you don't listen to the evil she'll likely spread to defend herself," she said, eyes narrowing. "Miss Dunne is a wretched liar. Next she'll be saying all sorts of things about Peg and me, to make her own self look good. Don't believe them."

"I asked you to leave, Molly, in case you didn't hear me."

Molly blanched and scurried down the stairs, toward the kitchen.

Miss Dunne's gaze was fixed on a spot halfway up the wall. Spine erect, shoulders squared, she awaited his sentence like a prisoner in the dock.

Dash it all, why did you do this to me, Miss Dunne? I wanted to remember you as perfect in every way . . . I wanted to hold on to you until the last possible second.

He walked nearer until they stood face-to-face. He attempted to gather his thoughts, but they kept slipping away from him, like he was trying to cup grains of wheat in his hands only to have them trickle through his fingers. He had to believe she was innocent of any crime, this woman he had come to respect so highly. This woman he had desired to embrace, to kiss. But it was clear now that she had kept secrets from him. Clearer still that his only option was to send her away.

A vast abyss, arid and wide as some distant desert chasm, opened in his chest.

When he spoke, his mouth was dry. "You should have told me what happened to you in Ireland, Miss Dunne. Now because Molly knows what you've concealed and the rest of the house will learn, too, I have no choice but to dismiss you from my employ."

"I am sorry for not telling you. Believe me, I truly am." Her eyes begged him to understand. "But the treatment I received in Carlow from people who had known me all my life led me to believe I had to keep quiet. They shunned me, Dr. Edmunds, went out of their way to avoid me on the streets, like I was a leper. They shunned my family as well. My mother's work as a modiste dried up like . . . like a puddle of water on a hot day, as if it had never existed. My brother, my little sisters, treated with contempt and cruelty though they were innocent . . ." Her voice cracked. "I concluded I would have no chance at honest employment anywhere if my past were known."

He started to reach out to grab her shoulders and shake her back to being the woman he'd believed her to be. "I entrusted you with the care of a patient."

"It is too late now to change what I did."

Too late. Much too late. "I wish you had told me anyway."

Rachel's eyes were on him. "I hope you will still give me the character reference I require. In spite of everything."

Without a reference, she would have no future in London beyond some menial job that would force her into poverty. He couldn't do that to her, no matter that disappointment weighed like a millstone on his heart.

"Your work for me has been exemplary. I will write to Mrs. Chapman and inform her of just that, nothing more." James swallowed hard, though the lump he felt wasn't in his throat. "I must ask you, though, to please pack your things and leave in the morning. The staff . . . they'll expect me to force you to go. I'll pay for hackney fare to whatever destination you choose."

"I am forever in your debt, Dr. Edmunds."

She bowed her head and left him to the emptiness of the hallway.

How long did I think I could keep this from him? Forever?

Rachel stared up at the bedchamber ceiling as if she might find an answer in the dips and hairline cracks in the plaster. Frankly, she should feel better that the truth had been forced into the open, but she didn't. Not when there were details of that awful day in Carlow that she'd kept from him.

Restlessly, Rachel shifted on the bed, her sniffles nearly drowning out the sound of a muted sob coming through the bedchamber wall. Rachel lifted her head and heard another sob coming from the chamber next to hers. The one shared by Peg and Molly, but only occupied by Molly now that Peg was in Finchingfield.

Throwing back the sheet, Rachel rose, tucked her feet into slippers, and pulled on her robe. Dark stillness stretched along the hallway, defiantly quiet. Rachel tiptoed down to Molly's door and listened. She hadn't imagined the sound; Molly was whimpering.

Rachel tapped on the door. "Molly, are you ill?" She whispered to avoid waking Mrs. Mainprice, who slept in the room at the end of the hallway. "What is the matter?"

"Go away."

"Are you ill? Have you . . ." Merciful heavens. What if the girl had taken another tonic to rid herself of her baby? "I am coming in."

"No!"

Rachel pushed open the door, which Molly had left unlocked. "Tell me what is wrong."

Dim moonlight bathed the room in silvery light, showed a form curled up on the far bed. "I said go away."

Rachel hurried to the girl's side. "Did you take something to get rid of the baby?"

Molly shook her head, the dark braid of her hair moving across her shoulder.

Rachel rested her hand against Molly's forehead. It was hot and frighteningly dry. She was at the height of a fever. "You have a fever, Molly. Let me fetch the doctor."

"No!" Molly twisted to face her. "Leave me alone. I'll be fine. I don't want your help, and I don't want him to know."

"I will not leave you to suffer here alone, because you do need help. Someone's help, if not mine. Tell me the truth. Have you tried to get rid of the child?"

Molly squeezed her eyes shut. Answer enough.

"Have you lost it?" Rachel asked. *It.* The same way the prosecutor had referred to Mary Ferguson. *"Did you harm it?"* A thing, a creature. Not a human being. Rachel flushed, angry at the memory, angry with herself. "Have you lost the baby?" she amended.

Molly shook her head, her cheek digging into the pillow. "I don't know. I'm bleeding, but not much anymore. Lord, how it hurts. My insides are going to come out."

Fear shot through Rachel. "I am going to fetch the doctor."

"Don't!" A sudden spasm convulsed Molly, her face pinching and making her look years older. She was too proud to cry out with Rachel standing right next to her. "I knew you'd tattle on me," she managed. "You'd like to see me on the street."

"I do not want to see you on the street any more than I want to be there. I really only want to help you."

Molly's hand shot out from beneath the sheets to grab her arm, the reaction plumbed from some deep reserve of frantic energy. "You can help by not telling Dr. Edmunds."

"I have to tell him. I cannot do this, Molly. I cannot tend you. I made a promise to myself . . ." A promise she had been forced to break how many times since that afternoon in Carlow? The jury might have found her innocent, but no one else had, least of all herself. She'd vowed never to sit at another sickbed after Mary Ferguson had died. Never be responsible for another's life. Yet here she was, yet again, her intentions as worthless as the false golden glow of pinchbeck.

Rachel broke Molly's grip on her arm. "I have to bring him, Molly. He is the only one who might save you!"

Rachel fled the room and hurried down to the next floor.

She pounded on Dr. Edmunds's bedchamber door. "Dr. Edmunds, it is Rachel Dunne."

He pulled open the door, a lit candle in hand. His hair was tousled and his legs were bare beneath the indigo brocade dressing gown that skimmed the top of his ankles.

He frowned. "I can't change my mind about letting you go. I'm sorry——"

"I am not here about that," she interrupted. "It is Molly. She is very sick. You must come and tend her."

"Let me get some clothing on." He shut the door in Rachel's face. It reopened in moments.

"What are her symptoms?" he asked, tucking in his shirt while they strode side-by-side toward the staircase. "Is she sick to her stomach? Does she have a fever?"

"She is feverish, but I do not think it is the cholera, if that is what you are asking." This might be the only time Rachel wished someone were ill with a deadly disease. He would forgive Molly the cholera. Pregnancy, he wouldn't.

He walked into the maid's cramped room, the slap of his slippers soft against the wood floor. "Now, Molly, what is the matter?" he asked, dropping his voice into a soothing baritone.

"You didn't have to come, sir. I'll be all right. Honest," she said, still curled on her side. "Miss Dunne shouldn't have fetched you." In the light of the candle, Rachel could see a circle of rusty red on the white sheet, down below her belly. Condemning evidence. Dr. Edmunds spotted it too.

"Molly, you're bleeding heavily. Are you having trouble with your monthlies?"

"I . . . unh." Another spasm overtook her and she pulled tight into a ball.

"Dr. Edmunds, she is pregnant," said Rachel. He may as well know now what he was facing.

"She's lying!" Molly protested between gritted teeth. "She hopes you'll dismiss me. She hates me."

The line of his jaw tightened and he stripped back the sheet. The bloom of red was clearer against Molly's linen chemise, crimson on cream. An exhalation whistled through his teeth. "Miss Dunne, bring warm water and a towel. Some fresh linens as well."

Rachel gaped at him. "You want me to help? After what I . . . after what you said?"

"You're here and I need you to help me. Molly needs you," he said succinctly.

Rachel did as he asked, running down to the kitchen to heat a kettle. She roused the fire to life, set water to heat, and fetched clean towels and sheets. Everything gathered, Rachel returned to the bedchamber. While she'd been in the kitchen, Dr. Edmunds had gone to his office to retrieve his medicines—a bottle of fever mixture, another of elixir of vitriol, the common brown bottle of laudanum.

His face was set with concentration, his hands moving steadily and assuredly as he laid out his paraphernalia. "Miss Dunne, mix a tablespoonful of the fever mixture in two cups of water while I prepare the medicine to ease . . . Molly's cramping."

Meaning her body's efforts to rid itself of the baby. He poured out drops from the elixir of vitriol into a glass of water—a good cut-glass goblet from the crate in the dining room—adding a small amount of laudanum to help Molly sleep. Rachel dropped the towels and sheets nearby, hastily poured the hot water into the empty washbasin, some of it splashing over the rim. Using the doctor's silver measuring spoon, she made up the fever concoction and set it at his elbow.

"Here, Molly, take both of these. They will help you." Gently, he lifted her head. She gagged on the taste but bravely swallowed both.

Meanwhile, Rachel dipped one of the smaller towels in the hot water and wrung it out.

"I think it best you wash Molly up, Miss Dunne."

Respectfully, he turned aside and shook out the sheets while Rachel washed the drying blood off Molly. The maid was too weak to protest, though she had sufficient energy to glare. Rachel slipped off Molly's stained chemise, found a clean one in the chest, and helped the girl into it. Dr. Edmunds handed her a sheet and Rachel replaced the old one, Dr. Edmunds assisting as she lifted the mattress to hold the sheet in place. Molly closed her eyes and drifted off to sleep.

Exhausted, Rachel's knees gave way and she dropped down onto the lone chair in the room. She clutched her robe tight around her neck. The maid's color had evened out, her breathing steadied. Molly had passed through the worst.

"Molly shall recover," she stated.

Dr. Edmunds finished saying a prayer and tucked the clean sheet around Molly's arms, untangling her braid from beneath it to lie out upon the dimity sheet, a rope of brown against white.

"She's strong." He ran his fingers through his hair, curling and wild. "Too strong, perhaps. She didn't lose the baby, which I gather was what she was trying to do."

"She purchased a tonic, and I think this was her second attempt to use it."

He gathered up the dirty towels and threw them atop the stained sheet.

"So you knew what she was planning." He tied the linens into a bundle for laundering later, his hands jerking the knot secure. "Is this household keeping any more secrets from me?"

"I was not completely certain until this afternoon what Molly intended to do," Rachel answered in defense.

He swiveled his head to look at her. "Yet you suspected she was pregnant. You suspected and decided not to tell me."

"I knew she had been meeting a man, but I promised her I would say nothing to you. In return for her not revealing what she had learned about my trial."

"If ever there was a time to break a promise, this would've been it, Miss Dunne. You might have saved her this failed abortion. If she'd taken more of whatever concoction she purchased, she might not be lying there asleep. She might be lying there dead from blood loss or poisoning."

"You think I do not realize that?" Shaking with anger, Rachel stood. "If I had told you, you would have dismissed her immediately and she would have gone off to rid herself of the child in some dark, squalid room elsewhere. The outcome would have been no different."

"I know of a small charitable institute for girls in her condition. I would've sent her there, which is what I still intend on doing once she has recovered. She'll be well taken care of and the baby will be adopted out. Presuming it lives, after what she's done."

"I suppose she will be thankful to be dismissed and have her child taken away from her," Rachel hissed, trying to keep from screeching and rousing Molly or the rest of the household.

"Is there something else you would rather I do for her, Miss Dunne?" Vexed, red-faced, the doctor towered over her. "Such as keep her on, take her to Finchingfield House with me? An unmarried house-maid large with child. How would the people of that town treat her, do you think? Don't answer, because I know how they would treat her. And so do you."

Rachel's face burned. "That was unkind, Dr. Edmunds."

His jaw flexed again, but he didn't apologize for reminding Rachel of her treatment in Carlow. "I'll try my best to ensure that Molly finds a position elsewhere, once the baby is born. Somewhere in the country, perhaps. Far away."

Far away . . . as far as London was from Carlow, perhaps. Distance seemed the only cure for women like Molly and herself.

"Sending Molly away is the best course open for her," he continued. "The best I can do. You'll see."

"I will not see. I am leaving in the morning, Dr. Edmunds. First light. Remember?"

"This episode with Molly changes everything. Someone will have to take over Molly's task of packing the bedchambers. Mrs. Mainprice and Joe are too busy with their work. You'll have to stay."

"What if I refuse? I have the right to. You have dismissed me, after all, and I am no longer in your employ."

The look he gave her was that of a father scrutinizing a disobedient child. She had lost so much that day—his admiration, his trust. All that was left of his caring.

"Please stay, Miss Dunne," he ground out. "As further compensation, I will pay you your entire salary plus another crown for having to do Molly's tasks in addition to your own. I think I'm being more than fair with you."

She sucked in a breath, let it out quickly. He was bribing her, but she had no reason to refuse, besides pride. Pride, however, had swayed her too often in the past and God had punished her for her arrogance.

"Yes, you are being fair," she replied, because pride was a luxury she could no longer afford.

CHAPTER 21

"The doctor is out, I said."

Joe's voice was clear, echoing up the staircase to reach Rachel in the library. He had been assigned to answering the door, in lieu of any maids left in the house, but hadn't had time to master any of the manners that went with the job. Rachel could easily imagine the look of exasperation on his face right now, furious with whoever it was who declined to leave, and almost smiled. Almost.

Finishing the final entry in the ledger, Rachel straightened and wiped her hands across her apron. The last of the books, recorded and packed away. The room looked undressed, the massive walnut shelves empty of their volumes.

Footsteps marched up to the library, and Joe poked his head around the door. He'd been given a new outfit to go with his new role, and he rubbed his bare head as if his nervous fingers missed his old tattered cap, banished to the stable.

"Miss Dunne, are you busy?"

Her work in the library was completed, but Molly's tasks . . . she still had those to do. She had been procrastinating with them. "I have just finished here, Joe."

"Good, 'cause there's a person," he paused to roll his eyes as though the title "person" was a bit too noble for the creature, "who says she 'as to see Dr. E, an' won't listen when I tell 'er that 'e isn't 'ere. Says she 'as to see 'im and won't leave until 'e appears. Bloomin' stupid woman. She came to the front door too! Bold as brass."

"You need me to talk to her?"

"Mrs. M is busy meetin' with the butcher to settle the bill, else I'd 'ave 'er give the woman the boot."

Rachel untied her apron and went downstairs. A lanky woman, as tattered and stained as a rag left in the gutter, fidgeted on the threshold of the open front door. Joe had stopped her from coming inside; she appeared used to such treatment.

The woman's eyes were dark and piercing and world-weary. Displeased as they confronted Rachel. "You ain't no Dr. Edmunds."

"The doctor is out, and I do not know when he will return. Joe here has already told you that."

"'e has to come."

"Is there something I can help you with?"

"You be a healer?" the woman asked suspiciously.

Not any longer. "I might be able to assist if I know what the problem is. Dr. Edmunds directs some of his patients to Dr. Calvert—"

"I needs Dr. Edmunds. 'im only. Someone's got to 'elp Moll, an' seein' as she used to work for 'im, afore . . . everythin', I thought—"

Rachel caught the name and the tension that went with it. "Molly? You have come because of Molly?"

She nodded. "She wouldn't like me to be 'ere, not one bit. But 'e'd help 'er. I knows 'e would. She's terrible sick."

Rachel's insides clenched. Something had happened with the baby again, and this woman had either walked a great distance or spent her last penny to get here to plead for help. "The matrons at the institute Dr. Edmunds sent her to should be able to adequately care for her."

"Moll left that stinkin' hole. She didn't like it there 'tall. She's wiv me." The woman heaved an exasperated sigh, her hands kneading together as if they sought to choke one another. "Are ye gonna come, then, or just keep yammerin'?"

Molly's friend turned to leave, confident Rachel would follow.

"Miss . . . ma'am, I . . ." She could not keep tending to people. *Why does this continue to happen to me?* Today, however, there was no Dr. Edmunds to rescue her from tending Molly alone.

The woman stopped on the second step, noting Rachel's hesitation.

"Are ye comin' or not? Moll's gonna die." Her voice was sharp with impatience and fear. "Die, ye understan' me?"

Rachel swallowed and her tongue stuck to the roof of her mouth. Molly would die without help. Might die anyway. *God—or somebody—help me.*

"Joe!" Rachel shouted. He was at her side so quickly she had to believe he'd been lurking close by. "I need to tend Molly at this woman's house. I need the gig."

"Cor, miss, the master'll 'ave me 'ead for takin' the gig

without 'is say-so. I don' suppose you can afford a hackney." He lifted his brows hopefully.

"No, Joe. I cannot."

"Well, I'll take ya then. I guess."

"I will meet you in back once I have collected some medicines."

Joe glanced at the woman waiting by the door. "Come round back, miss . . . come round back, will ya? But not through the 'ouse. Cor."

Rachel ran to Dr. Edmunds's office. The door was open, but his medicine cabinet was locked. She couldn't get to his bottle of fever mixture. She would have to make do with what she could find in the kitchen, which might not be adequate. In minutes she procured two bottles—one of spirit of niter and one of laudanum, borrowed from Mrs. Mainprice's personal stores. Gratefully, the housekeeper had asked few questions as she'd handed the items over, too busy with the butcher to take much notice of Rachel's request.

Rachel met Joe and Molly's friend in the mews, the gig waiting and ready. Bottles safely tucked into her pocket, she climbed up alongside Joe. Her stomach roiled, but she would rather toss her luncheon of cold sliced beef and potatoes than turn back now like a craven coward.

"Hurry, Joe." *Before I change my mind.*

Rachel realized, as the gig clattered down the bustling thoroughfare of Oxford Street, how little of London she had seen. Each passing yard brought buildings a bit wearier, a bit more forbidding. They had driven past the big park near the house and the road that led to Mrs. Chapman's school, clattered away from the prosperity of the neighborhoods that Joe referred to as Mayfair. Quicker than she expected, Oxford Street ended and they squeezed into a narrower road, a sensation much like coming out the bottom end of a funnel. The buildings closed around them and Joe slowed the gig. The tart stench of decaying vegetables—and worse—hung in the air. Rachel fisted her nose while nausea rolled anew.

"Yeah, the smell of St. Giles," said Joe, his mouth twisting sourly. "Don't breathe in too deep. The air'll kill ya, it will. Drops 'em like flies around 'ere."

Molly's friend grunted, a noise of either affirmation or protest. It was difficult for Rachel to distinguish.

Joe brought the gig to a halt and the woman clambered down first. She sprinted toward a narrow archway spanning two buildings.

"Through 'ere," she called back over her shoulder.

"Good luck there, miss," said Joe as Rachel eased onto the slippery pavement.

"Do not tell me you are not coming with me," Rachel said.

"I leave the gig and it'll be gone in an instant." He snapped his fingers to accentuate his point. "Sorry, miss. If you leave before it gets dark, you should be okay. I think."

Small consolation, that.

"Tell Dr. Edmunds the moment he returns where I have gone, should I not get back before he does. Tell him . . ." *I need him to do the doctoring.* "Just tell him to come if I do not return soon."

"Aye, miss. Be quick."

"I doubt I can promise that. Thank you, Joe."

Molly's friend had disappeared. Lifting her skirts to keep them out of the filth clogging what passed for a gutter, Rachel hurried through the archway. It led into a courtyard. A man smoking a pipe leaned against a nearby doorpost, watching as she emerged. Decomposing matter filled corners, black mold grew up cracked plaster walls, and stained laundry hung from open windows. Two scrawny boys with dirty faces and tattered trousers halted their game of checkers and set down the bits of bone they used for playing pieces to stare. The air reeked of ordure, and bile choked Rachel's throat. The poorest quarter of Carlow was better than this place.

"Have you seen a woman come through here?" Rachel asked the man.

His gaze scanned her, assessing like a backstreet shopkeeper whether the information might be worth some money. The clothing on her back might fetch a pound, which would be a month's wages to a fellow like him.

Instinctively, Rachel clutched her arms about her. He finished his assessment and decided to take pity. She and her clothing were safe.

"Yep." He pointed a thumb toward a doorway two houses away, his pipe clicking against his few teeth as he clamped down again.

She thanked him and hurried forward, picking her way around mangy dogs and piles of rubbish. Impossibly, the smell intensified the deeper she moved into the dreary space. She clapped a hand to her nose.

A thimble-sized girl with dirty hands huddled inside the open door, bundling watercress. Rachel smiled at her and lifted her skirts over the threshold, slick with old grime.

"'ere, miss." Molly's friend signaled from a room just to Rachel's right. A sickly sweet scent, a mix of sweat and rot, drifted out. The woman jerked her head over toward the corner. "There's Moll."

Oh, you poor creature. That this might become the last place Molly knew.

The space was nothing more than a single room. Light struggled to pierce the web-encrusted window, and the air was damp and moldy, pressing heavily on her lungs. The plaster had cracked and fallen, revealing the decomposing lath behind. A pallet had been shoved against the far wall, a ragged sheet tossed over a rope to act as a curtain. Molly was a huddled bundle beneath a threadbare sheet no longer white but sheer as muslin from years of use.

Her eyes, glitteringly bright, glowered at Rachel. "Why are you here?" she asked, her strength insufficient to voice the resentment clear in her gaze.

Why *was* she there? To serve more penance? "Your friend came looking for Dr. Edmunds to tend you, but he has been gone all day. I said I would come instead. Until he can come himself."

The glare shifted to her friend, who had taken down a chair from the wall and set it adjacent the bed for Rachel to use. "You shouldn't have sent for either of them."

"Don' be ungrateful now, Moll. She's 'ere for free." A meager offering.

"I am all you have for now," Rachel said. "Please let me do what I can to help."

Molly tried to hold onto her resentment, but she lacked the strength for it. The hatred retreated from her eyes, leaving behind only the fever and the fear.

Sitting, Rachel lifted Molly's hand, felt along the girl's wrist, hot as a warming pan. Molly's pulse raced. "You should have stayed at the institute Dr. Edmunds sent you to."

"I couldn't listen to their lectures anymore. I'd rather die than stomach any more of their preachy jabbering."

You might get your wish . . . Oh, Lord, can You not heal her? Rachel rested Molly's hand atop the sheet. He would not help either of them, two sinners. Poor creature. "Has the bleeding started again?"

Molly nodded. "It was bad a bit ago. I thought it'd stop, like the other day. But it didn't."

"Soaked seven rags, she did." Molly's friend stood against the wall at the head of the pallet. A hard veneer protected the woman's emotions, but Rachel was confident the woman was frightened for her friend. She should be.

"Has the bleeding stopped now?" Rachel asked.

"Yes, but the cramping is bad. I'm so cold."

Rachel drew out the bottle of spirit of niter and the laudanum. "I need a cup of the cleanest water you can find and more cool cloths," she instructed Molly's friend.

Molly shivered and closed her eyes. "I'm scared of going to hell. I've been trying to pray but I can't seem to remember the proper words." She sobbed, but no tears fell. The fever was slowly wringing every ounce of moisture from her body, leaking it through every pore, leaving none for sorrowing. "I'm going to die, aren't I?"

Rachel brushed tendrils of the girl's hair off her forehead. *Yes, Molly, you are, and I cannot stop it from happening.*

"I will not let you die, Molly," Rachel said instead of the words pounding in her brain. Her mother had always insisted that the patient must believe they could heal, even if Rachel did not. "Do you hear me? I will not let you die."

Rachel raised her eyes to the peeling plaster of the ceiling while despair hollowed out her strength, draining it away like grains of sand slipping through an hourglass.

"God, do not do this again," she muttered wearily. So weary.

Molly's eyelids fluttered open. "What's that?"

"Nothing, Molly." Rachel patted the girl's hand. "Nothing at all."

Molly's friend shuffled back into the room, cradling a mug in one hand and a torn bit of cloth in the other.

Rachel diluted the spirit of niter. "Help me lift Molly." Her friend gripped Molly's shoulders to raise her up so she could drink. She lifted easily. Molly was light as a rag doll, a shadow of her former self, and just as limp. "This is for the fever."

The girl spluttered, half the liquid dribbling down her chin. When she finished the spirit of niter and a portion of the laudanum, she settled back on the lumpy tick. Molly moaned and curled into a ball. Her cheeks were splotched unnaturally crimson, her breathing fast and shallow.

"Will she live?" her friend whispered, laying the dampened cloth over Molly's forehead. The girl had fallen into a fitful sleep, insensible to the question.

Rachel shrugged. Dread weighed so heavily she thought it would drag her straight through the floor into the basement.

"I'll pray for 'er, beg God's mercy. She wasn't always a sinful girl, but that fellow she's been with . . . ." The woman shook her head regretfully. Her face was pinched and tears shone in her eyes. "'e ruined her, 'e did. An' now she's payin' the price."

"Yes. Pray for her," Rachel replied mechanically.

"I will. An' when Moll wakes up, she'll ask forgiveness, repent. Jus' like the preacher what comes roun' 'ere tells us to do. God won't punish 'er."

Won't He?

"I am sorry," Rachel murmured, not certain who she was saying sorry to.

CHAPTER 22

What is Miss Dunne doing in St. Giles at this hour?" James pulled out his gold pocket watch. Half-gone eight. His final meeting with Dr. Calvert had taken longer than expected, turned into a dinner invitation, then more conversation. About the cholera, mostly.

He scowled at Joe. "Why would she be in St. Giles? You must have misunderstood her destination. She must be at her cousin's." Although James thought he'd heard that Miss Harwood had abruptly left for Weymouth.

"Aye, I took—eh, I saw 'er take a hackney and, clear as I'm standin' 'ere, tell the bloke to take 'er to St. Giles. Fair surprisin' and all she'd venture out to take care of Moll, but there ya 'ave it. Miss Dunne's a good un."

"Molly isn't in St. Giles. The institute is in Marylebone."

"Moll's not at the institute, sir. Done left it, accordin' to the woman what come to fetch you. Stayin' in St. Giles. Miss Dunne says come as quick as you can, tho'."

"What time did she depart?" A sick feeling burrowed in his gut. "How long has she been gone?"

Joe's eyes wandered to a high corner of the entry hall, as if the answer to the question resided in the crown molding. "I'd say five . . . six hours at most, sir."

"She should have been back by now." The sick feeling intensified, transformed into a tingling panic. "Where in St. Giles, Joe? I need an address. And the mare saddled."

Joe provided an address that only increased James's alarm. "You should have stopped her. You know how dangerous that area is."

"Too late now, sir, pardon my sayin' so."

Dearest Jesus, do not let it be too late. Don't let her come to any harm.

Joe was quick to saddle the mare. James jumped up onto the horse's back and trotted toward St. Giles as fast as traffic would permit. Not fast enough for him.

Along Oxford Street, inky darkness slithered through the alleyways, seeking the low and hidden crevices. A horrible place for a lone woman to be, a target for predators. Laughter spilled through the door of a pub, rolling into the street like a splash of filthy water from a washbasin. A lamplighter hobbled along the pavement, his ladder over one arm and his flint box and supply of cotton wicks secured on the other, the sparsely spaced streetlamps springing to life as he advanced. The lamps were spaced far apart and stretches of the roadway remained in shadow, providing cover for criminals.

Rachel was out in this, attending to Molly because he had been using his meeting with Dr. Calvert as an excuse not to return home at a reasonable hour. Sharp words had passed between him and Rachel over Molly, and neither had figured out a way to restore the relationship they'd had before. It had been easier for him to avoid Rachel completely. A coward's actions.

James kicked his mare into a canter and stretched his neck to scan the road. There were plenty of people on the streets—shop workers heading home, a couple of ragged men dodging carts to collect dung from the roadway, girls selling the waste of the day's vegetables. Not a one of them Rachel. Sweat trickled beneath James's collar to itch along his neck and back. He might have missed her, passing in an omnibus or a hired coach as he came out to search. Or she was still up ahead in St. Giles.

In a fit of agitation, he jabbed his heels into his horse's side, making the mare shy sideways. James clutched the pommel and cursed his stupidity. Getting tossed onto the cobblestones and bashing his brains out would help no one.

Out of the corner of his eye, he caught sight of a familiar figure walking along Oxford Street. He let out a breath. *Thank You, God.*

Setting his features sternly, he guided the horse over to her. "Miss Dunne, you should not be walking the streets of London at this hour."

"I do not have the fare to do otherwise." Her shoulders drooped beneath the shawl she had thrown over them, as though she were weary of the world and everything in it.

"It's dangerous in St. Giles. Perhaps you were unaware, but any manner of evil could have befallen you. And here you are, alone, unchaperoned, easy prey," he barked, angry at her, at himself. She could have been assaulted. Because of his cowardice.

Because of him.

"I completely understand how dangerous, how awful St. Giles is, Dr. Edmunds," she said with sudden rancor. "Absolutely, completely understand. Oh God." Her chest heaved with a shuddering breath, and she began to sob.

James jumped off the horse and took her shoulders in his hands. Her entire body trembled and the vibration moved through his palms, down his arms. "What is it? Something has happened to you. Did someone harm you?" He would kill them. God forgive his sinful thought, but he would hunt down the man who would dare to hurt her.

"No one assaulted me." Rachel pressed her lips together, released them again. "It's Molly. She is dead."

The word rang out, echoed in his head, though she had only whispered it. "No."

"Indeed, she very much is." She looked up at him, her eyes frighteningly intense. "I could not save her. She died. She lost the baby and she died. No matter what I gave her, or how often I bathed her forehead. Her passing was so quick too. It should have taken the entire night, but she was gone barely hours after I arrived. Now she is cold and stiff on that filthy pallet. Oh God. She never woke up to beg forgiveness . . ."

James gathered her into his arms. "Shh," he breathed against her hair, the softness of it caressing his lips. She had left her bonnet somewhere, he thought irrationally. "Shh, Miss Dunne. It isn't your fault. I should have been there."

He gathered her closer, drew her head against his shoulder. *You don't need to cry.* It did no good. People died whether your heart broke for them or not. He murmured to Rachel, nonsensical words and sounds to ease the sobs that echoed in his own body. *Please, don't ache like this.*

"It isn't your fault," he repeated, feebly.

"No. It is God's fault."

Dr. Edmunds crooned soft reassurances, his embrace strong and secure, propping her up. Rachel wanted to stay there, have his arms tighten around her until the feel of them blocked out the thoughts of Molly fading, sinking into the pallet, her last breath easing out of her to be followed by eternal stillness. Hearing the sound of keening in the room, the shrill noise emanating from the throat of Molly's friend.

"Don't cry, now."

He pressed his lips to her hair, feather-light, quick as the drumming of hummingbird wings. She longed for that kiss to lower to her face. Her previous pride vanished in the face of sorrow and helplessness, wanting his lips to draw away the tears streaming from her eyes. In a meadow in Finchingfield, he had claimed to care for her. She needed that caring more than anything right now.

However, all that had passed between them since that summer-ripe afternoon made her fear she'd lost any chance at having him care for her.

A passerby uttered a rude remark and Dr. Edmunds released her. He swiped a finger across her cheek to dry her face. "It doesn't do to be standing in the roadway, Miss Dunne. I should take you home."

Home? Home was Ireland and she could no longer go there.

With strong yet gentle hands, he lifted her onto his mare and took the reins. Rachel peered down at him, the brim of his hat shielding his face. *I am in love with him.* A man she could not have. A good man, after all. A decent man.

At the house, Joe waited for them. She caught his fretful gaze and knew her expression told everything as readily as a placard carried by a newspaper boy. Molly was gone.

"Tell Mrs. Mainprice to come and help Miss Dunne, Joe," directed Dr. Edmunds, handing over the horse's reins.

He helped Rachel down from the saddle. His hands lingered at her waist for a few seconds.

"I want to tell you, while I have the strength, that I regret sending Molly away. I thought I was serving justice with my actions, but the beggar I'm supposed to clothe and feed was right inside my house, at my doorstep, and I rejected her. Gave her to someone else to take care of her. I made a terrible mistake, and because of my actions, I exposed you to danger."

Rachel blinked at him, standing so close. "You did what you thought best."

"I did, and I was wrong." Something gave way in his eyes, his emotions bared, his remorse exposed like rocks scraped clean by relentless winds. "I can't ask for Molly's forgiveness any longer. I need someone's. I need yours."

"I wonder," she murmured, "if the forgiveness you truly seek is your own."

Dr. Edmunds let her go without another word and Rachel wandered through the dark garden, heading for the lamplight shining through the rear door that Joe had left ajar.

Mrs. Mainprice met her just inside the doorway.

"Molly . . ." The name was all Rachel could manage. If she uttered another word, she would shatter.

"Joe told me you went to her. Come down to the kitchen, lass, and we'll get something warm into you."

Would something warm help? She wasn't cold; she was vacant. Soup or heated cider would not fill the void. Still, she let the housekeeper slip a comforting arm around her shoulders and guide her down the stairs, through the hallway where, not so many days ago, Rachel had huddled and overheard Molly's first condemning words. The memory stung, sharp as the thorn of a rose. Molly—vengeful, desperate—had been alive then.

Mrs. Mainprice lowered her onto the bench fronting the kitchen table. The bench was firm, the table solid as ever, yet the room seemed to twirl about Rachel's head, a spinning top in her brain. She sucked in a breath to stop the dizziness.

"Here you go." The housekeeper smiled, setting a mug in front of Rachel. The contents steamed. "It's some tea."

Rachel wrapped fingers around the earthenware. Heat seeped into her skin. "Nothing helped, Mrs. Mainprice. Not the spirit of niter or the laudanum I borrowed from you."

"You cannot expect to perform miracles."

"I should have been able to save her." She had failed again to help someone who'd depended upon her. First Mary Ferguson, then Mr. Fenton-Smith, now Molly. Proving one more time there was no point to her trying. She should have clung to the promise she'd sworn to herself and never have bothered to go. "Molly lost the baby and was feverish, but still I should have been able to help. I used to be able to."

The housekeeper clucked her tongue against her teeth. "Molly had been taking all manner of potions to rid herself of that baby. Who knows what sort of foul concoctions she drank in the past days? As sure as I'm sitting here, it was one of those potions that took her life. Not something that you didn't do. 'Twas her foolishness that caused this."

"But Mary Ferguson was not foolish. She was merely poor."

"Did she have something to do with your trial in Ireland?" Mrs. Mainprice asked gently. "I'm afraid we've all heard about it, Miss Dunne."

"She perished under my care." Rachel lowered her head. "She had only had a cough, some swelling in her throat. I thought I knew what to do to help. It seems I was wrong, and far too prideful about my abilities." Clinging to that pride like the last leaf of autumn unwilling to release the tree.

"We all make mistakes, miss."

"Most people's mistakes do not end in someone dying." Rachel pinched her eyes closed. "When they accused me of murdering her, I was shocked. Angry, even. I had tended many of my accusers, too poor to afford even an apothecary's remedies, yet they were so ready to find me at fault. However, I could not easily defend myself against their accusations. Mary died while I was asleep at her bedside—asleep!—and I could not say precisely what had happened."

The cruelest blow of all. She didn't even know what had gone wrong. With Molly, though, Rachel had been awake for every second, watching the girl's life flow from her like water seeking a drain. The fever had worsened, she had become confused and restless, then she was suddenly motionless. Her friend's prayers turned frantic. God didn't listen to her either.

Mrs. Mainprice gathered up Rachel's hands. Her touch was tender but firm, the skin raspy where her calluses rubbed. "Don't blame yourself for Molly's passing."

"Molly should have been under a physician's care. Dr. Edmunds should have been there." Even he knew he should have.

"You think Dr. Edmunds is always successful? You know better, Miss Dunne. It's killing him. His failures are eating him up, like rats feasting in a corn bin. He couldn't save his wife. Imagine how that feels."

Dreadful? Hollowing? Black and frigid as the maw of hell?

Rachel withdrew her hands, dropped them to her lap. "He still believes in God, though. He has not lost all hope."

Mrs. Mainprice considered Rachel for a long time. She chafed under the woman's gaze. "Holding on to hope in God is all we ever have in this world, Miss Dunne."

CHAPTER 23

Rachel's mouth was dry as a week-old oatcake, and her head . . . the sooner she reached the kitchen and found Mrs. Mainprice's store of headache powders, the less chance her skull would cleave right in two in the hallway. Rachel groped her way down the stairs. She had been too insensate last night to realize the housekeeper had laced her tea with laudanum. Enough to put down ten women, if the pain in her head was any indication. Without the laudanum, however, she wouldn't have slept, and sleep had been preferable to reliving Molly's last minutes on this cruel earth.

Slowly and quietly, Rachel pushed open the kitchen door.

"I was expecting I might see you about now, miss." Mrs. Mainprice brushed her hands across her apron, retrieved a knife from its storage block, and sliced a loaf of bread waiting on the broad oak table. "I was just preparing a bite for you to eat."

"I've no appetite." Rachel dropped onto the bench. "Though I could use a generous pinch of headache powder."

"By itself? Nonsense. You need toast and coffee to fix you right up."

Mrs. Mainprice poured a cup of coffee as proof and set it in front of Rachel. The smell, hot and bitter, churned Rachel's stomach and she grimaced.

"No turning your nose up, Miss Dunne. Don't make me stand here and watch you to make sure you eat, when I've so much to do."

"I would much rather hide in my bedchamber the rest of the day than take a bite of anything."

"And when did hiding do anybody a bit of good?"

"It might this time."

"*Wheesht.* Stop your silliness."

Rachel obediently took a bite and swallowed some coffee. The first sip made her tongue recoil and her stomach as well. The headache powder—a mixture of willow bark and slippery elm and wormwood with ginger and pepper, diluted in a cup of water—tasted no better.

Mrs. Mainprice patted Rachel's shoulder and returned to the bread, slipping it into a rack for toasting. "Molly's passing is hard on all of us, in one way or another. You're not alone in your suffering, but time will pass and you'll feel calmer. Trust in the Lord."

Rachel curled her fingers around the stoneware mug. "I wish I could, Mrs. Mainprice."

The housekeeper tutted. "He'll wait for you until you can, miss." She deposited a plate in front of Rachel. "Here's some toast, Miss Dunne. Won't help to starve yourself either."

Mrs. Mainprice settled across the table from her. The perfectly browned bread, dripping with an extravagant dollop of butter, waited next to the coffee. She watched until Rachel bit off a corner; Rachel didn't even taste it.

Mrs. Mainprice nodded, looking pleased about Rachel's meager cooperation. "I've been thinking about a bit of work for you, miss, if you're up to the task. It would be nice to have some trimmings for our bonnets, for the funeral. As your mother was a seamstress, I thought you might have some skill with the needle."

"I can sew a little. I would be pleased to help." A positive task to occupy her mind. "I lost my bonnet, though, in St. Giles."

"I've a spare you can have," she offered generously. There is black crepe in the attic storage. In one of the crates. Left over from when the household mourned for Mrs. Edmunds, God rest her soul. Feel free to search up there when you're recovered."

Steps sounded on the flagstones in the hallway and Dr. Edmunds came through the door.

"I thought I might find you down here, Miss Dunne." He nodded at Rachel then turned to look around the kitchen as if he hardly recognized the place.

Mrs. Mainprice hopped up from the bench, surprised to see him. "Are you needing something, Dr. Edmunds?"

"I just wanted to see how Miss Dunne is faring." His gaze traveled over Rachel, and she knew he was remembering last night, how close, how tight he had held her.

"As well as might be expected, Dr. Edmunds. Thank you for asking." *Thank you for caring. Though it does neither of us much good.*

"Good." He took a step closer. "I wanted you to know that I have arranged for a funeral for Molly. A proper funeral."

"Oh, sir," exclaimed Mrs. Mainprice, "that is most generous of you."

Dr. Edmunds's eyes didn't leave Rachel's face. She suspected he hadn't even heard his housekeeper. "I had to, Miss
Dunne. It was the least I could do."

"I understand." Understood everything about guilt.

Just then, Joe burst into the kitchen. "Sir, Mrs. Woodbridge and Miss Amelia are at the front door."

"They're here?" Dr. Edmunds asked, his body going
tense.

"Aye, sir. Sure as I'm standin' in the kitchen."

"Then I suppose I'd better greet them. Miss Dunne." He
inclined his head and left, Joe on his heels.

Mrs. Mainprice shot Rachel a glance and frowned. "Now
why did they have to come today, of all days?"

"Whatever is the matter?"

The housekeeper clucked her tongue dolefully. "'Tis
the day of reckoning, Miss Dunne. You stay right here,
miss, and finish up your coffee and toast. No need for
you to get snatched up by the whirlwind that has just
blown in."

<hr />

"What is going on, Sophia?" James asked, his voice reprehensibly harsh, his eyes not on his sister-in-law but upon
the young girl beside her on the threshold. Upon the gold-
en curls of her hair, the eyes blue as summer skies. Just like
Mariah.

Sophia's face was as pallid as the lining of her bonnet.
She carried a valise and used it to push James aside. "Agnes

is ill. With the cholera. Let us in, James. Unless you want the neighbors to see your relations out on the steps, arguing with you."

Amelia blinked up at him, her small hand tightly clutching Sophia's. *Do not leave me here,* James imagined her thinking. *Not with this angry man.*

Sophia shoved into the entry hall, Amelia stumbling to keep up. "Amelia, say hello to your father."

Amelia sidled up to Sophia until she was half-hidden by her aunt's voluminous black skirts. Scared to death of James. As scared as James was of her.

"Good day, Papa." She had such a tiny voice. Its impact was far from tiny, however. The child wielded it, unknowingly, as sharp and large as a scimitar James had once seen in the British Museum.

"Hullo, Amelia," James stiffened his back against the cuts bleeding away his composure. "Would you like to see the kitchen? Have a bite to eat? I would guess a young person your age is hungry."

"James, she doesn't need to eat right now. She has already taken her midday luncheon, like she always does at this time."

Should I have known that? "That may be the case, but I insist." He signaled to Mrs. Mainprice, who had hurried up from the depths of the kitchen, anticipating his need.

"Kiss your Aunt Soph before you go," said Sophia, bending down for the girl's swift peck on her cheek. "Be a perfect miss, like you know how to be."

"I will, Aunt Soph." She smiled adoringly at her aunt. Amelia didn't need a mother when she had Sophia. Might not need anyone else at all.

"Come now, lass," encouraged Mrs. Mainprice, "we've all sorts of good food to eat in my kitchen."

Smiling, she took Amelia's hand and led her away. The girl steered clear of James as she passed. A natural response, James reassured himself. Caution was good when you only saw your father a scant few times a year.

The scimitar cut deeper, right down to his heart.

"I would not have brought her if the situation weren't desperate, James," Sophia explained unnecessarily. "I had to get away from the house. I have instructed my housekeeper to burn sulphur in Agnes's room and to wash down the walls with carbolic acid. I could hardly stay with that going on."

"Are they sure Agnes has the cholera?"

"Quite sure. She's . . . she's terrible. It's terrible." Sophia freed her hair from the monstrous bonnet she wore, all feathers and ribbons. "I sent her to the hospital. Tell me that was the right thing to do."

Sophia, asking his approval, when the only person she had ever taken advice from was her husband. If she took advice at all. The world had turned on its head. "Dr. Castleton would have attended Agnes at your house."

"Forcing me and Amelia to stay there with her, nursing her, exposing the sweet girl to the consequences of such a frightful disease." She tossed her gloves and bonnet onto the entryway table with a slap. "Agnes must have contracted it over at her sister's. She'd been there to visit recently—you remember me telling you that. And I heard that her sister died from the cholera. Right out on St. James Street, if you can believe it! In the middle of the pavement!"

"In front of a chophouse?" James asked, certain he knew the answer. He'd wondered why he had thought he recognized that woman. Years ago, Agnes had introduced him to her sister, not many weeks after Agnes had been hired to act as Amelia's nursemaid. "Thatched House?"

"Precisely the place! How utterly dreadful. To breathe your last in front of an uncaring mob. I can't be certain, though, that Agnes caught the cholera at her sister's house. Maybe she had done so in my own home. If you consider, New Bond Street is really not much of a barrier to protect us from St. George's. I told you about that fellow passing away who lived in that neighborhood. The winds have been so hot, and blowing toward our house from that direction . . . the mere idea we could contract cholera by staying has kept me awake all night. I couldn't imperil Amelia like that. So I sent Agnes off and now we are here." Her voice rose with each word until she reached an impossible soprano squeak. "I have nowhere else to turn. You must take us in."

"I . . ." How could he face Amelia every day, in this small house with few places to avoid the child? This reunion was supposed to wait until Finchingfield, where there was more space for them all. That was what his carefully laid plan had been. "I . . ." he stuttered.

"Besides, what if Amelia or I fall ill?" Sophia persisted, battering him with her rationale. "The good Lord forbid, but you would want to tend to us, wouldn't you?"

Please, Lord, do not let it come to that.

"Then stay, Sophia." In the end, he had no legitimate rebuttal against her arguments. "Amelia can use Molly and Peg's room. You can use Mariah's old bedchamber. We've begun to pack it, but the bedding is still in place."

"Amelia will not be a bother to the household, but I

know how hard her presence here is going to be for you. Each passing day she is coming to look more and more like my beloved Mariah. I find the resemblance a comfort, though I know you do not. I am sorry for that."

There were others who would be reminded by the resemblance. James counted on them not to mention it. His sister-in-law, however . . .

"Sophia, I do have one request to make of you—please don't discuss Amelia with Miss Dunne. She doesn't know about our arrangement. I'll explain the situation to her."

Sophia's eyebrows twitched scornfully. "Believe me, I have no intention of discussing family matters with a servant."

"Miss Dunne is not a servant. She is my assistant, and her cousins are the Harwoods, which makes her grand-father a gentleman."

"She has fallen very far from such heights, hasn't she?" Sophia pursed her lips. "It continues to disturb me, James, that you seem to care about Miss Dunne's opinion. I cannot fathom why her sentiments are of any value."

He met his sister-in-law's hard gaze. "Because, Sophia, I care what she thinks. This poor Irish girl you so enjoy despising. I won't have her believing that I am a heartless coward." Less than the man he should have been.

Sophia exhaled sharply, a sound filled with disgust. "The shock of our arrival has befuddled you. Clearly. I am going to take my rest now, and hopefully when I see you later you will not be speaking such nonsense. Troubled over a servant's sentiments. Bah."

"Don't count on me being any less troubled when you see me next, Sophia."

"Mariah . . . your father . . . they would both be severely disappointed in you."

The scimitar sliced his heart in half. "I know."

Rachel was scraping off her plate in the scullery when Joe entered the kitchen with a young girl. Miss Amelia, she presumed.

"Here ya go, young miss," Joe said, guiding the girl to the table. "We've toast already and I think I know where there's a bit o' currant jam."

While Joe rustled about in the pantry, Rachel stepped into the kitchen. The girl looked to be around three years old, not much younger than Sarah and Ruth. She was much better scrubbed than they ever would be, however, and pertly pretty in her navy blue checked frock banded with a thick ruffle. Raised to keep her back painfully straight, Miss Amelia folded her hands in her lap and lifted her chin haughtily. It didn't take long for the gentry to learn their superiority, it seemed.

"There you are, Miss Dunne," said Joe, surfacing with the jam before ducking back into the pantry for a jug of milk. He thrust a chin in the girl's direction when he returned, his foodstuffs balanced precariously in his hands. "This 'ere is Miss Amelia. Mrs. M's given me charge of the girl this mornin' until Mrs. Woodbridge is settled. An' this, Miss Amelia, is Miss Dunne."

"Good day, Miss Dunne," the lass replied, her voice cultured as fresh cream. "Aunt Soph said we had to come. Agnes is sick. She went to the hospital."

"Oh, I see." So the child was Mrs. Woodbridge's niece,

not her daughter as Rachel had initially presumed. "Is Agnes your nurse?"

"Yes," Amelia said, delicately biting into the bread. "She's awful sick and Aunt Soph says we must pray for her."

"Ah . . ." Rachel paled. She met Joe's gaze over the top of the girl's head. He frowned and poured out some milk, thumping the jug heavily onto the table when he finished. For the both of them, Molly's death was too raw. "I am sorry she is ill, Amelia. I hope she gets better."

"She's got the chol'ra. I heard Aunt Soph say that Agnes is going to die."

"I believe I need more coffee," interjected Rachel, cutting off the conversation. "Joe, do you want some?"

"Nah. Can't stand the stuff."

Rachel didn't much care for it, either, but sticking her nose in a mug was better than gaping at Amelia or trying to think of what further to say that didn't involve disease or death.

The rapping of footsteps on the flagstone flooring of the hallway saved her from her dilemma. Within moments, Mrs. Woodbridge marched into the kitchen.

Her gaze skipped over Rachel and ignored Joe altogether. "Amelia, here you are. Would you like to go outside to the garden for a while? I've decided I'd rather rest out in the sunshine. My room is a trifle . . . musty. Maybe you could play with the dolls I brought along while your Aunt Soph reads. What do you say? Hm?"

Without saying farewell, Amelia rose from the bench and strolled off, hand firmly grasping her aunt's.

"That there is one o' God's curiosities, Miss Dunne. That it is," said Joe, his eyes tracking their departure. He leaned across the table and swiped the crust of bread Amelia had left behind, downing it before continuing the pursuit of his line of thought. "Can never understand why Dr. E doesn't take the little lass into 'is own 'ouse." He licked his thumb and blotted up crumbs.

"Why would he bring her here?"

"I b'lieve Miss Amelia's 'is daughter. Not positive, as she's never talked about, all 'ush-'ush an' all, but I think she is."

"His daughter?"

Rachel glanced toward the doorway, as if she might still see Amelia there. Dr. Edmunds would have mentioned having a daughter, wouldn't he?

"Born right afore the missus died, I'd wager."

"Surely Dr. Edmunds is not so coldhearted as to keep his daughter away from him, not when he has a widowed sister-in-law to help raise the girl in this house."

"I'm only sayin' what I've 'eard, miss."

"You do not truly think that is possible, do you?" she asked, bewilderment making her head ache worse than before. "Amelia is probably a niece of Mrs. Woodbridge's deceased husband and you have misunderstood the situation."

"Sounds right logical, miss, but—"

"It is wrong of us to continue to speculate."

"As you say." Joe shook his head and let out a whistle. "Can never understand the gentry. No, I can't. They jus' don' think nor act like normal folk. Cor, there's the front knocker again. Sure 'ope Dr. E finds 'imself a right good maid in Finchingfield. I 'ates the job!"

He scuttled off, brushing breadcrumbs from his new waistcoat, before he could make any further comment on the incomprehensible Dr. Edmunds.

CHAPTER 24

The next morning, Mrs. Woodbridge sailed into the garden like a ship of the line scuttling before a gale wind. Amelia toddled behind, arms overflowing with dolls, her dandelion-colored dress a moving beam of sunshine.

Rachel rose from where she had been squatting among the herbs and garden greens. "Good morning to you, Mrs. Woodbridge. Amelia. I was just collecting some maiden-hair to make up a tea for Mrs. Mainprice. She awoke a trifle hoarse today, and this will help—"

"Yes, yes. Most interesting. Though I'm sure James could prescribe a pill that would be far more effective than your Irish country remedies." Mrs. Woodbridge took a seat on the bench beneath the plum tree, its shade dappling her coal black dress with darkness and light. "Amelia, dearest, your dollies might like to play by the fountain."

Amelia obeyed and arranged her dolls in a half circle on the ground.

"Your dolls are very lovely, Amelia," said Rachel.

"Would you like to play with them, Miss Dunne?"

"She is too busy, dearest." Mrs. Woodbridge's tone froze the warm summer air.

Rachel knelt to pluck a handful more of the maidenhair from the edge of the kitchen garden. She would quickly dry the leaves over the fire then steep them in hot water. As good a remedy as any pills.

The other woman fluffed her bombazine skirts. "I recollect that you are related to the Harwoods, Miss Dunne. Am I right?"

The correct amount of herb gathered, Rachel stood. "They are my cousins."

"As I thought." Mrs. Woodbridge produced a book from the deep pocket hidden within the folds of her skirt and peered at Rachel over its top. "I admit I've been curious as to why they did not take you in upon your arrival in London. Having to do servant's work must be humiliating for a young woman with such respectable connections."

Rachel tucked her basket tight against her waist as though the woven straw might shield her body from Mrs. Woodbridge's contempt. "I would not dream to ask them. I want to make my own way in this world."

"Your own way?" she scoffed, making Rachel's intentions sound ludicrous and pitiable. "As what?"

"I have interviewed for a position as a teacher."

"Noble enough, I suppose. I also suppose you expect my brother-in-law to provide you with a character reference." Mrs. Woodbridge gazed along the length of her patrician nose, her eyes two chips of obsidian honed to slice. "Ah well, James is a good man and likely shall. Sometimes, though, his heart is far too soft. He has a tendency to pity the unfortunate and downtrodden. The wretched of this world."

Rachel bristled. "He is not providing me a character reference out of pity, Mrs. Woodbridge. I have done good work and deserve his recommendation." Though she had feared he would refuse for reasons she would *never* tell Sophia Woodbridge.

"I cannot judge the quality of your work. I must leave that to James, but I do worry—you must understand, Miss Dunne—about the soundness of his judgment when it comes to a pretty face like yours." Her eyes flashed like the edge of a blade. "He can be lonely in this house and deeply misses the companionship of his wife. James loved Mariah, my dear sister, more deeply than words could ever describe. She was the best of women, the loveliest, the most accomplished. Any other woman could only pale in comparison."

Such as me?

Rachel returned Mrs. Woodbridge's stare. "I have occupied too much of your time, Mrs. Woodbridge. I have a tea to make."

Gathering her skirts in her fist, Rachel hurried back into the house. *Awful, spiteful creature.* The woman was just being mean because she despised the Irish. Delighting in telling Rachel that she was inferior to Mariah Edmunds. So smug, so cruel. Didn't she realize Rachel already knew she could never expect to gain Dr. Edmunds's affection?

Rachel raced through the back door and collided with Joe on the other side, her basket slamming into his chest.

Joe reached for her arms to hold her steady. "'ey there, miss, now, what's wrong 'ere?"

"That woman is dreadful," Rachel spat through gritted teeth.

His brows jerked high and his mouth quirked. "Miss Guimon' used to b'lieve so too."

There. That made the last.

James closed the file and packed it in the box with the others. He had updated every patient file and placed each one in its appropriate stack—some bound for Dr. Calvert, some for Thaddeus, some even for young Hathaway. He would appreciate that.

Standing, James rubbed the stiffness out of his back and made a circuit of the room, inhaling the long-familiar smells with a twinge of nostalgia. Foolish, really, to be bittersweet about the room. Soon he would never again have to worry if the aroma of camphor bothered his patients, especially the more delicate ones. Or if the settee was comfortable enough. In three days, London would be fading into the distance and the clear skies of Finchingfield—not misty soft like those of Ireland, but blue enough for him—would be on his horizon.

He glanced at the boxes of notebooks and ledgers, rising on his desk like headstones to his medical career. The moving agency was collecting the first crates today and everything was ready. The momentum propelling him forward was unstoppable now, a force like water rushing over a falls, months' worth of planning fully engaged. He was going to walk away from it all. He was going to become a gentleman farmer at last.

So why the unnerving certitude that, just around the

next bend in the path of his life, he would encounter a brick wall?

Lord, help me come to peace with this decision.

James shut the office door behind him and tossed the key upon the entryway table. It would go with the other keys Thaddeus would be collecting soon, when he came to take temporary control of the house until the new tenant arrived.

Mrs. Mainprice was humming as she scrubbed down the hallway wainscoting in Peg's absence—probably the last time that task would be required of any member of his diminishing staff. She lifted her head as he passed.

"Miss Amelia's in the garden, sir," she said, a statement he could either interpret as a warning or encouragement.

"I should see how she is doing today."

"Do you wish me to bring lemonade out to you, sir?"

"I won't be out in the garden that long, Mrs. Mainprice." He wouldn't push himself just yet. One step at a time. And with the grace of God, each step getting easier as he took it.

Sophia was reading beneath the pear tree while Amelia danced her dolls across the rim of the fountain, the sunlight warm on her bright curls. They composed a lovely familial tableau, as charming as any painting. Yet here he was, little more than an observer. Excluded from the tiny circle Sophia had drawn around her and Amelia. The circle he had permitted her to draw. Asked her to draw.

"James." Sophia looked up from her reading. "It is most pleasant out here. I'm glad you could join us. Aren't you, Amelia?"

"Yes, Aunt Soph," she said, eyeing James with cautious curiosity. Determining that her father wasn't going to scowl at her and wasn't going to hug her either, Amelia resumed playing with her dolls, singing an off-key tune for their awkward dance steps.

An urge to crouch down next to the girl—*his daughter*—rose in James's body, twitched along his feet to move him forward. He should go play with her, ask about her dolls. He had every right. A right he had never bothered to exercise before, though. Those brief visits at Christmas and for Amelia's birthday had been staid affairs where James had maintained his distance, close enough to observe Amelia but not close enough for the girl to penetrate his heart.

The earlier urge withered like a spring flower beneath summer's hot sun. There would be time enough in Finchingfield to play with Amelia. If the girl even wanted his attention, something she had done without all of her life. James looked away, over to Sophia, but his ears continued hearing—the tiny childish murmurings Amelia made while she pretended to hold ladylike conversation, the pauses when she stopped to have the dolls curtsy or shift their positions along the gravel pathway.

"I thought I would come out and see how you two are getting along," James said.

"Well enough, though I'm not sure Amelia slept well in that chilly attic room. She seems a trifle out of sorts this morning. I am somewhat peaked too." Sophia sighed and pressed a palm to her forehead. "Perhaps your little assistant could make up a healing tea for me."

"Are you intent upon discussing Miss Dunne with me again?"

"No, James. That topic of conversation has been suitably dispensed with."

He frowned and tucked his thumbs into his waistcoat

pockets. "Mr. Jackson informs me he has located rooms at an inn near Finchingfield House for you and Amelia. You'll find them to your liking."

She lifted an eyebrow. "An inn to my liking?"

"You would not enjoy sleeping in the drawing room, Sophia, while repairs are underway."

"True."

James doubted she would even enjoy sleeping in the bedchamber he'd chosen for her. All of them at Finchingfield House were smaller than what Sophia was used to. "He expects all the work to be finished within the month. Good progress."

"Excellent." Sophia gave one of her thin-lipped smiles. "Amelia shall be so happy in the countryside. Won't you my dear?"

"Em, yes, Aunt Soph . . ." A sudden grimace twisted Amelia's face. "Em . . ."

"What is it, sweeting?" Sophia asked, setting down her book.

Amelia wobbled, as if the ground had gone liquid beneath her feet, and she sank to the gravel. Her doll slipped from her fingers. "I feel bad."

James rushed to his daughter's side.

"Amelia!" Sophia dropped to the ground next to her, black skirts ballooning, swallowing up the doll. Her fingers swept across Amelia's forehead. "Sweeting, what is it?"

Easily, James lifted Amelia, her small body trembling against his chest. The heat of fever radiated off the child through his sleeves to scorch his arms. The trembling became contagious and spread to James. "She's burning up, Sophia. Why didn't you tell me?"

"She was restless but ate breakfast this morning," she said, her gaze never leaving Amelia. "I would have told you if I thought she was unwell."

Amelia's watery eyes blinked up at him. "I feel sick."

"You'll be all right, Amelia. Trust me." But why should the lass trust him at all?

Sophia's face crumpled with panic. "Agnes has infected her with the cholera. My precious darling."

"Let's not presume the worst."

James stumbled back into the house, carried the girl up the stairs, his sister-in-law hurrying to keep up. Fear chasing them both.

"How is Amelia, Dr. Edmunds?" Rachel peered into Molly's old room. The cramped space smelled of sickness. "I heard from Mrs. Mainprice she was taken ill."

Dr. Edmunds slouched at the child's bedside, his waistcoat and cravat discarded, the sleeves of his linen shirt rolled up to his elbows. His face had aged, the weight of anxiety carving grooves across his face like a heavy downpour gouging fissures in soft dirt.

"She's resting easy." He flattened his palms against his knees and stood. "The fever she had earlier has abated and she's not been ill again."

"So it is not the cholera."

That was what Mrs. Mainprice feared. She'd said Mrs. Woodbridge was so certain Amelia was ill with cholera, the woman had fainted in the drawing room and needed to be helped up to her bedchamber.

"I keep telling myself it isn't." Dr. Edmunds swept his hands through his hair, mussing it.

"Do you need any help?"

"Are you offering to sit with her, Miss Dunne? I know how difficult that would be."

For you . . . I would sit with her for you. She had guarded her feelings from Mrs. Woodbridge, but Rachel could not hide them from herself. James Edmunds scattered her wits like the first fall of leaves upon a stream, carried away to the farthest reaches of the sea, and made her fear she would never be rational again.

"If you need me to tend her, I would."

"I won't ask you. There's no need for both of us to suffer." He grabbed up his cravat and waistcoat, came out into the hallway where Rachel waited, his movements as slow and laborious as a prisoner climbing a treadmill. "Until my sister-in-law feels up to the task, Mrs. Mainprice has offered to stay with Amelia for the remainder of the day."

Up close, the lines were even deeper, extending into the corners of his eyes. He had to be Amelia's father. There would be no reason for him to be so distressed otherwise.

"You are very concerned about Amelia," Rachel said, prevaricating. *Ask the question you really want answered.* But she was afraid to hear the truth, for what it might reveal about his failings.

"I am concerned about any young child stricken with this horrible disease. Watching a child die . . ." His Adam's apple bobbed as he swallowed. "There is no worse torment."

Rachel's memories, bristling like a thistle, caught and snagged her heart. "None worse."

"You understand me, Rachel."

The sound of her Christian name on his tongue made her shiver. She didn't correct him.

"I understand loss and trials and difficulties, Dr. Edmunds. I understand struggling to hold onto hope that tomorrow will be better than today. I understand how hard it is to watch a child suffer and feel powerless to help her. I understand wanting to believe that God will perform a miracle and feeling lost and disillusioned when He does not." Old, sad bitterness tainted her words. "That is what I understand, Dr. Edmunds."

His gaze searched her face, looked directly into her eyes, straight into her soul. "So what do we do now?"

Confused by his question, Rachel answered the only way she could. "We go forward."

"But what if you don't have the strength to go forward? What if you don't have the courage?"

"Somehow, you have to find it."

Slowly, he nodded, lifted a fingertip to trace her jaw, the contact both sweet and agonizing. "You are strong, Miss Dunne. I envy you for it."

Before she pressed her face into his hand, closed her eyes, and let the contact linger, Rachel stepped back. "I promised to help Joe bring down the trunks from the attic. Please excuse me, Dr. Edmunds, but I must go."

"Eh, what is it now, miss?" Joe cocked his head, the lamp they'd brought up to the attic dancing shadows over his face like the lamplight of a busker's show, making his expression of concern almost comical. "Still upset over

Moll, are ya? Or maybe Miss Amelia? Ya look sorta sick, or somethin'."

"Perhaps I am." *Heartsick, if nothing else.*

Joe jerked back as if what she had might be contagious. The lantern swung drunkenly. "Truth an' all?"

"It's nothing catching, Joe. It's just . . . so much has been happening lately. I wonder that I can make sense of life at all anymore."

"Me mum would say not to bother. Jus' live it, s'all we can do."

"And she was right." Rachel smiled at him to erase the worried frown from his face. "Now do you want me to help you move these trunks, or shall I go about doing what I had originally planned and search for that box of black crepe?"

"Now don' get all touchy on me. 'ere. Take this one."

She grabbed the handle and shuffled backward, depositing the trunk in the hallway beyond the door.

"You'd think we was movin' lead bars," Joe complained as they shimmied the next one across the floor. "All jus' to give what's in 'em to charity before we go. Shoulda left 'em with the 'ouse for the next tenant to deal with." He grunted as his shoes slipped on the dusty floorboards. "I mean, who'da thought clothes could weigh so much?"

"You have obviously never worn stays, petticoats, and a woolen gown before, Joe."

"Well, I 'ope not!"

The trunk caught on the lip of the doorframe and they doubled their efforts to give it a mighty shove. It toppled over, the latch breaking and the lid flying open to spill its contents.

Rachel fisted her hips. "Do help me put this back to rights, Joe."

"It's all women's underthin's, miss!"

She glanced up at him. Joe was blushing. "Then I shall protect your sensibilities and repack the items myself. Search for black material in the trunks while I am doing this."

Rachel clambered over the trunk to its opposite side. Chemises, corsets, and stockings lay in a tangled mess of pale silk and linen, the private clothing of a woman she had never thought much about. Other than Mrs. Woodbridge's pointed mention of her sister, it had been easy for Rachel to overlook the late Mrs. Edmunds. Aside from the furnishings in her room and the untended garden, the house had been as thoroughly purged of her memory as if a maelstrom had obliterated them. Here she was now, though, revealed by the most intimate items, the ones she had worn next to her skin.

Rachel lifted a corset, the faded aroma of patchouli clinging to it. The scent was sweet, musky, spicier than she'd imagined the wife of Dr. Edmunds to be. The sort of woman he would marry would be God-fearing, a woman of his class, handsome and respectable. Much as Mrs. Woodbridge had described her. A woman who would never stand in a dock in an Irish courtroom or feel hunger or have stains upon her gown.

He truly must miss his wife. Only deepest sorrow would explain why he had allocated every memento—here was a padded velvet box for jewelry, her silver brush and combs, the gem-studded pins for her hair—to a dark room where he would never encounter them.

Rachel bit her lip and stuffed the clothing into the trunk as quickly as she could. She was making a mess of it. The clothes had been tightly packed and weren't submitting to being clumsily forced. A gold chain dropped out onto the floor, tangled in a stocking. She unwound it from the silk, cautious not to rip the material. It was a locket, engraved with the letter M. The latching mechanism had been jostled, and the lid wasn't completely closed. Rachel fumbled with the tiny latch, trying to get it to catch, and accidentally sprung the lid. Within, the locket framed a miniature portrait of Dr. Edmunds when he'd been younger and less careworn, his expression full of pride and anticipation. Had his wife worn this near her heart, where she could lift the locket to gaze upon his face whenever the need took her fancy? Had she rubbed her thumb over the smooth gold surface, a meager replacement for the feel of his cheek beneath her fingers, as Rachel did now?

"Is this 'ere what yer lookin' for, miss?" Joe dangled a length of black crepe from his hand.

She blinked at him through tears that stubbornly filled her eyes. "Yes, Joe. That is perfect."

"Ya know what else I found? Come 'ere." He beckoned to her to join him. "A bunch o' family pictures, it looks like."

Lifting her skirts out of the way, Rachel stepped over the trunk, the locket gripped tightly in her fist. Against the wall were stacked a handful of paintings. They'd been exposed when Joe had pulled one of the trunks into the center of the room. She leaned closer, her stomach dropping out beneath her, her head seeking to deny what her eyes so clearly saw.

"What do ya think?" Joe asked.

The woman in the painting was young and dainty in her high-waisted dress of deepest cobalt blue, her hair the color of goldenrods around her face. The best of women, the loveliest, the most accomplished.

With a face so like Amelia's only a blind man could miss the resemblance.

"I think Mrs. Edmunds looks precisely like her daughter."

CHAPTER 25

hy did you not tell me?" Rachel asked Dr. Edmunds, seated behind the office desk piled high with boxes and brown-paper-wrapped stacks of books. His wife's locket dangled from Rachel's fingers, trembling at the end of its chain. She had forgotten to leave it in the trunk.

He set aside the medical text he had been reading, pulled from one of the stacks, the paper torn off. "Do you wish to sit?"

"I prefer to stand."

"Very well." He curled his hand, resting atop the book, into a fist. "I presume you're asking why I never told you about Amelia. Well, Miss Dunne, I never told you she was my daughter because I didn't want you to know."

"You didn't want me to know?" Rachel's pulse thudded in her chest, pounded in her head, hammer falls of pain. "All the while you were cajoling me to be honest with you, scolding me for keeping secrets, you were hiding such a thing from me?"

"You aren't alone in not knowing about Amelia. I didn't tell you, and those others, because I was ashamed."

"Ashamed of your daughter?" He was heartless. Truly, he was.

"I would never be ashamed of Amelia." His eyes turned cool and dark, gray as the stones lining the stream that gurgled down from the hills near Rachel's house in Carlow. Devoid of the warmth she had seen just a scant hour ago. He was ever changeable, unpredictable as clouds scudding before a storm—bright one moment, black as coal dust the next. "I was ashamed of myself."

"You should be." Rachel gripped the locket's chain, pressing the metal into her palm. "You have neglected her. Do you ever see her? In the weeks I have been here, she has never visited until now. When there was desperate need."

"Amelia has not been neglected. Sophia loves the girl like a mother would and has taken very good care of her. Believe me."

"But how could you . . ." *My storybook hero, the man whose embrace brought me peace and calm. The man I thought I loved.* "You were so tender with that apple girl when she was injured by the carriage, so sympathetic after Molly's death. How does a man with that sort of compassion ignore his own child? Bear to be apart from her? Your very flesh and blood. My father would never, even in the worst of times, have sent a child of his away."

"Then he was a better man than I am," he replied, flatly, as if his words were truth that merely needed a signature and a seal to become law. "When my wife passed on, permitting Sophia to take Amelia seemed the best and most sensible course. Sophia's husband was still alive then and they had no children of their own. Besides, sisters often step in to replace a lost mother. Even in Ireland, I'm sure."

"In Ireland, only fathers who do not care or are good-for-nothing let those sisters raise their children away from their house." He made his actions sound utterly logical; Rachel refused to be swayed.

"Then maybe I am good-for-nothing, because I wasn't fit to be Amelia's father. Not at that moment, maybe ever." His fist clenched and unclenched. "Right before my father died, though, he made a request that Amelia be brought to Finchingfield House and raised there. Sophia will be living with us, to help me, so you should be happy to learn we'll all be together and my daughter will no longer be neglected."

Rachel dragged in a breath, which shuddered through her chest and failed to calm the whirling of her emotions. She had fallen in love with him, a man she had completely misjudged. How much of who he seemed to be was actually a lie?

"You claimed I understood you, and I confess I thought I did. A little." She was proud that her voice shook only a trifle. "But I see I was wrong. You are so full of contradictions, you're impossible to understand. You act as though you are happy to become a gentleman farmer, when anyone with eyes in their heads can see you have no more than a passing interest in it. You want me to believe you are finally going to play the role of good father, when it took the request of a dying man to force you to reunite with Amelia. And then only belatedly."

His face had gone very pale, but Rachel pressed on. "Worst of all, you tried to get me to believe you cared for me, when I wonder that you know how to truly care for anyone." Rachel's fingernails dug into her skin. "I wanted to believe in you, but how can I after this?"

The locket swung as she thrust it toward him. He stared

at it, a blood vessel visibly throbbing in his temple. Rachel held her breath and waited for him to profess how much he did care and that she could still believe in him. Waited for him to prove he wasn't a lie.

"Anything else, Miss Dunne?"

"No, Dr. Edmunds." The locket slithered from Rachel's grasp and fell unheeded to the desk. "There is nothing else."

The locket and its chain lay coiled on James's desk like a serpent ready to strike. He had stared at it for the past hour, not particularly eager to touch it and be stung by the rush of memories the piece of jewelry held.

With a groan, he finally stretched out his hand and lifted the locket. Springing the latch, James stared at the miniature of himself contained within. The painting came from happier days, right before he and Mariah had gotten engaged, when he had been more certain of himself, certain he was on the verge of a promising future. The sort of man who would never have denied his child and then hidden her existence like a blemish. The man he used to be, as Thaddeus had claimed ages ago. Before loss and failure had stripped him of his confidence.

James dropped the locket onto the desk and stood. The office blinds opened with a squeak of protest, their unused hinges stiff from lack of use. Beyond, the tangle of leggy green weeds he'd been expecting to see had been tamed. Joe's handiwork. Had it been years or only days ago that he had instructed the lad to clear the garden? James peered through the slats, the sun slanting low over the top of the house to light the shaggy-headed trees. The garden lacked its former glory, though vestiges hung on its bones like the fading loveliness of an aging beauty's face. He was certain if he stared long enough he could summon the image of Mariah moving among the roses. She would not be there, if he succeeded, any more than heat shimmering off scorching pavement was truly water.

"Do you love me, James?"

He had respected Mariah, cared for her, certainly. But love? In those early days, he had loved his practice far more than he had cared for anything or anyone else. Mariah had been pragmatic enough to turn her affection to tending her flowers. The relationship might have looked successful to their acquaintances, but at its core lay unfilled need and emptiness. She hadn't been the answer to his heart's needs, and he surely hadn't been hers. In the end, he had failed Mariah just as surely as he had failed his father. As he continued to fail Amelia.

James pressed his hands against the slats, shutting the blinds against the scene beyond the window, rested his forehead against the wood. The three years since Mariah's passing had only brought him one revelation—that the emptiness still marked his soul, like the imprint of a footstep in the sand.

And he was still waiting for something, or someone, to wash it away.

Rachel stared up at the School for Needy Boys and Girls. The building looked abandoned, the windows closed and shuttered, an air of neglect clinging to its bricks. Not even a wisp of smoke billowed from the chimneys. Had the school been shut down because of the fear of the cholera?

Rachel hugged her arms to her waist to keep from shivering with panic. *Good luck comes in tricklets; ill luck comes in rolling torrents.*

"Oh, Papa, I could do without thinking of one of your sayings every time life hands me another misery," she whispered. Although this misery could turn out far worse than discovering Dr. Edmunds was not the man she had wanted him to be.

Rachel squared her shoulders, marched up the steps, and pulled the bell. Many moments passed, long enough to draw the attention of a passing shop boy.

"Got the cholera there, miss. Don' think anyone's gonna answer," he called out to her.

"Thank you, but I might wait a few minutes longer to discover whether or not that is true."

"Suit yerself."

Once he'd gone on, Rachel dragged the bell pull more insistently and, with relief, heard noise beyond the door. It opened a crack and the sharp odor of quick lime wafted through, so strong it smelled as though they had doused the building in it. An attempt to conquer the dirt that caused diseases like the cholera.

A young woman with a pox-scarred face peered around the door. She was not the unnamed girl with the hole in her shoe who had answered the bell the last time Rachel had visited. "What do you want?" she asked.

"Where is the girl who usually answers the door?"

"She's not here."

The young woman started to shut the door. Rachel shoved her boot between it and the frame to stop her. "Is she ill? Does she have the cholera?"

"I dunno. She's been told to stay away like the rest of the students. Why do you care? What do you want?" she repeated, squinting suspiciously at Rachel.

"I need to speak with Mrs. Chapman. I interviewed for a position as a teacher and we had another appointment scheduled. I must talk to her today about the situation."

"Ain't no one here going to talk to you about nothing today, miss. The headmistress is gone with the others. Leaving just me and Megs to clean this filthy place." She kicked at Rachel's foot. "Now let me shut the door. No one better spy me talkin' to you. People been comin' and threatenin' to burn us out, saying we're harborin' the cholera and infecting the neighborhood. If they figure out I'm here, they'll drag me away to hospital and I know I'll get sick and die there. So just go away."

"Can you at least provide me with Mrs. Chapman's address so I may contact her?"

"She lives with her brother on Clifford Street, but you won't find her there. She's skipped town. Lucky her."

"Here. Wait." Rachel poked through her reticule and found the piece of paper Claire had included in her last note. It contained the address of a lodging house Claire had recommended to Rachel, and where she would very soon be living. "Tell Mrs. Chapman, when she returns, that she may contact me at this address. I shall be staying at the lodging house beginning day after tomorrow. Tell her I am still very interested in the position and will not fail her. I must have this work. I need the money."

The other woman looked unimpressed. "You and a thousand others," she said, though she took the paper and stuffed it into an apron pocket. "Now, go away!"

Rachel removed her foot and the woman slammed the door in her face.

The sound of hopeless finality.

"Oh, it's terrible," sniffled Mrs. Mainprice into her handkerchief. "Such a pitiful gathering. Poor Molly."

"It is far better than she might have expected, given her situation," said Rachel.

"Rightly so, miss. A place in a nice graveyard with a tiny headstone and all. But so far away from Hampshire and her family . . ."

Rachel scanned the assembly, the sun—shining so brightly in defiance of the sorrow—dappling their faces, shifting blocks of light across their shoulders and bowed heads, white against dark. Only a small crowd gathered around Molly's gravesite, the number a testament to the narrowness of her world. Joe, subdued and grim, shifted on the balls of his feet, his cap crushed in his fingers. Mrs. Mainprice gripped her Bible close to her chest and held out a clean handkerchief for Rachel to use. Molly's friend, a tattered cipher in a borrowed once-black frock, huddled near the wrought-iron fence, staying clear of the household staff. The sexton and his boy, standing not too far from her, leaned on their shovels while they waited for the brief ritual to end. Peg had remained in Finchingfield, and Mrs. Woodbridge had stayed at the house with Amelia.

Though Rachel suspected the woman would not attend a servant's funeral even if she had no good reason to be absent.

Rachel's eyes settled on Dr. Edmunds. He stood apart from the rest, the planes of his face set into immovable angles, attention fixed on a spot above the minister's head, somewhere in a direction beyond the churchyard, out into the streets of London. His wife might be buried in this yard somewhere. Perhaps that was why he stopped his gaze from slipping too low.

"Miss Dunne." Mrs. Mainprice nudged, her crying under control. "Do you need another handkerchief? I've a spare."

"No. This one is still adequate," Rachel answered, pressing it, crumpled and damp, to her eyes. Where were the tears coming from? She'd thought she had used them all up last night, soaking her pillowcase with a torrent of salty self-pity.

Dr. Edmunds's eyes shifted at the sound of Rachel's voice, but they didn't meet hers. It was just as well he didn't look at her, when he was the greatest part of why she had wasted all those tears.

The minister was delivering the final prayer: "O God, whose mercies cannot be numbered, accept our prayers on behalf of the soul of thy servant departed, and grant her an entrance into the land of light and joy, in the fellowship of thy saints; through Jesus Christ our Lord. *Amen.*"

"Amen," Rachel murmured along with everyone. She hoped God would show more mercy toward Molly in death than He had in life.

The sexton and his boy moved forward while Rachel and the rest of the staff filed out of the yard, onto the street. Dr.

Edmunds surged ahead and they were left to follow in his wake, like a line of dark-clothed ducklings. Molly's friend disappeared into the usual crowd filling the street like any other day in London. In Carlow, everyone would know of a town member's death, even someone as ordinary as Molly. They would share in the mourning. But here, life would proceed with the clamor of ants rebuilding a destroyed mound, oblivious to the chaos in others' hearts.

"Now that was the saddest thing I do believe I've ever been a part of," said Mrs. Mainprice at Rachel's side. "Not even Molly's . . . her beau come to see her off. Though I gather he's left London. How I would've liked to give him a piece of my mind."

"That would not have done Molly any good, Mrs. Mainprice."

"'Tis true, but it would've done *me* good." Mrs. Mainprice blew her nose with force and tucked away her handkerchief. "Such a wretched past few days."

Rachel stared straight ahead. Beyond Joe's head, the crown of Dr. Edmunds's top hat bobbed as he led them all back to the house.

Mrs. Mainprice took note of Rachel's attention. "A very difficult few days for the master, Miss Dunne."

Rachel's fingers tensed around the handkerchief. "If his daughter had been living with him all along, her sudden arrival would not have added to his difficulties."

"*Och*, well now, miss. Can't say I'm surprised you've finally found out." Mrs. Mainprice sighed. "Likely a shock to you as well, I'd guess. I would've told you, Miss Dunne, but I promised him I would never tell a soul unless he wanted me to."

"It seems a pointless promise when he is going to live with Amelia in Finchingfield and everyone will know then."

"But not before, which is what he wanted." Mrs. Mainprice's gaze was direct and resolute. He had won her loyalty. "Don't think it's been easy for the master, miss. After the missus passed on, Dr. Edmunds was very distressed. His father blamed him for her death, you see. They had a horrible row. The words exchanged . . ." The housekeeper tutted as they hurried across the street, dodging carts and horses. "Chased our old parlor-maid, Hannah, right out of the house. Said she wouldn't put up with such ungodly cursing and she quit."

"His father blamed him for Mrs. Edmunds's death?" *Falsely accused . . . "So it is, your lordship, gentlemen of the jury, that the unfortunate prisoner at the bar, Rachel Dunne, stands charged upon the coroner's inquisition with the willful murder of Mary Ferguson."* Rachel's pulse thrummed. "He was not responsible, of course. His father was just upset."

"More than upset, miss! After their argument, Dr. Edmunds was so distraught he couldn't bear to see the little miss, and so he let Mrs. Woodbridge raise her. He made clear the girl wasn't to be spoken of again." The soft folds of the housekeeper's face tucked in on themselves as she frowned. "'Twas easy for the others to follow his orders. Molly, Peg, and Joe were hired after the mistress passed away and didn't ever see the girl, would never even think of her. But it was a burden for me, Miss Dunne. I had to respect Dr. Edmunds's wishes, however, honor his desire for privacy. I prayed he would tell you. 'Twasn't my place to reveal his secrets, though. No more than you wanted yours told, or Molly wanted hers revealed. Though I fear we've all paid the price for our silence, may the good Lord forgive us."

"I merely wish I had not been forced to discover the truth about Dr. Edmunds's daughter on my own."

Mrs. Mainprice gently squeezed Rachel's arm. "One day, lass, I hope you'll think better of the master. He's drunk deep of the cup of bitterness and is still searching for a cure."

The house loomed, halting their conversation. Dr. Edmunds permitted the servants to enter through the front door.

"Mrs. Mainprice, see that everyone is served lemonade and cakes in the drawing room," he instructed. His gaze turned to Rachel. "I would like to speak with you, if I may."

"I'll just be getting that lemonade, sir," said Mrs. Mainprice, scuttling past, pushing Joe ahead of her and into the house, leaving Rachel and Dr. Edmunds on the street.

Rachel waited while his gaze swept over her face before settling on her eyes. "Miss Dunne, this is good-bye. I have been called away to attend Lady Haverton's daughter, a most important patient, during the delivery of her child—the first grandchild for the Havertons—and I might not return before you depart tomorrow. I have left your fee in your bedchamber."

Good-bye, and the last time they would see each other. It was wrong to be parting on sour terms, but there was no helping that.

"You would leave Amelia right now?" she asked, selfishly satisfied to see him flinch.

"Sophia is with Amelia, and she was sleeping well before the funeral. Her fever is abating. So it is safe for me to go. Besides, Lady Haverton will have no one else in attendance besides me. Her daughter is frail and will need the best of help."

"Lady Haverton will miss you, then, when you are gone to Finchingfield and no longer doctoring."

"Someone shall miss me, at least."

Was that comment meant for her?

Rachel held out her hand to shake his. "Good-bye, Dr. Edmunds."

He raised her fingers to his lips, his mouth warm upon her bare skin. She flushed to her toes.

"Good-bye, Miss Dunne," he murmured and then he was gone.

CHAPTER 26

he only words that came to James's brain were curses, and he released one softly before the door opened to his knock. He presented his gloves and hat to Lady Haverton's utterly proper footman and followed the man up to the bedchamber. *I might never see Rachel again. Never. Never.*

As had always been planned. But still . . .

"There you are, Dr. Edmunds." Lady Haverton's booming voice echoed down the staircase. "Come at once, sir. My daughter is in much pain and she needs your assistance."

The urgency in her voice focused his attention. He grabbed the walnut staircase railing and propelled himself up the thickly carpeted stairs. This would be his final case and he had to do the best he could for Lady Haverton's daughter.

Lady Haverton waited impatiently outside a door open at the end of the hallway. She led him inside. The room was stuffy, windows shuttered against the outside air, and smelled of sweat. The odor mingled sickeningly with the scent of fading roses, a bouquet of which had been left to perish on the mahogany dressing table. A monthly nurse was stacking towels alongside a basin atop the washstand, while another servant hurried past James with a pile of stained sheets. Lady Haverton's daughter, wan and frail, was nearly lost among the snowy-white pillows and thick mattress of her curtained bed. Her face shone with perspiration, and two eyes the blue of Delft china blinked fearfully.

"Oh, Doctor. Thank the good Lord you've come," she said weakly, her hand reaching for his. It was clammy to the touch.

James set down his medical bag and pulled up a chair. Dorothea Haverton Blencowe had always been a frail woman, even before she'd married. Carrying a baby had sapped whatever vitality she once had. "Mrs. Blencowe, how are you feeling?"

"Tired. Very tired. I do wish my dear husband could be at my side, but . . . but I know that's not proper. He is in the library with Father. Maybe drinking port. He's so afraid." A contraction overtook her, and she gulped down a cry until it passed. "I told him to pray. For me. Rather than drink. Though . . . though it's the wages of Eve's sin that we suffer so."

Lady Haverton leaned around James and gently patted her daughter's hand. "Do not fret, my dear, and do not try to talk. The doctor does not need conversation, and you will only make matters worse for you and the baby."

"Now, Mrs. Blencowe, I do not wish to make you uncomfortable, but I need to examine you a little to see how the baby is progressing. I shall feel your belly and listen with my stethoscope."

She nodded and he pulled the stethoscope case from his

bag. The sight of it recalled the day he had proudly shown the stethoscope to Rachel and she'd nearly fainted. *Will everything I do from now on remind me of her?* Even in Finchingfield, he wouldn't be able to escape the memories. He would see her in the meadow, the kitchen, the library. Forever, he would remember.

Mrs. Blencowe primly turned her head aside as James lifted her chemise and rested the stethoscope on the swell of her abdomen. He found the baby's heartbeat. It weakened, dipped too low as a contraction tightened her muscles. The fetus was in distress, and unless it was born soon, might not survive.

James ran his hands over her abdomen, the skin as hard and tight as the surface of a drum. The contractions were coming but not fast enough. The delivery might last too long. He'd attended other women like her, fragile as young birds, used to soft living and insufficient exercise. The challenge of childbirth was too difficult. As it had proven to be for Mariah.

His focus blurred and suddenly the woman lying there was Mariah, sweating with the strain of delivering Amelia. He had rushed from morning rounds at the hospital to find his father pacing the length of the Blue Room and old Hannah bathing Mariah's forehead. She had been strong enough to deliver the child. Just not strong enough to survive the subsequent childbed fever and his ineffectual attempts to eradicate it. Had he let her die? Had he cared so little that he hadn't thrown his whole heart into healing her?

"Do you love me, James?"

"You are a failure, James. My son, a failure."

He wasn't concentrating on Dorothea Blencowe. He was

letting his memories clog his brain like refuse damming a sewer, and he had to stop.

Lowering Mrs. Blecowe's chemise, he drew up the sheets and returned his stethoscope to its case.

"Well? How is the baby, doctor?" asked Lady Haverton.

"The placement of the baby is good, so that helps. You've not given your daughter anything except weak tea or broth, I hope? No cordials for the pain." Cordials or any such liquors would slow the contractions. The last thing Dorothea Blencowe and her baby needed now.

"No, most certainly not!" huffed her ladyship.

"Good. I would recommend that a supply of warm, damp cloths be applied to her belly. They might help hasten the process. I've also found, if you have the strength, Mrs. Blencowe, that if you get up and try to walk around a little, it speeds matters."

"Walk around?" asked Lady Haverton. "Dorothea hasn't the strength to lift her head."

"Mama, I shall try. If the doctor thinks I must." Impatience showed in her eyes. That she had the strength to argue with her mother was a good sign. At least, James hoped it was.

"I shall observe for a while and then we'll see," he said. "Thank you for being courageous."

James smiled reassuringly at Mrs. Blencowe, who attempted to return the expression. She had to hold on and work hard. If she didn't, he would have to send for a surgeon to save the baby. Mrs. Blencowe, however, probably wouldn't survive the cesarean.

Warm cloths arrived and were placed on her belly. Feeble contractions came and went. Time ticked by, the mantel clock chiming musically, regularly. The baby made no progress.

Sweating from the heat of the room and his own nerves, James stripped down to his waistcoat and shirtsleeves, rolling them up out of the way. "It's time to walk, Mrs. Blencowe."

Taking hold of her shoulder, James assisted her to sit up. Her breath came in labored gasps, sweat beading on her forehead. *She can't do it. I'll have to send for the surgeon and I'll lose her . . .*

"If you feel faint, Mrs. Blencowe, you must tell me immediately." He hoisted her onto her feet. She groaned in response. "Most importantly, you have to concentrate on bringing that baby into the world."

"Doctor, really," Lady Haverton protested. "She is too weak for this."

"She must walk, m'lady."

A maid rushed into Mrs. Blencowe's bedchamber. "Dr. Edmunds, sir, there's someone at the door to see you. Says it's most urgent."

"I can't leave Mrs. Blencowe at the moment."

"Most urgent, sir," the maid repeated.

"Make her walk, Lady Haverton," he said, letting her take control of her daughter.

Mrs. Blencowe sagged against her mother's supporting arm. "Please hurry back, Dr. Edmunds." Air wheezed between her clenched teeth. "I . . . I . . . will keep trying to concentrate."

"I'll be only a minute. Please excuse me."

He bolted down the stairs and found an agitated Mrs. Mainprice waiting. James's steps slowed as he crossed the hallway to where she stood by the front door.

"Dr. Edmunds!" she cried. "You must come. It's Miss Amelia, sir. She's sick again. Worse this time. Much worse." She glanced over his shoulder and whispered to prevent the footman from hearing, "Oh, sir, I do think it's the cholera for certain."

The brick wall James had feared now reared up to slam him in the face. "But she was better this morning." Had he misread Amelia's symptoms intentionally? Blindly?

"She isn't any longer, sir."

"I can't leave Lady Haverton's daughter right now. There are serious complications." Sweat slipped along his collar, suddenly tight enough to choke him. "She might perish."

Mrs. Mainprice's eyes widened with disbelief. "So you won't come now, sir?"

"Send for Dr. Castleton, Mrs. Mainprice. He's seen far more cases of the disease than I have and he's often tended Amelia in the past. Besides, she will be more comfortable with him than with me." *Heavenly Father, let Thaddeus be able to heal Amelia, because I don't know that I could. I might only fail her . . .* "And send Joe to bring Dr. Hathaway here immediately. He can tend to Mrs. Blencowe. I will return to the house as soon as he arrives."

Her mouth twitched with reproach she dare not voice. "Aye, sir."

"Mrs. Blencowe is in a critical state, Mrs. Mainprice. I can't leave her. You must understand."

Her pitying gaze nearly undid him. "Aye, sir."

Nodding, he spun on his heel and vaulted up the stairs. "Send for Dr. Castleton and Dr. Hathaway." He called over his shoulder. "I will be home as soon as I'm able."

After Dr. Edmunds had left for Lady Haverton's, a few pence and some useful instructions from Joe enabled Rachel to take the omnibus to the lodging house to introduce herself to the landlady. The woman scowled and tutted during Rachel's visit, her small dark eyes skittering over Rachel like a pair of frantic bugs—she only took ladies of "select character" and had to be most careful—but was happy enough to accept eleven shillings as advance payment on the first week's rent. The rent of a tiny furnished bedchamber and miniscule sitting room with a smoky chimney-piece and cracked plaster walls that made Rachel glad she would not be living there in the winter months.

Rachel had then stopped to post a letter to Claire to inform her of the news concerning Mrs. Chapman and the school. Not that Claire could do much from Weymouth, but her cousin would want to know. While she'd been posting the note, Rachel recalled the name of another charity school Claire had mentioned in her letter. She would inquire there about a position later today, once she'd had a chance to collect her thoughts and have a bite to eat. Rachel was not in a rush to hurry back to Dr. Edmunds's. Nothing remained for her to do at his house except chance coming face-to-face with him.

A small meat pie purchased, and the stretch of lawns and lime trees that marked Green Park beckoning, Rachel strolled to a secluded location. She dropped onto the grass, heedless of the damage she might do to her dress. Equally heedless of the well-dressed ladies strolling nearby that sneered at her. Let them deride her poor clothing and common man's meal; she was getting used to being judged and found wanting.

She finished her pie and discreetly wiped the crumbs from her fingers. The weather had continued fair since the funeral, and Rachel let the fading early evening sun dance on her cheeks, warm her face. If she closed her eyes and shut out the noise of the city that rumbled past on distant Piccadilly, she might pretend she was in Ireland, the ground cool beneath her, a bird trilling in a tree.

Folding her arms around her shins, Rachel rested her chin on her knees and stared at a tangle of children throwing a ball near a reservoir, the water of its fountain splashing brightly. So happy and carefree, like she had been when she was their age, seeing life through a sparkling prism. Before reality had dimmed the glass.

Rachel swiped a tear from her face. She would not cry. She would be strong, because she had to be strong. For Mother, for Nathaniel, for Sarah and Ruth. No matter how hard life continued to be, she must hold up her spine and work hard. For them.

"You are strong, Miss Dunne. I envy you for it."

If Dr. Edmunds only knew how fragile her strength really was, he would not have bothered to envy her at all.

"Cor, miss, 'ere you are!" Joe shouted across the lawn.

Rachel shielded her eyes with her hands. "Joe? Why are you here?"

"Been lookin' everywhere." He slid down from the doctor's mare and started striding toward her, pulling the horse behind. "Went to the school, the lodgin' 'ouse—what a queer hen ya got there, miss—yer cousin's 'ouse, come back down 'ere and, cor! 'ere you be. Mrs. M sent me to come fetch you back 'mediately."

"Whatever for?" She jumped up, brushing grass from her skirt.

"Miss Amelia is sick. Poor lass 'as got the cholera. Mrs. Woodbridge 'as gone and fainted in her bedchamber, an' it's all Mrs. M can do to 'elp the child. She needs you bad and right now."

"The cholera?" Rachel's stomach danced like she had swallowed a flock of frantic moths. Would Dr. Edmunds stop believing in God if He took Amelia away? "I do not understand why Mrs. Mainprice has to tend Miss Amelia. Is not Dr. Edmunds caring for her?"

"Dr. E's still at Lady H's place, tendin' the daughter. Had Mrs. M send for Dr. Castleton, but Dr. C is too sick with the cholera 'imself. Then, right afore I left the 'ouse, that rummy cove Dr. Calvert come on behalf o' Dr. Castleton." His thin lips pinched tight.

"No doubt he will tend to Amelia properly," she answered, willing herself to believe what she said. "I do not know why you expect I could do better than Dr. Calvert."

"Dr. Calvert's told Mrs. M that 'e's goin' to purge the girl, get all the illness outta 'er, and I don' think I've seen a little tyke look sicker than that lass."

The moths in Rachel's stomach transformed into geese flapping frantically. Purging was not what her mother would do at all, but Rachel knew too many doctors and surgeons thought it proper. Help the body rid itself of the poison, they reasoned, when all they were truly doing was draining away life. It might work for a normally healthy adult, but for a little child?

Rachel marched up to Joe. "He cannot purge her. You and Mrs. Mainprice must stop him."

He shook his head. "Sorry, miss, but no. Dr. Calvert's not goin' to listen to me. You hafta come."

"What makes you think he will listen to me?"

"For one, you talk prettier than either Mrs. M or me," he pointed out. "An' you look a whole lot prettier too. That bowl-o'-puddin's a soft touch around women."

"I am sorry, but I cannot help." Rachel clutched her skirts to stop her hands from trembling. "Truly, Joe, I am sorry."

"'Sorry'?" Joe released a stream of curse words, the first time she had ever heard him utter anything stronger than 'cor.' "'Scuse me, miss, but you can be bloody stubborn. You 'ave to come right now."

"Have you forgotten what happened to Mr. Fenton-Smith? To Molly? I could not heal her. How could I help Amelia?" A child. A little child. She killed little children. Joe could just ask Mr. Ferguson.

"Forget Moll! What you done for 'er was care when she was beyond 'elpin. So no more feelin' sorry for yerself, miss." He jabbed a finger into her shoulder. "No more feelin' sorry or tellin' me 'sorry.' You 'ave to help Miss Amelia. Do it for me and Mrs. M. Do it for Dr. E, if nobody else. C'mon. C'mon, you silly . . . jes' c'mon!"

He was breathing hard as he stared at her. Joe believed in her still. She would have to believe too.

Be strong.

Rachel released her grip on her skirt. "All right. I will come."

CHAPTER 27

Relief registered on Mrs. Mainprice's face when she came down the stairs and saw Rachel standing just inside the front door, removing her bonnet. "Thank heavens Joe found you, miss."

"Joe said you needed me," Rachel said, her voice quivering less than she thought it might.

"The lass needs you, Miss Dunne." Mrs. Mainprice gave a gentle smile. "Dr. Calvert has been purging the child, and he's sent for a surgeon to bleed the lass. Poor wee thing."

"We have to stop him."

"Don't think I haven't been trying."

A man, round and soft—rather like a mound of pudding, as Joe had said—appeared at the top of the stairs.

"Mrs. Mainprice, we need more blankets." He peered at Rachel. "Better yet, send the servant girl there. I need you at the patient's bedside."

"My name is Rachel Dunne, Dr. Calvert. I am Dr. Edmunds's assistant. I have come to nurse Miss Amelia. If you require my aid," she added with a humble smile, summoning all that charm Joe seemed to think she possessed. Hoping the expression masked her tremors.

Dr. Calvert looked down his considerable nose at her, his heavy sideburns bracketing the uncertain frown on his face. "You have some experience in these matters?"

"I have an extensive knowledge of herbal remedies and have been sitting at the bedsides of the ill since I was ten. I have nursed people through dropsy and typhus and croup." With only one death—no, three—that haunted her.

His thick eyebrows rose in unison. "You sound most accomplished. Edmunds never told me he'd hired an attendant to replace Miss Guimond."

"He was afraid someone might snatch Miss Dunne away if they found out, sir," interjected Mrs. Mainprice. "You know how hard it is to find a good attendant, and Dr. Edmunds was a wee bit possessive of our Miss Dunne."

"Was he now? Well then, in that case, I believe I can trust you with the care of our patient. I left a very important function at Lord Wellsley's and must return immediately. My duties here are concluded for the moment, anyway. It is time for the surgeon to ply his trade."

"You can trust me to follow whatever instructions you provide," Rachel replied. "I shall attend to Amelia's care until the surgeon arrives."

"Mrs. Mainprice knows what needs be done. My directives must be followed to the letter. Am I understood? The child must not come to harm because of incompetence."

"I understand completely, Dr. Calvert," said Rachel stiffly, keenly aware that if he lost a patient, he would never suffer the accusations she had endured.

"I see I've made myself clear, then. Good evening, Miss Dunne. I shall return once my schedule permits." He retrieved his medical bag and marched out of the house.

Rachel hurried up the stairs as soon as the door closed behind him, the housekeeper wheezing as she hastened into Amelia's room with her. Mrs. Woodbridge was nowhere to be found.

Rachel stripped back the heavy blankets covering Amelia, beet-red from fever, pulled out the warmed brick at her feet. The child stirred and moaned. She didn't open her eyes, though. She had obviously been dosed with laudanum.

"The doctor said sweating her was the proper thing to do," Mrs. Mainprice explained.

"She is already burning up. She needs less heat on her body, not more." Rachel dropped a nearby clean rag into the basin of water. "When was the last time you thought to cure a fever by laying heavy blankets and hot bricks all over a person?"

"Exactly never. Cordials, spirit of niter, and cool wet cloths usually work best. If anything does." Her eyes softened, moistened with tears. "Poor lass."

"We had best make some of my tonic." Rachel wrung out the cloth, the excess water splashing into the basin. "We have to get some down Amelia as soon as we can rouse her from her sleep. Tonic and cordials and anything else you can think of."

"I agree, Miss Dunne." Mrs. Mainprice punctuated her assent with a crisp nod, her cap ribbons flapping.

"We should also tell Joe to prevent that surgeon from crossing the threshold of this house. Instruct him to tell the man anything, that we've had an outbreak of the plague if necessary, but keep him away. And we should not let Mrs. Woodbridge in this room. She would not approve of my tending to Amelia."

"Dr. Calvert dosed Mrs. Woodbridge with laudanum as well. She was rather hysterical when he arrived. I've a feeling she won't be rising for many an hour." A wry smile twisted the housekeeper's mouth, and she hurried off to fetch the tonic.

Rachel turned back to Amelia, and her heart sank as fast as an anchor tossed over the side of a ship. The poor child was so very ill. She squirmed from the fever and the pain that gripped her. Damp cloth in hand, Rachel gently wiped it over Amelia's limbs.

"Amelia, do try to wake up. Please. You need to take some medicine."

Mrs. Mainprice returned, a steaming mug of tonic in her hands. She helped Rachel spoon a small amount past Amelia's lips. The child spluttered, the liquid dribbling onto Rachel's arms.

"Please drink some, sweeting," Rachel cooed and clamped her fingers around the spoon to stop their trembling. Amelia's eyes drifted in and out of focus, fighting against the effects of the laudanum. Rachel noticed anew that they were the most incredible blue, a rich color, like precious sapphires. Her heart swelled until she thought her chest would burst. "Yes, Amelia. Good girl. Concentrate on me and try to swallow some of this. It will make you feel better."

"I can't. I hurt." Amelia moaned, a piteous sound that tore at Rachel's heart. Mary Ferguson had moaned just the same that afternoon, in between wrenching coughs . . .

She spilled tonic onto the sheet, a circular stain of greenish liquid.

"Here, miss." Mrs. Mainprice leaned across her, wiping at the spill with a clean cloth. "Let me get that."

"I want Aunt Soph." Amelia's legs churned beneath the sheets, fighting off the pain consuming her, wasting her away. "I want Papa. Papa now!"

James, you need to come home. Your daughter is dying.

"He will be here very soon, Amelia." Rachel forced a smile, the tears swimming in her eyes to blur the child's features. If she let them fall, they would drain away her last ounce of courage. "But until he gets here, I will take good care of you. I promise."

Amelia sipped more, until the effort to drink exhausted her beyond where she could resist the laudanum. Rachel rested the child's head, its mass of shiny curls, onto the pillow and let her sleep.

"Oh, miss." Every wrinkle in the housekeeper's face creased. "She looks so dreadful sick."

"She *is* dreadful sick."

Wearily, Rachel stood, her back stiff, and went to the room's window. It looked out over the garden, late afternoon shadows mantling the paths, the fountain, the pear tree in darkness. A face peeked through the stable window. Joe. He would patiently wait to hear what happened with Amelia, no matter how late it grew or how bad the news.

"We should pray, Miss Dunne," said Mrs. Mainprice.

Would prayer do any good now, when it had failed before?

"Do you know what I used to pray for as a girl, Mrs. Mainprice?" Rachel pressed her fingers against the window frame as if she might shove the glass away and fly through, freed from this room. "I used to pray that God would make us rich, that God would help my father learn how to make money." *Rather than fritter it away.* "Well, that never happened. When I was older, I prayed God would not let my father die. But of course, he did die. Then, so many times, I prayed for the people I tried to heal. Sometimes God listened. Many times He did not. When He let Mary Ferguson fall ill and then die . . ." Her fingers pushed against the wood. Pushed hard. "She was only a wee child, Mrs. Mainprice."

"Mary Ferguson was a child?" Rachel heard the surprise in the housekeeper's voice, the sudden worry.

"Younger than Amelia. So frail and helpless. She had an angel's face and the greatest misfortune to be born in Craigue, near the stink of the tanneries and the filth of the streets." Rachel's breathing came in ragged shudders. "She was innocent and sweet, in spite of her drunken father's mistreatment, a resilient blade of grass springing up after being repeatedly trod down. I prayed hard for her. Neighbors came and prayed too. When she died, I knew God was not watching over the least of His sparrows. And when I was accused of her murder, I knew He had abandoned me for good."

Silence stretched. Rachel's fingernails dug into the wood frame, risking a splinter.

Skirts rustling, Mrs. Mainprice stood and rested her hand, a touch light as purest down, upon Rachel's shoulder. "God has never abandoned you, child. But He doesn't always answer our pleas the way we expect. It doesn't mean He doesn't love us."

Rachel met the other woman's gaze. "Forcing me to witness another death hardly seems like love. Especially the death of another innocent child."

"Who ever promised life would be easy?" Her dark eyes flashed with the challenge she was laying out. "God gave you and Dr. Edmunds a special gift—the gift to care for the sick. The gift to heal. I saw what you did with Joe's arm. I remember how you rushed to help the apple seller when she was injured in the street. A young girl, mind you! You're a healer and you cannot turn away from that calling. That's why God sent you to us. That's why you're here now, why you had the courage to chase Dr. Calvert off. You know you're a healer. Help the lass. She needs you."

"I cannot," Rachel insisted. "I do not have the ability or faith anymore to help Amelia."

"I think you do. If only you would let yourself realize it." Mrs. Mainprice's hand squeezed, willed strength into Rachel. "If only you'd release the anger, the disappointment. If only you'd forgive yourself for what happened in Ireland. For what happened with Molly. If only you'd give yourself over to God."

Rachel looked into the other woman's eyes. Could she forgive herself? Could she trust a God she had blamed for so long?

She turned to gaze down at Amelia, the girl's limbs stiffening from the cramps that seized her body, her breathing strained, her plump cheeks flaring with red. She was so small, so helpless, lost in the middle of that bed. The tiniest of human creatures. A mustard seed in the crush of humanity. *God, can You even see her?* "I am so very afraid."

"'Tis natural to be afraid, miss, but God is with you. Whom shall you fear?"

Myself. I fear myself.

Trembling, Rachel laid a hand upon Amelia's chest, felt her racing heart thrum beneath her fingertips, the source and echo of life. She had to help this child. There was no other course. She was a healer, like her mother had been. And if she failed . . . she had to accept that. Stop blaming herself. Stop blaming God for not listening. Leave the outcome in His hands.

Where it belonged.

God, forgive me. I have been so filled with arrogance and pride. They have blinded me from the truth. Help me now to be strong. And, if You choose, through the work of my humble hands let Your healing flow.

Rachel reached for Mrs. Mainprice's hand. "Stay with me. Pray with me. I cannot do this alone."

"You can do all things through Christ who strengthens you, Miss Dunne."

"Then let us pray to Him."

She closed her eyes and began to recite every prayer she could think of. She was joined by Mrs. Mainprice until both their voices grew hoarse and the hours ticked onward into the dead of night.

❧ ☙

"Dash, Edmunds, I'd have come sooner if I'd known." Hathaway fingered his top hat. The buttons of his overcoat were misaligned and his cravat disheveled. "I was at the club celebrating my engagement, but I neglected to tell my landlady where I'd gone. Not that she'd have remembered even if I had."

"It's quite all right. The worst is over." For Mrs. Blencowe, if not for Amelia.

Mrs. Blencowe's labor had taken hours, but she had delivered the child. A tiny boy, alive, if puny and blue-tinged. A rough massage had revived the infant, though James feared for his long-term health, as well as the health of his mother. Drained, she had bled fiercely. James and the monthly nurse had swabbed her with vinegar-soaked rags until the flood had stopped. If she didn't fever, she might live. A large *if*.

James tugged his gloves over his fingers. "Congratulations on your pending marriage, Hathaway."

"Say you'll come to the wedding. Oh, bless me, Edmunds, she's a veritable angel and my parents adore her. I couldn't have found better."

Memories pressed, their load like ropes dragging James down. "Be true to her, Hathaway, and don't fail her. Don't fail anyone."

"I'm not intending on failing her." Hathaway blinked, his bliss dimming like a candle flame ruffled by a breeze. "Are you quite all right, Edmunds?"

No. God in heaven, no. "My congratulations again, Hathaway, but I can't delay. I must go. Good luck here."

James slipped out of the house. From nowhere, a fog had lifted off the streets to muffle the sounds of carriages passing in the dark night. What hour had it become? He withdrew his watch. Almost eleven in the evening. The hour's lateness ached in the small of his back, painfully stiffened the muscles at the base of his skull.

He pocketed the watch and marched on, down Pall Mall toward Belgravia and whatever awaited him at home. Hackneys passed without stopping at his signal, filled with customers bound to happier prospects. James passed the rows of clubs, candlelight yellow in their windows, their front doors exhaling smoke and the baritone rumble of men's voices. The one he occasionally frequented was just a few doors down. He might step inside and say a final good-bye to the colleagues he would find there, enjoying their chops and the endless gossip about theater women or politics or the mean-spiritedness of their wives. Drift along on a current of topics far removed from his own problems.

Be an idiot.

The fog swirled in his path as he strode along, like ghosts chasing him. The ghost of a woman he had married in order to please his father, a man impossible to please; the specter of his medical career, which he'd pursued with a single-minded ambition that excluded everyone around him, until the losses grew so great he couldn't bear them anymore; the apparition of his only child, held at such a safe distance that she feared him and treated him like a stranger.

I was going to make it all up to you, though, Amelia . . . tomorrow.

Always tomorrow.

The bell of a church tolled, followed by another and another, all of them striking eleven. They sounded like a death knell to James. He had received the news about Amelia over five hours ago—forever to a cholera victim, who could perish in hours or just minutes, like Agnes's sister who had collapsed and died outside the chophouse. Even Thaddeus, with all his training, would find it hard to halt the momentum leading toward collapse. One moment the patient would be only vaguely ill, the next . . .

A shudder overtook him, and James jerked his coat collar up around his neck, the wool rasping across the stubble sprouting on his chin, unable to fend off the chill. Impossible to get warm when the chill was coming from deep within, crystallizing like hoarfrost to coat his heart with ice. *God, grant me Your mercy; give me strength.*

He tripped over a break in the pavement and grabbed the iron railings surrounding a churchyard to arrest his fall. He was exhausted, couldn't recall when he'd last eaten, and now he was stumbling about like a drunken man. The gate to the yard hung open and James went inside, collapsing onto a bench set against the iron fence. He would pause for just a moment, long enough to quiet the pounding of his heart, jittering like a fly entrapped in pitch. Ancient trees and twisted headstones rose ethereal and white, picked out by the light of the moon, monuments to others' losses, others' heartbreak. He rested his head against the fence and closed his eyes, pressed his skull into the hard metal as if the pain might serve as atonement.

Heavenly Father, I have failed everyone who counted on me. All those patients he hadn't been competent enough to save; Mariah; Rachel, whose friendship he had sacrificed rather than reveal his miserable truth; Amelia. It had to be over for the child, and he hadn't been there. So very likely she had drawn her last breath without him to witness it, her tiny hand clutched in Sophia's, her aunt's name the last word she would likely utter.

Because James had made so very certain the girl would never call for him.

Just as my father had not called for me.

He sobbed out his sorrow, tears that coursed hot on his face, the cold moonlight doing nothing to ease the burn. *I have even failed You, God. I've attended church, done my duty as a good Christian, but where has my heart been?*

"Merciful Father, help me though I'm undeserving," he pleaded, turning his gaze to the heavens, dark and indecipherable above his head. "Help me see my way through these trials, as only You can. I am sorry for everything I've done wrong, all the people I've hurt. Forgive my stupid selfishness, my weakness. Give me the strength I lack. Help me accept Your will if it's Your decision to let Amelia pass into the kingdom. Help me . . ." His voice broke as tears strangled him.

No God, don't take Amelia. I couldn't bear it. I couldn't lose her too.

Dashing his tears from his cheeks, James pressed his palms against his thighs and stood. No more delay. The time had come to face what he had avoided for too long.

James turned down the next road and headed toward Belgravia, his feet moving him inexorably toward home. He picked up speed the closer he got, his pulse racing in time with his steps, until he was running, his heart thudding in his head.

Lord, dearest Lord, let it not be too late for Amelia. Get me there in time to hold her close one last time . . .

CHAPTER 28

"Calvert, what are you doing here?" James asked, reaching his front door a few seconds after his colleague. Joe, rumpled and bleary-eyed, had just opened the door to Calvert's knocking. "Where is Castleton? I sent for him."

The other man sniffled, extracted a handkerchief, and blew heartily into it. "Castleton thinks he's contracted the cholera. Sick as a dog. Sent me here to tend to the young girl in his place. Just got back from Lord Wellsley's fete to check on her." He pursed his lips and gave James a sweeping, censorious look. "Whoever she is."

"She is my daughter." He said the words firmly, without remorse. For the first time.

Calvert's bushy eyebrows jogged upward. "Daughter? You've a daughter?"

"I pray I still do." James shoved past the fellow's corpulent frame, which reeked of cigar smoke and a long evening. "Joe, how is Amelia?"

"I haven't 'eard anythin' meself, sir," the boy answered. "But it's been awful quiet up there."

Which could mean any number of things. James shot a glance back over his shoulder. "Thank you, Calvert, but you're not needed any longer."

"But . . ." the man spluttered, "but I had to pay the hackney double to rush back over here!"

"You've my apologies," James called back as he ran up the stairs, taking them two at a time. He'd already reached the first floor when he heard the front door slam shut.

He kept running until he reached the attic rooms. The hush was tangible, the quiet heavy as the air in a church. Or a graveyard. The door to the bedchamber Amelia used stood partly open, and a thin sliver of orange light cut a rectangle on the wood planks of the hallway floor.

A floorboard creaked as he eased the door open, and Rachel, seated at a chair by the bed, spun her head to look at him. The mixture of emotions on her face was unreadable. His gaze didn't linger long enough to decipher them. His eyes skipped over both Rachel and Mrs. Mainprice to the girl lying still on the bed, her face and body concealed by the enveloping sheets. He was too late.

Heavenly Father, don't let it be so. Do not let her be lost to me.

"Is she gone?" His legs somehow continued to support him, though at any second his knees would certainly buckle.

"No," Rachel answered quietly. "But she is not past the worst of her illness just yet. It is good that you are here. At last."

He went to her side and looked down at Amelia, the flush of a fever still hot on his daughter's cheeks. He pressed a finger to her wrist and felt . . . life. A pulse, weak but steady. Love, deep and powerful and possessive, crowded his heart.

"Thank God she's still alive," James murmured. He bowed his head, sent a prayer of thanksgiving to heaven, and closed his fingers around Amelia's wrist. Tiny, fragile. Precious to him.

"She has been fighting hard." Rachel brushed a strand of wheat-gold hair back from Amelia's forehead. "There have been moments when I feared the worst, but Mrs. Mainprice would not let my spirits or my faith flag."

She smiled at the housekeeper, who'd been busy gathering up damp used cloths.

Mrs. Mainprice lifted a weary smile in return. "'Tis glad I am to see you, sir. Miss Amelia needs you both to help her make it all the way back safely." She slipped out of the room, leaving James and Rachel alone together.

"Rachel . . ." Where did he begin?

"Yes?" She was surprisingly composed, though her eyes were red-rimmed with weariness, her hair coming undone from her braid, her dress crumpled from her efforts. Even in precious jewels and silks, she couldn't look more like an angel to him than she did at that moment.

"I'm sorry I didn't come earlier. Dr. Hathaway was delayed in arriving at the Havertons'. . ." James raked his fingers through his hair, as if ordering the strands could force order to his thoughts, his emotions. "Inexcusable, really."

"All that matters is you are here now." Rachel's eyes held no recrimination, only understanding. And forgiveness. "Mrs. Mainprice and I have done everything we know to do for Amelia—forcing liquids down her, keeping her cool and clean, quieting her fears. Praying. But when she called for you, there was no way we could answer that."

"She called for me?"

Rachel nodded and reached for his hand, her fingers sliding to rest in the cup of his palm. "She needs her father. What child does not?"

Amelia needed him. Astonishment and awe spread warmth through his chest.

James pressed Rachel's hand to his chest, held it close to his heart. "Thank you."

"I did nothing."

He lifted his other hand to tuck an errant strand of hair behind her ear, her skin warm against his fingertips. "You have done more than you could ever know."

Sunlight slicing through the blinds struck Rachel directly in the eyes, making her cringe. She squeezed them closed and wondered, hazily, why the morning sun was hitting her in the face. Normally, it did not.

With a jolt, she lifted her head. Normally, she was not asleep in the upstairs attic room that faced east either.

"Dr. Edmunds?" Unfolding herself from where she slumped across the side of the bed, Rachel rubbed her eyes. She was alone in the room. When had he left? He had been at her side all night, bathing Amelia's tiny limbs, lifting her head and encouraging his daughter to sip the tonic. Holding Rachel's hand as they prayed together.

On a sigh, Rachel twisted in the chair and leaned over Amelia. "Amelia, sweeting? Are you awake?"

The child whimpered, softly, a noise of protest, and shifted in her sleep. Rachel swept a tangle of curls from her forehead. Amelia's skin was cool. Finally, cool. And her color was more even, her breathing more relaxed.

"Oh, dearest Lord," she whispered. The crisis was finally, truly over. Amelia was going to live.

Wonder spread through her like sun filling shadowy nooks long unused to light. *God. Blessed God . . .*

"Mrs. Mainprice!" she shouted, rushing out of the room, stumbling over the skirt hem snagged upon the heel of her shoe.

The housekeeper was already headed up the stairs, a tray conveying a bowl of thin soup in her hands. "Hush, I'm coming. Don't wake Mrs. Woodbridge. She's snoring down in the drawing room where I left her hours ago, sprawled across the settee like a drunken sailor. Never thought I'd see that."

"But Mrs. Mainprice, it's Amelia, she is . . . she is . . ."

"Going to be well." Mrs. Mainprice grinned, a smile so large it pushed the folds of her face up around her eyes. The housekeeper balanced the tray in one hand, rested the other alongside Rachel's cheek. "Our heavenly Father answered our prayers by working through you, child."

Through me.

"I could not have done it without you. You made me see how arrogantly blind I have been."

"Then God has worked through us both," Mrs. Mainprice said. "We should be grateful for His mercies. Here and now."

Rachel smiled. How difficult she had made her life these past months by concentrating on the difficulties, letting the hardships rule.

She returned to Amelia's side. Tenderly folding the sheet beneath Amelia's chin, Rachel bent to brush her lips across her smooth forehead, soft as the sweep of a feather to keep from disturbing her. "I am indeed grateful for God's mercies, Mrs. Mainprice. Here and now."

"'Tis glad I am to hear it." Mrs. Mainprice set the tray on the dressing table. "I'll tend to the child for now, miss. Try to get some soup in her when she wakes. You should go down to the kitchen for a bite of breakfast, take your food out into the garden. The master's there. He might like to see you this morning."

A flurry of nerves danced along Rachel's arms. She swiped a hand over her tangled hair. "I shall not be gone long."

The housekeeper smiled knowingly. "Take as long as you need, miss."

The cup of coffee was cold in James's hands, but he hadn't taken a sip from it in a half hour, so it hardly mattered what temperature it was. He scratched his stubbled chin, set the cup on the bench next to him, and stretched out his legs. The day would be hot, last night's damp lingering in the air, but he was chilled from lack of sleep and weariness and happy for the heat. He stared at the fountain, the stone scrubbed and ready for the new occupants. For once, for the first time since he'd accepted his father's bidding that he move to Finchingfield, he could look on this tangible sign of his departure and not feel creeping dread.

Last night, as he'd sat at Amelia's bedside, stroking her flaxen curls while she slept and Rachel dozed in a nearby chair, he had begun to feel a peace that had eluded him for too long. Odd, to feel peace at the sickbed of his only child, but tranquility had descended like a warm cloak to shield him. He'd permitted his anxieties, his feelings of inadequacy to rule him for so long, he had managed to fulfill his greatest fear—that he would not live up to his father's expectations. The only person he had truly failed, though, was himself.

He had smiled over at Rachel then, the candlelight falling softly on her sleeping face. After Molly had died, Rachel had claimed that she blamed God, yet she remained. She kept returning to do the things that caused her the most pain, in the end never flinching from her calling. She'd had more faith in God than he had, all along, even if she hadn't realized it. The faith that made her do what was right.

And he had nearly let her go, walk out of his life forever. What a fool he'd been.

"Please, Lord, help me again . . ."

Just as he gave voice to the prayer, Rachel was there, coming down the gravel path.

The sun glinting on her red-gold hair, her pale eyes watching him, made him catch his breath. She was lovely. In more ways than mere physical beauty.

"Good morning, Dr. Edmunds," she said in that lilting voice that had enraptured him from the beginning. "You do know that Amelia is better and will fully recover?"

James stood and gestured for her to take his seat. He leaned back against the fountain to keep himself from pacing.

"Thanks to you, Miss Dunne."

"Thanks to God, not to me." She yawned into her hand. "I am happy to have been able to help, though, and have my efforts work. Like they used to."

A healer. Of course that's what she had been back in Ireland. It explained why she knew how to attend to the apple seller, why she'd been willing to go to Molly in St. Giles, and why she'd felt responsible when the girl had died. He had so much to learn about Rachel, a woman becoming more amazing by the minute.

"The woman you were accused of . . . harming. She was a patient of yours?" he asked.

"My mother and I never referred to them as patients, but you might think of them that way." Rachel smiled fleetingly. "And Mary was not a woman; she was child. A wee girl whose greatest afflictions seemed to be poverty and neglect. I do not know what went wrong or why she perished. That has haunted me most of all. To fail and not understand the cause."

The old, familiar pain tightened James's chest and then, miraculously, lifted. "The price we sometimes pay as healers, Miss Dunne. The not knowing."

Understanding—true understanding—lit her eyes. "It made you want to give up medicine."

"I hate to admit this aloud, but I was a coward." His heart was thumping hard in his chest as though he'd run a race. He knew, though, he still had so much farther to go. "But not anymore."

"You will not be giving up your practice?"

"This morning, I made the decision to continue as a physician in Finchingfield." He felt relieved saying it. How blind he had been. "Which should make my tenants—and my steward—happy. Nothing worse than an incompetent gentleman farmer interfering in their business."

She smiled. "You would never be incompetent at anything you set your mind to."

I might be, because I'm blundering this conversation quite miserably . . .

"I hope that's true, because I've set my mind to addressing a problem I have let fester for too long." The gravel crunched beneath his shoes as he leaned toward her. He looked down into her eyes, the color of a coastal sea lit by sunlight, and wished he could drown in them forever. "Last night I finally learned that I must become the father Amelia deserves. A real father. And provide her with a proper mother."

The smile fell off Rachel's face. "Miss Castleton will be pleased."

"Miss Castleton? What has she to do with . . . You think I mean her?"

"Who else?"

James dropped to his knees in front of Rachel, gathered up her hands. They shivered like a leaf caught upon an autumn's chill wind.

"I have been a heedless fool for so long, Rachel. It has become the only way I know how to behave." Rachel tried to tug her fingers free but he only held them the tighter. "I have had many fine pearls cast before me and you are, by far, the greatest. The most precious pearl of all. From the moment I first saw you at St. Katherine's Docks, you called to my heart, though I was too deaf to hear."

Her hands stilled.

"I don't deserve your affection," James continued. "I can be aloof, abrupt, sometimes harshly judgmental, and clearly able to withhold my attention from those who need it the most. I intend on reforming, God willing, but I'll need help. Your help. Please tell me that you're willing to try. Tell me that you care for me. Please."

C H A P T E R   29

*R*achel gazed on his face, saw the bright light of hope in his clear, gray eyes.

"You haven't thought matters through, Dr. Edmunds," she protested, her heart hammering. She loved him too much to let him be hasty, to let him regret choosing her, a poor Irish nobody.

"I believe I have. Quite thoroughly, and for the first time in a long time."

"But . . . but your happiness over Amelia's recovery has blinded you to the practical truth—I would never be welcomed among your friends and family. Even though the Harwoods are my cousins, I am not of your class, and I have a stain on my past that will forever leave a mark."

"I don't care what class you think you are or what happened in the past." He squeezed her fingers so tightly they began to hurt. "I only care about you."

"What about Mariah?" *Think, James. Think clearly . . . because my heart is riding on this.* "Her memory still haunts you. It kept you from this garden, made you hide her portrait in the attic. What woman would want to come between you and the abiding love you still have for your deceased wife?" In a day or so, once it was clear Amelia was past all threat, he would remember his love for Mariah. And rethink his grateful affection for Rachel. She knew he would.

He released her fingers. "All this is about Mariah?"

"I do not want you to ever have regrets. I want you to be certain you know what you are asking."

"I was certain." He rocked back on his heels. The light in his eyes guttered out. "It's you who apparently has doubts."

"I just know how much your wife meant to you."

"You do, do you?" James straightened and began pacing. "Maybe I should tell you what Mariah meant to me so you really understand."

Rachel couldn't bear to see him upset, and she certainly didn't want him to notice if she began to cry, so she looked away, down at the gravel, at an insect crawling along in the detritus of scattered dead leaves. As vulnerable as she was.

"I knew Mariah since she was a little girl," he began, like he was commencing a storybook tale. One with an unhappy ending, though. "Our families were close acquaintances and my father always adored her. After all, she was perfect —lovely, pristinely respectable, accomplished, demure. Well bred."

"She does sound perfect."

"Hm. Perfect." He paused. He might have run his fingers through his hair. She didn't look up to check. "The perfect and only possible wife for me. There was only one problem—she didn't love me, and I didn't love her. That's no great sin; many people marry without love, I know. I didn't dwell on the inadequacy of our feelings for long. Once I was financially able to set up a household, I asked for her hand, even though it meant giving up my plans to spend time in Scotland and on the Continent furthering my studies. The marriage proposal greatly pleased my father, which almost made up for my sacrifices. For once, I didn't fail him. Instead, I failed her."

His voice cracked. Rachel held as still as her wobbling spine would allow.

"I respected Mariah," he continued. "I cared for her, and she was a good wife to me, but our relationship was always cool. I thought it might change when she got with child, but we'd grown too distant by then. I had spent so much time building up my practice, I hardly ever saw her. The worst of it was I didn't realize how difficult her pregnancy had been, how weak she'd become. I was honestly surprised when she came down with the childbed fever. Mariah, afflicted? She had always seemed healthy. And then she was gone, too quickly."

He stopped talking, and she wondered if he had concluded his tale. The clatter and hum of the city intruded in the silence, reminding Rachel that the day was advancing and she still had to wash up. Pack. Leave.

His feet came to a halt in front of her. "When Mariah died, my father was fiercely angry, utterly disgusted with me. We fought terribly for days until he stormed out of the house and never crossed the threshold again, leaving me with a newborn child and a shattered heart. Poor little Amelia, who looked exactly like Mariah from the minute she was born. Every time I saw her, I knew I would be reminded that I had failed to be the husband I could've been. That I couldn't even be a good enough physician to heal my own wife. And that my father despised me for it, which made me despise myself."

He squatted on his heels, bringing his face level with hers, forcing her to look at him. "I hid from this garden and from Mariah's portrait for the same reason I hid from Amelia—self-loathing. However, last night I learned that I'm ready to move past my pain. That God will give me the strength to start a new life if I'm willing to reach for it. But I want that life to include you."

From somewhere, Rachel found breath. "I do not know what to say, Dr. Edmunds."

"First, you can stop calling me Dr. Edmunds and call me James." He gathered her hands to his chest. She could feel his heart beating through the layers of his waistcoat and linen shirt. "Listen, Rachel, I love you. Say you love me too. Say you'll come with me to Finchingfield. Be Amelia's mother. Be my wife."

Her pulse beat in time with his, swift as a fiddler's jig. She was tempted to fall into his arms, whisper her love, but she had to say what was in her head, not in her heart.

"There are too many obstacles. For instance, there is still my family to consider," she said. "What of them? Would you have them live with us in Finchingfield?"

"Can you only think of obstacles, Rachel?"

"It is frighteningly easy, when there are so many," she answered. "Such as Mrs. Woodbridge. If you still intend for her to live at Finchingfield House, how could I live there as well? She despises me and would make our lives miserable."

His jaw set and he pulled Rachel up from the bench. He tugged her toward the house. "Come with me. We'll attend to this right now. I did not spend last night praying for forgiveness and strength, asking God for a second chance, to have you doubt my commitment to you."

"Where are we going?" she asked, tripping behind him.

"To talk to Sophia. Mrs. Mainprice," he shouted, spying his housekeeper on the kitchen steps, the empty soup bowl in her hands. "Can you take a moment from tending Amelia to bring the smelling salts to the drawing room? We may have need of them."

James pushed open the drawing room door. Sophia dozed on the settee, a lap rug thrown over her legs, loose hair straggling across her wan cheeks. He had never seen her look so exhausted.

"Maybe we should come back later," Rachel suggested, halting in the doorway.

"Oh, no. I'm not waiting any longer."

Leaning over the settee, he gently shook Sophia's shoulder. "Sophia, wake up. I must speak with you."

"James? When did you return?" She rubbed her eyes, stuffed her pins back into her hair and slowly sat up. "Amelia isn't worse, is she? When I last spoke to Mrs. Mainprice, she was doing better, but that was hours ago."

"She will be quite fine. Thanks to Rachel's loving care." He signaled for Rachel to join him. When she came to his side, he slid his arm around her waist and tucked her close. Her slim, small body fit perfectly, as if made to be a part of him.

Sophia's gaze flicked over them. "What is the meaning of this? And what is she still doing here? I thought she was supposed to be moving to a lodging house or some sort of place."

"That's not going to happen now. I want you to be the first to know." James held onto Rachel and felt her warmth spread, fill him like a balm to his soul. "I intend to take Rachel as my wife."

He waited for the storm to break over their heads. It was not long in coming.

"What?" Sophia screeched, throwing the lap rug off of her. Rachel jerked nervously, her hip bumping against his. "You can't be serious, James. Have you gone utterly mad? What has she done to persuade you? I shudder to think."

James clutched Rachel's arm to keep her from marching angrily out of the room. "There was no subterfuge, Sophia, no persuasion, other than me finally recognizing how much she means to me. I love her and want to marry her."

"How could you even contemplate such a thing?" Sophia asked, her eyes turning dark as jet as she glared at Rachel. "You claimed you never wanted to marry again, James, yet here you are, telling me you intend on replacing dearest Mariah with this Irish nobody. A servant with a dubious past. You are a gentleman, and she is beneath you. Mark my words, I will find out everything there is to know about her and prove to you she's unworthy."

Rachel eased out of James's embrace. "I shall tell you, Mrs. Woodbridge, everything there is to know and save you the trouble."

"Rachel, you don't have to," he said, trying to drag her back to the security of his arms.

Her eyes sought his. "Yes, I do. I cannot hide any longer." She interlaced her fingers with his and held on while she faced Sophia. "All you need to know is that my father was an Irish shopkeeper and my mother is the daughter of an English rector, a gentleman's daughter. That her eldest brother was Anthony Harwood, whose widow lives in Mayfair, which I have seen to be a genteel neighborhood. That we led a decent and upright life in Carlow, Ireland. Until I was accused of murder."

"Murder!" Sophia's shout rattled the windows.

"I was accused but found innocent, because I was innocent," Rachel continued, her voice gaining strength. "Unfortunately, the gossip damaged my mother's business as a modiste and the work she did as a healer. I was forced to leave Ireland and come here to find work. Your brother-in-law did my cousin a great service and took me in." Her fingers pressed his and she smiled all her gratitude at him. "A more generous act than the respectable Harwoods were willing to perform for me. You are a good man, James."

His heart swelled with love for this incredible woman. He tucked her into his embrace once more and dropped a kiss onto her head. "You make me good, Rachel."

"Oh no, James, no." Sophia collapsed onto the sofa. "You cannot marry this girl. You'll be drummed out of proper society. No one will speak to you. No one will look at you. Think of what you'll be doing to Amelia, to her future. To all of us. Ruined. Utterly ruined."

"The only way I'll be drummed out of proper society is if you tell people what happened to Rachel back in Ireland," James said pointedly.

"But others know," Sophia sputtered.

"Miss Harwood and the rest of Rachel's family would never breathe a word."

Sophia sank into the cushions as if her bones had lost their ability to hold her up. "You can't do this. I won't let you."

"It isn't up to you. I'm lost and lonely, and Rachel can heal my heart. I love her more than life." He smiled down into Rachel's face and saw the answer to every prayer he had ever breathed in the line of her cheek, the curve of her lips, the warmth in her eyes. Here was God's plan for him. This woman. Their future together. "I do, Rachel. I do love you more than life. All this time I've been beseeching God to show me the way, He was bringing me you. My hope for healing, my very soul."

"Oh, James," whispered Rachel, tears in her eyes.

"Oh, James," Sophia echoed, a sob choking her words, "you've ruined everything."

Mrs. Mainprice tapped on the door, the bottle of smelling salts in her hand.

"Here. Give those to me," commanded Sophia, snatching the bottle out of the housekeeper's hand. She uncorked it and inhaled, flinching from the sharp scent.

"Thank you, Mrs. Mainprice," said James, excusing her.

He took the bottle from Sophia, set it on the table at her knee, and clasped her hands between his. They were cold and quivering with anger. "Please be at peace with my decision. I'll never be happy without Rachel."

"You will make us the laughingstock of all of England, James." Desperation deepened the faint wrinkles that fanned out from her eyes. "Why cannot life stay as we'd planned? You and I and Amelia together in Finchingfield? It would have been perfect."

"Because it isn't enough for me any longer," he replied. "I need Rachel."

"You will be miserable, James," said Sophia, her voice gone small and tired. "She isn't the right one for you."

"Yes, she is. God has been kind by bringing me Rachel, and I won't turn away from His gift." Sophia's garnet wedding ring jabbed into his palm, but he wouldn't let go until she understood just what Rachel meant to him. And if it required another hour—another day, weeks—of explaining, so be it. He wouldn't be a coward any longer. "I want you to continue to be a part of my life, for Amelia because she loves you so; but that life has to include Rachel from now on."

Sophia frowned and let out a sigh, all the fight exhaling on her breath. "It seems my brother-in-law insists upon having you as his wife, Miss Dunne."

Rachel beamed at him. "It seems he does."

"Then take him," she said with a flick of her wrist. "Because I've had enough of his nonsense."

"I believe she has given us her approval, Rachel," said James, grinning. When was the last time he'd done that? Years. Maybe a lifetime. "Would your father have a saying for this moment, my dear?"

"The only one that comes to mind is something about a man's wife being either his blessing or his bane."

"You shall definitely be my blessing." He glanced over at Sophia and took Rachel's hand. "If you'll please excuse us, Sophia, I need a private moment with my betrothed."

James guided her down the hallway. Rachel's heart fluttered like the wings of birds, and her head was so dizzy with love and hope and excitement she had to concentrate hard to keep from stumbling.

"Where are we going now?" she asked, laughing, the sound pouring out of her, fresh and happy.

"Do you know, Miss Rachel Dunne, I don't think I have ever heard you laugh before. It reminds me of the tinkling of bells, or the sparkle of dew on grass."

"I do believe, Dr. James Edmunds, you might wish to read more of the poetry you own," she teased. "Your own verse is a little cliché."

"Ah, Miss Dunne, I pray I'll be spending far too much time with you to have time to read," he replied, winking.

Her body flooded with delicious warmth. "You have not answered my question, though. You have not told me where we are going."

"In here should suit," he said, and tucked her into the library. The room where her life had begun in London. "I don't think we need Sophia eavesdropping on this particular conversation."

"And what conversation is that?" she asked, her blissful dizziness making her feel as though her feet might lift off the floor.

Arms embracing her, he crushed her to him. His eyes, the shade of a dove's feathers, sparkled with a brilliance to outshine all the constellations in heaven. "A very short one, I hope. Say you love this weak and foolish man, Rachel Dunne. Say you'll marry me."

"I thought I have already agreed to marry you."

"Not officially."

"All right then." She pulled in a breath and inhaled . . . him. *He will be mine forever. My storybook hero.* "Yes, I do love you, James Edmunds. With all my heart and all my soul. And I shall marry you."

"Thank the Lord!"

His hands moving to gently cradle her head, he lowered his lips to hers, and she yielded to the force of their insistence, the press of his love, wished every particle of her body could meld with his. He was turning her knees to liquid, taking the air from her lungs, removing all thoughts from her mind until she could only feel and breathe and think of him.

Shakily, James lifted his head, dropped tender kisses upon her eyelids, her brow, the tip of her nose. "If I do not stop, I may not stop at all, and you're not my wife yet."

"Do not stop just yet, James," she said, boldly, her breathing rushed.

"At your command, madam."

He bent to kiss her mouth again, each kiss promising a love she had never imagined. A love she had hardly expected to find when she'd been standing on a London dock, fresh off an Irish steamer, her life in tatters. In spite of her doubts, her disbelief, God had worked a miracle for her.

A miracle whose name was James Edmunds.

CHAPTER 30

*A*fter a whirl of hasty preparation, they held the wedding a month later. Rachel's only regret was that her mother had written to say that her family wouldn't be able to attend. After postponing their arrival to wait for the cholera to subside in London, they now had to untangle the last of Father's business dealings. At least they'd been spared any more threats from Mr. Ferguson. He had suddenly left Carlow not three weeks past, without a word of explanation, in the dark of the night. More of God's mercies. James had kindly offered to postpone the wedding until her family could arrive, but Rachel knew what that suggestion cost him. It was hard enough to be separated for the sake of propriety, him moving to Finchingfield House, her staying in London. Any more time apart would be too hard for either of them to bear.

But soon—in less than an hour, to be precise—she would be his wife, to love and to cherish, to honor and obey, until death did them part, and her happiness surged until she feared her heart would stop from the power of the emotion.

Rachel smiled at Claire, adjusting the ribbon of Rachel's butter-yellow silk bonnet one more time. "You can stop fussing, Claire."

"I don't believe I can! There," she declared at last, stepping back from her handiwork. "I have never seen a lovelier bride. Especially when you blush like you're doing right now. He is a lucky man, you know."

Rachel's mother had declared much the same thing, that day Rachel had climbed onto a post chaise bound for Cork and the beginning of a life-changing journey. But Mother hadn't known what the future would bring or who James Edmunds would turn out to be—the love of Rachel's life. The other half of her soul.

"I am a lucky woman, Claire."

Claire clasped Rachel's fingers. "I think I envy you."

"Someday, Claire, you will find someone wonderful too."

A shadow of a memory dimmed the light of her cousin's eyes, like a figure passing before a lantern, muting for an instant its glow. "Just to see you happy and in love is all I want right now. But I do want you to be certain that you don't mind giving up your plans to teach. That you will be content to merely be his wife."

Rachel smiled at her cousin. Claire only wanted the best for her and the recognition warmed Rachel's heart.

"I will not merely be his wife, though I promise you I would be most content to have that role alone. He wants me to be his attendant, since he's going to start a small practice in Finchingfield, and I have agreed. Not that I think the role will be easy for me, but with God's help, I am ready to try to be a healer again. I know that James and I shall make a marvelous team. So you see, you have no reason to worry about me."

"I suppose I don't." Claire sighed, tears welling in her eyes. "Oh, Rachel, here I've just gained you and now I must let you go again."

"You shall have Mother and the rest." In the few days Claire had been in London, she had secured the rent of a space for Rachel's mother to use as a dress shop, along with assistance from James. The letters that had passed back and forth between Ireland and London had made clear that Mother didn't want to interfere in their life in Finchingfield and that she would prefer to make her own way in the city. Reluctantly, Rachel had agreed. "London is not so far away that there cannot be frequent visits."

"You are very sensible, Rachel."

"James has always thought so," Rachel agreed.

"He must be more intelligent than I ever knew."

Rachel rocked forward on her toes to press a kiss to her cousin's cheek. "I am so grateful you came from Weymouth to be here with me."

"An entire battalion of soldiers couldn't have kept me away, Rachel. My mother's protests and Gregory's frowns of disapproval had no chance of succeeding at all." Claire lifted her eyebrows. "Are you ready?"

"How is one ever ready for this?"

"Having never been a bride, I'm sure I don't know." She blinked away the tears and smiled. "Let's get out there before they think you have abandoned your handsome husband at the altar."

Mrs. Mainprice was waiting for them at the rear of the church. She dabbed a handkerchief to her eyes when she spied Rachel. "Oh, bless me, miss, I knew I was right to hope for this moment."

"You hoped I would wed Dr. Edmunds?"

"Of course I did. From the instant I realized the master was starting to think about something other than his own problems, I knew you'd caught his heart. And there you stand, the loveliest thing I've seen since I spotted my blessed departed husband coming up a country lane on an October morn. *Wheesht*, you are." Tears spilled and she applied her handkerchief again. "Here, I've something for you."

She handed Rachel a book of prayer and a small bouquet of crimson roses. Rachel lifted the flowers to her nose, the scent sweet as a spring morning in the Irish countryside, and she had to swallow down tears.

"I know you didn't bring your Bible from home," Mrs. Mainprice was saying, "so you can borrow my prayer book to carry. And the roses came from the garden. The summer's last good bloom. Joe is ever so proud that his tending has encouraged them to be so lovely again."

"They are lovely. I shall have to thank him."

"Wait until well after the ceremony, miss. I think he's bawling out in the church like a baby, right now."

The organ began to play, signaling to Rachel it was time to begin. Mrs. Mainprice hugged her close before scurrying to her seat. Claire kissed Rachel's cheek and turned up the aisle. Rachel stared at the length of the church, the apse looking a thousand miles distant, its stained-glass window glittering with rainbow light, the small gathering that occupied the pews pressing in on her. There was the now-healthy Dr. Castleton and his unobtrusive wife. But not his sister, who had begged off for fear of the cholera still sparingly present in London, though Rachel knew her reason ran so much deeper. Joe, his face blotchy from tears, insistent on being allowed to attend. Peg, still learning to cope with Rachel's sudden elevation to mistress, was absent so that she could stay at the house to ready the food for the breakfast afterward. Sophia sat in the front-most pew, honoring the occasion by wearing a deep burgundy gown instead of her usual unrelieved black, her expression stern but accepting. Amelia's nursemaid Agnes, recovered from her bout with the cholera, sat on one side of Sophia. At the other side was little Amelia, her cheeks rosy and curls bright, smiling at Rachel. They had become good friends in the past month. She prayed she could become a good mother to the girl as well.

Claire was halfway down the aisle when Rachel's gaze turned to James. He waited eagerly for her at the rector's side, a smile on his face. Love tingled along every nerve ending, coursed through every blood vessel, thrilled the deepest part of her heart. Washed away the last of her pain and anguish.

Oh God, I will bless You all my days for bringing me him.

Then Rachel smiled her love at James and took a step forward.

Into tomorrow.

Into forever.

Acknowledgments

No author can write a book without the support of others. Great thanks go to my wonderful agent, Natasha Kern, who never ceased believing in me, and to the fabulous staff at Worthy—especially Jeana Ledbetter, who loved my words.

I am deeply blessed to have had the insight and encouragement of many fellow authors, the most important my long-time critique partner and a fabulous author, Candace Calvert. My rock!

Lastly, I would like to acknowledge my family for never once letting me quit. Much love.

The Irish Healer is **Nancy Herriman**'s debut novel. An award-winning writer, she received an engineering degree from the University of Cincinnati. After retiring from a career in the high-tech industry, she pursued her love of writing. Nancy lives in the Midwest with her husband and two teenaged children, and performs with various choral groups in her spare time.

WORTHY

PUBLISHING

IF YOU LIKED THIS BOOK . . .

- Tell your friends by going to: www.theirishhealer.com and clicking "LIKE"

- Share the video book trailer by posting it on your Facebook page

- Head over to our Facebook page, click "LIKE" and post a comment regarding what you enjoyed about the book

- Tweet "I recommend reading #TheIrishHealer by @Nancy_Herriman @Worthypub"

- Hashtag: #TheIrishHealer

- Subscribe to our newsletter by going to http://worthypublishing.com/about/subscribe.php

**WORTHY PUBLISHING
FACEBOOK PAGE**

**WORTHY PUBLISHING
WEBSITE**